It Happened in Barcelona

Colin Guest

Published by Tigerman, 2023.

IT HAPPENED IN BARCELONA

First edition. August 18, 2023.

ISBN: 979-8223767824

Written by Colin Guest.

Also by Colin Guest

1
Desperation Rules the Day
Suzy's Dilemma

Standalone
Desperation Rules the Day
Fatal Love
An Unforgettable Cruise
A Dangerous Love Affair
An Expats Experiences of Living in Turkey
Impending Disaster
Terror Holiday
It Happened in Barcelona

Watch for more at https://www.colinguestauthor.com.

Chapter 1

John Philips, thirty-eight, a successful architect speciating in house designs, arrived home devastated. He had been to the funeral of his wife who had died in a traffic accident. Even the welcome he received from Lucky, his golden retriever did little to help. John went to the cabinet, poured himself a large vodka tonic, then wandered into the lounge and sat down. Lucky came and lay next to him.

"You are a good boy," he said, ruffling his head. Lucky looked up at him. He knew something was wrong, but did not know what.

John took a slug of his drink, then gazed around. The lounge had a cathedral ceiling with a walk-around on the first floor. He and Jasmin had designed the house between them, with a specialist company building it. Before she died, it had been a pleasure sitting in the house. Now, burdened with memories, it was as though he carried a weight around his neck.

'I can't go on living here,' he said. 'If I stay here, I'll go mad. No, I have to get away.' A knock on the door announced Gilbert, Wendy his wife, along with, George and Joan his other friends and neighbours.' They had accompanied him to the funeral, and returned to try and ease his distress.

Once all were sat with a drink in their hands, Gilbert raised his glass. "To absent friend." All raised their glasses and echoed his words.

After they had gone, saying call if you need us, John clipped on Lucky's lead. and took him out for a walk. In the past, it had been a pleasure to go out and return home to be welcomed by Jasmin.

Over the next six months, from once a smart dressed man, John now looked like a tramp. His once sparkling hazel-coloured eyes looked dull and lifeless. He seldom bothered to shave, while his hair hung down to his shoulders. It was only Lucky who kept him sane. Each day, they would go out for long walks before returning home. Now, with the memories it held, the house was like a millstone around his neck.

After a restless night's sleep, John's thoughts turned to how things used to be. Due to his despair, he cancelled all new projects. Then with a supreme effort, completed the one he had been working on.

Despite his weariness to go on, before the winter began, John ordered a load of logs for his open fire. To sit with a glass of wine at hand and some smooth jazz playing in the background, would help take away his feeling of loneliness. However, he was not alone; he had Lucky, his faithful golden retriever

While working on his computer one day, John stopped and looked down at Lucky lying beside him.

"There must be more to life than this," he mumbled. Lucky looked up and cocked his head as if to say, "I'm sorry, but I can't answer you."

He bent and rubbed his head. "I know if you could, you'd say you miss Jasmin as much as me." The thought of her brought tears to his eyes as he looked upwards. "I miss you so much. Why did you have to go and leave me."

Come Christmas; unlike in the past, John did not erect a Christmas tree or hang any decorations. Apart from a wreath he hung on the door knocker, the house was devoid of anything related to Christmas. He did, however, buy a turkey that once cooked, would feed not only him, but provide a treat for Lucky.

On New Year's Eve, with frost covering the front lawn, John sat huddled by the fire with a glass of whisky in hand. Finally, on the stroke of midnight, he lifted his glass.

"Well, Jasmin, that's another year gone." With his shoulders slumped, in a half choking voice, he said, "I'm sorry, but I have to get away from here. There are too many memories in this house for me to stay." He paused, then nodded. "I know, I'll go and live abroad."

As he brushed a hand through his shoulder length hair and rubbed his whiskery unshaven face, he made a decision. "Right, that's it. Once Alex is open again, l will get my haircut. I've looked like a tramp long enough."

His frown turned into a half-smile as he glanced down at Lucky lying asleep on the rug.

"Happy New Year, Lucky, I have a nice treat for you tomorrow, a leg of Turkey."

The next day, as John sat brooding, he heard a knock on his door. On opening it, he found Gilbert standing there. He wore a thick coat, with his cheeks red from the cold.

"Morning, John." He shrugged. "Sue and I thought you'd rather not want company last night, so we left you alone."

"You were right. I was not exactly in the party mood. Anyway, come in and have a drink. Or is it a bit early for you?"

"No, I could manage one, if it's alright with you?"

"Of course, come in."

As Gilbert walked into the lounge, he undid his jacket and rubbed his hands. "It's nice and warm in here" He chuckled at the sight of Lucky sprawled out on the rug by the fire, then went over and stroked him.

"Happy New Year, Lucky." He looked up at John and asked, "Did daddy give you a treat?"

A flicker of a smile crossed John's face. "Yes, I gave him a leg of Turkey for his breakfast."

Gilbert grinned. "Well, who's a lucky boy?"

Lucky raised his head. He looked at Gilbert, gave a woof of welcome, then lay back down.

John handed Gilbert a glass of whisky. "Sorry, but it's all I have. I've drunk all the other booze in the house."

Gilbert shook his head. "In the circumstances, I don't blame you, but don't get in the habit." Before John could answer, he added, "it won't help."

John gave a half smile. "Don't worry. I mean, if I was always drunk, who would look after Lucky. No, life must go on; Jasmin would come back and haunt me if I gave up the ghost." He looked down at Lucky. "What do you think, boy?"

Lucky sat up and wagged his tail. John grinned. "See, he knows what I said."

"He always was a clever boy. Anyway, I came to see if you would like to have dinner with us? Now, before you say no, we have a goose and a chunk of beef."

"In that case, what can I say but yes, thanks."

Perfect! We'll be expecting you at 1 pm. Wendy should have dinner ready by then." After a chat and finishing his drink, as Gilbert left, his final words were, "Don't forget, we will be waiting for you."

Chapter 2

As the door closed behind him, John looked at Lucky. "Yes, another walk will help blow away the cobwebs." When he picked up his lead, Lucky

jumped up, wagging his tail.

He grinned. "Okay, we are going." After he put on his boots and a thick jacket, he then clipped on Lucky's lead.

As they walked outside, John sighed as he breathed in the crisp morning air. Then with the temperature less than he had thought, he pulled the hood of his coat up.

"Yes, this is what I needed," he muttered.

Lucky barked as though in agreement as he ran around on his extending lead. Now and again, ice cracked as John's boots broke the thin covering over some frozen puddles. He smiled at the sight of icicles hanging from branches here and there. Although later than usual, it showed winter had arrived.

After about a 45-minute walk along frost covered lanes, they returned to the house.

Once inside the front door, as a matter of habit, Lucky sat while John

wiped his feet before letting him run into the kitchen. The next minute, he could hear him slurping up a well-deserved drink. A glance in the hallway mirror made John smile, his nose was red from the cold.

He removed his boots, hung up his jacket, then with his slippers on, went to the kitchen and made himself a cup of coffee. He took it into the lounge, put it on the coffee table, then put another log on the dying fire. Once satisfied it would catch, John switched on the TV, then settled down to catch up on the news.

Apart from showing the firework displays worldwide, there was little else of interest. Once he had finished his coffee, John went upstairs and showered. As he caught his reflection in the bathroom mirror, he shook his head. Not only did he need a haircut, it showed he had not shaved for some time. As he was going to Gilbert and Wendy's, John decided he should at least make an effort to look presentable.

Once shaved and dressed, a further look in the mirror made him nod in satisfaction. From now on, he would keep himself smart and not look like some down and out. He chuckled. It would have horrified Wendy had she seen him a short time earlier.

Later, after checking Lucky had water and food, John rubbed his head.

Right, you be a good boy; I'll be back later."

After he locked the door and walked to the gate, he stopped and looked back. The view of his house was not as per the norm. A company specialising in barn conversions had built it. The house had three bedrooms, a good-sized kitchen, and a spacious lounge with a cathedral ceiling. John shrugged. Those were happy times, but since Jasmin's death, being there brought back memories he could not face.

At Gilbert and Wendy's house, he rang the doorbell, which opened to reveal Gilbert standing there. When he noticed John's clean-shaven face, he grinned. "Now, who's a pretty boy? You look much better than you did earlier." Standing to one side, he beckoned John to enter. "Go into the lounge; lunch is not quite ready."

After removing his coat and boots, he put on a pair of slippers before going into the lounge. As he entered, the sight of a large Christmas tree covered with fairy lights and decorations made John blink.

"This looks great." He shrugged. "I never bothered this year."

Gilbert nodded. "I'm not surprised." As they stood looking at the tree, Wendy walked in. She flashed John a smile and kissed him on the cheek.

"Hi John, I'm glad you came." A hint of a smile crossed her face. "We thought you might not want company last night, or we would have invited you in."

Gilbert laughed. "If you had seen him before he shaved, you might not have wanted him to come for lunch."

Wendy's eyebrows shot up. "Oh, were you that bad, John?"

He rubbed his chin. "I must admit, Gilbert is right. Still, I decided Jasmin would not have liked to see me as I was. I'll have my haircut once the barber's shop is open."

Wendy nodded. "Good for you. I'm sure you made the right decision." Turning to Gilbert, she said, "Now, what's going on? Where are our drinks?" She shook her head. "It's hard to get good staff these days, John."

The three of them laughed, then Gilbert said, "What's it to be, John?"

"A glass of wine, please."

"White or red?"

"Red."

Once everyone had a drink, Wendy raised her glass. "To absent friends," to which John and Gilbert echoed her words.

Although he felt down being there without Jasmin, Wendy had cooked an excellent lunch. Also, with Gilbert cracking a few jokes, it made a nice change for him.

After moving into the lounge, once they were all sitting, John said, "I've decided to sell up and move abroad." On seeing their shocked expressions, he shrugged. "It's time I started to get my life back on track."

Gilbert nodded approval, while on recovering, Wendy said, "Well, although it came as a shock, I understand why you decided on this." She cocked an eyebrow. "Still, if you are sure, what about Spain? There are plenty of Brits living there, so you wouldn't feel lonely,"

John nodded. "Yes, Spain could be suitable. I guess I should take a look at some places over there."

"If you went there, apart from some language problems, you might get free or reduced-cost medical health treatment," Gilbert said.

"Yes, and property prices are less than a few years ago. Plus," Wendy added, "the weather in Spain is usually better than here." She rose and left the room, then returned with a pen and paper that she gave to John.

"Now let's see where you could go." After some discussion, John made up a shortlist of potential places to check out. Apart from Valencia and around the Alicante area, he had added Barcelona.

Before he left, John thanked Wendy and Gilbert for the delicious meal and their suggestions about Spain. He then returned home far happier than when he had left.

Chapter 3

WITH HIS MIND MADE up, John had several real estate agents came and valued his house. To his delight, he could buy a suitable property in Spain at less cost than what he would get on the sale of his house.

After he found a dog sitting couple to stay in his house and look after Lucky, John took them to meet Gilbert and Wendy.

After introductions, he said, "They will help if any problems arise with Lucky or the house. Oh, and they might visit the house once in a while."

Gilbert chuckled. "Don't worry, we won't come too often."

"No problem," the man said, then turned to John. "We love dogs, and like us, we could see you keep your house clean and tidy. "A smile flashed across his face as he added, "It will be the same on your return."

"You can take that for granted," his wife said.

With this settled, they shook hands with Gilbert and Wendy, then left.

To John's annoyance, the day before his flight to Alicante, he received a phone call. The husband of the dog sitters had broken a leg while playing football, so they had to cancel. Thankfully, due to having travel insurance, John could rebook without losing any money. A further check and he found an experienced house sitter who loved dogs. After they agreed on a date, the woman arrived the day before John's flight out to Spain. He showed her where everything was, then took her to meet Joan and Gilbert.

The next day, John shakes the woman's hand. He ruffles Lucky's fur, telling him to be a good, then leaves for the airport.

Later, while sitting relaxed in his seat on the plane, John's only interest is finding a place for him and Lucky to live.

On his arrival in Alicante with clear blue sky and warm sunshine, it helped dispel his doubts about why he was in Spain. A taxi took him to a small hotel he had booked online. Once checked in, he took a taxi to see Stefan, the real estate agent he had spoken to on the phone while in England.

After greeting, Stephen showed John photos of a few more properties he thought John might like. He had earlier told Stephen he wanted either a two or a three-bedroom apartment/house. Also, as he intended to bring his dog with him, the property must allow animals. Given these details, Stefan had made arrangements for them to visit three houses and one apartment.

After they had checked them out, John thought one house and the apartment were suitable. However, he told Stefan that he would also be looking at properties in Valencia and Barcelona. When Stefan learnt it was his company in Valencia where John had seen a few possibilities, he called and spoke to a colleague.

THE NEXT DAY, JOHN flew to Valencia, where he met Clarissa, who Stefan had spoken with. After she took him to look at three properties, two houses and one apartment, John thought the apartment the most suitable. Then he discovered that the apartment did not allow animals.

After he thanked Clarissa, John booked in at a hotel she had recommended. Once showered and changed, he went out and enjoyed a tasty mixed grill. As he ate, John shook his head. It disappointed him at not finding a suitable property. Still, he looked forward to going to Barcelona, where he hoped for better luck.

On his arrival, from bright sunshine down on the Med, it overcast the sky with dark clouds threatening rain. John was glad he'd packed a collapsible umbrella.

After clearing customs, he went to collect his case. When it did not appear on the carousel, John goes and reports his missing case.

"I'm sorry sir," an official says. "If you leave me your phone number, we will call you once it arrives."

Although not happy, John has no choice but to accept the situation. As he had not booked a hotel, John decided to take a taxi to the real-estate office. Once there, no doubt they could recommend where he could stay.

As he entered, a glance showed two women and a man sat at desks. The man looks up, then comes and welcomes him.

"Good morning, sir, can I be of help?"

John flashed him a smile. "I've been talking to a lady named Mia, is she here?"

"Yes, I'm Carlos, her secretary. I'll tell her you are here." He then turned and entered a separate office. On his return, he said, "She won't be a minute."

While John is looking at some brochures of properties for sale, he hears the clip clop of high heels. He turns to see an attractive woman approach him. John holds out his hand "Good Morning Mia, I'm John Williams, we spoke on the phone."

Mia, whose eyes had lit up on seeing John, flashed him a beaming smile, then took hold of John's outstretched hand.

"Yes, good morning, Mr Williams." The warm touch of John's hand had sent shivers down her back. He looked just the kind of man she had always wanted to meet. Reluctantly, she released John's hand and said," Please come into my office.:

Once inside, she gestured to a chair by her desk. "Please sit."

Before sitting at her desk, Mia put a hand to her mouth. "Sorry, would you like tea or coffee?"

"Coffee please, thank you." Mia went to the door, rattled off a string of Spanish, then returned and sat in her chair behind her desk.

John's eyes had lit up with admiration when he noticed Mia's trim figure.

Mia who had noticed his change of expression gave a silent chuckle, then said, "Right, Mr Williams. I have contacted the owners of the properties you were interested in." She shook her head. "One property sold, but the others are still available. I have the keys, so we can check them out whenever you like."

"If you have time, I'm ready when you are," John replied.

"Right, once you finish your drink, we will go."

A short time later, a taxi dropped them off outside an apartment block. As the driver drove away, John heard him muttering.

"The driver did not seem too happy with the tip that you gave him," he said.

Mia shrugged. "No, it does not seem to matter how much you give them, they always want more. Still, here we are. The apartment is on the third floor."

A glance showed John the apartment in a quiet area with the building in a good condition. Ongoing up to the apartment, Mia opened the door and stood aside for John to enter. He flashed her a smile. "After you."

Once inside, after he had checked it out, John nodded in satisfaction. "Yes, this looks okay" However, the sudden blast of loud music made John shake his head. "Well, it was, but if that's a taste of what the neighbours are like, then I'll pass on this apartment."

Mia, who had gasped at hearing the loud music, nodded. "Please accept my apologies, Mr. Williams, but I have to agree with what you said." With that, as they left the apartment, Mia locked up behind them.

They then went and checked another two apartments before Mia suggested they stopped for lunch. With this over, they visited another two apartments before returning to Mia's office. While they sat talking, John mentioned about his lost case. He shrugged. "Also, could you recommend me a hotel."

"Right, first I'll phone to see if your case has turned up. As for a hotel, there is one nearby." Mia phoned the airport, then after talking with someone, she turned. "Good news, your case is there. We can go and fetch it."

John let out a sigh of relief. "Thank heavens, I'd be in a right state had it not arrived."

Mia nodded. "Now I'll phone the hotel." After she spoke and put down the phone, she said, "That's another thing sorted out. I've booked you in."

"Oh thank you Mia, that's great."

"You are welcome." She rose and flashed another of her dazzling smiles. "Let's go and get your case, then go to your hotel."

After collecting John's case, their taxi driver then took them to John's hotel. Once checked in, John turned to Mia. "Please don't think me cheeky, but you have been so helpful." He paused, then said, "Would you be free to join me for dinner.?"

To his delight, Mia flashed him a broad smile. "I'd love to, and thank you." Under her breath, she said, 'I had hoped to see more of you, and you have obliged.'

John, his eyes bright at the thought of them having dinner, together could not have been happier. The first sight of Mia had made him realise he was alone. She not only looked attractive, but during the day had seemed happy to be with him. Nodding his head, he expressed his satisfaction. Not only had he looked at four of the properties he had seen online, but now had his case. With a twinkle in his eyes, he said, "So, where shall we go and what time?"

Mia gave a short laugh. "Well, as you don't know your way around, I'll come to your hotel, say at 8-30." On noticing John's eyebrows shoot up, she said, "From your expression, the time is late for you." She then continued saying, "In Spain, we never have dinner until 9 pm, but as I thought it might be late for you, I said 8-30."

John nodded. "You're right. 9 pm would have been too late, but I guess I can survive until 8-30."

With this agreed, Mia shook John's hand then left. After a last glance at her retreating figure, John went to his room. He had been up early, so after setting the alarm on his phone, crashed out on his bed. Before going to sleep, John's thoughts were on Mia. He had not journeyed to Spain in pursuit of romance, yet sensed an attraction between them. Minutes later, John was fast asleep.

On waking, John shut off his alarm. Once showered and dressed, he went downstairs to await Mia. As she entered the lobby, John's eyebrows shot up at the vision of beauty. Her long black hair, no longer up, hanging loose, it gleamed under the lobby lighting. With green eyeshadow emphasing her large black eyes, John could only stand and gasp. "Wow, what can I say except you look fabulous."

Mia blushed and replied, "You look pretty good yourself" As she walked over to him, without thinking, John gave her a quick kiss on the cheek. The touch of his lips made Mia tremble with excitement. Unlike Manfred, her last boyfriend, John was a gentleman. He also appreciated the time she had spent getting ready to go out.

As they stood close together, it took all of John's resolve not to pull her close and kiss her. Mia sensed his longing, so said, "it would be best if we go."

John nodded. "Yes, we should, before I do something I might later regret," he said, laughing. His words made Mia blush. She knew what John meant. To his surprise, as they stepped outside, Mia linked her arm with his. When she felt John tense, she said, "Sorry, I hope you don't mind. I'm not used to wearing high heels outdoors."

He shook his head. "With you looking like this, I'd have to be mad to object." Then with both laughing, Mia stopped a passing taxi. On the way to a restaurant, Mia's closeness made John tremble inside.

When the taxi pulled to a stop outside a restaurant, he climbed out then helped Mia. She flashed him a smile. "Thank you, John." Had it been her old boyfriend, he would have got out and gone inside, leaving her to pay the fare. She could tell that John was a real gentleman. He paid the metered fare, adding a tip, then opened the restaurant door for Mia to enter.

Once seated with a menu in hand, John asked, "What do you recommend?"

She winked. "It depends on what you fancy," she said.

John blushed at her unsaid meaning. He gave a short laugh, then said, "I meant on the menu." Mia's cheeks coloured at his reply. "Okay, you win," she said, then added, "I can see we are going to get on well."

"I'd like to think so," he said. As he spoke, John thought, 'What am I doing? We are flirting. He flashed her a smile, then said, "I've decided to stay a few days more. I would like to take a look around the city."

Trying hard not to show her delight, Mia said, "If you like, I'd be happy to show you around."

John's eyes lit up at the thought of this.' Anyone who turned down an offer from an attractive woman like Mia, would be mad.

Mia, who had noticed his change of expression, said, "I hope I'm not embarrassing you, John? If so, I didn't mean to."

"There's no need to worry, it's not a problem for me.: As he gazed at her eyes across the table, he said, "What about you?"

"No problem, I'm enjoying talking with you."

"Yes, as am I with you." John then mentioned how his late wife had died in a traffic accident. At this, Mia said, "Oh, I'm so sorry John." She then thrust a hand to her mouth. "I'm sorry, I should have said, Mr Williams."

With a disapproving look, he shook his head. "After spending the day together, John is fine."

On finishing their meal and a bottle of Merlot that John discovered Mia also liked, Mia stopped a taxi and dropped John back at his hotel.

While saying goodnight, Mia reached up and gave John a fleeting kiss on the cheek. Before he could respond, Mia turned, "I'll be back tomorrow, John." She then left and set off home.

After taking a shower, John climbed into bed. As he lay there restless, his thoughts kept going back to Mia. One thing he knew, if he bought a place in Barcelona, he would have no need to seek a female companion. Mia filled all the boxes in a man's wish list of what they wanted in a woman. She was attractive, intelligent, and knew what she wanted in life. Also, as the boss of her own company, she had no need to hook a man.

Chapter 4

IN THE MEANTIME, MIA took a slow walk home. It helped take away the disappointment of John no longer with her. She had enjoyed the time spent together. No man had ever made her feel like this before. With these thoughts swirling around in her head, Mia climbed into bed and was soon asleep.

When she awoke the next day, the thought of spending the day with John made her face light with glee. After she had taken Aza out for his morning walk, she checked to ensure he had food and water, then set off to John's hotel.

As she did, John smiled at the thought that Mia would be downstairs soon to take him out sightseeing. Sure enough, after finishing breakfast and entering the foyer, there she was. His emotions rose when Mia beamed him a broad smile as she walked toward him.

She held out a hand. "Good morning, John, did you sleep well?"

He grinned. "I did when at last I went to sleep."

Mia's cheeks flushed. "Oh, did you have something on your mind why you couldn't?" He grinned. "Never mind, shall we go?"

Once out of sight of the hotel, Mia linked her arm with John's. "You don't mind, do you?"

"No, but it's something I could get used to. Any man who did not, would need his head examined."

Mia sighed and squeezed his arm. "It's a pity we had not met before." She cast her eyes downwards. "I can't believe it, but I'm going to miss you when you leave." A hint of a smile then crossed her face as she gazed into John's eyes. "It means I'll have to persuade you to stay on longer."

As he bent and skimmed his lips across her neck, he said, "Look, I'm attracted to you, but we have only just met." He shrugged. "For now, let's enjoy our time together. Tomorrow is another day."

A satisfied smile crossed Mia's face. "Yes, you are right." With her arm hooked in his, she asked, "So, is there anywhere in particular you would like to visit?"

"How about the fabulous La Sagrada Cathedral? From what I've seen on the television, it's an incredible sight."

She bobbed her head in agreement. "Yes, it is. Had you not mentioned it, I would have taken you there." Her smile widened as she said, "You may not believe it, but the authorities say it's still only three quarters finished." She then went on to say, "As building works have been ongoing for over 140 years, it is unbelievable. Nevertheless, at this time of year, we shouldn't have too much problem getting tickets to go inside.

On their arrival, as John looked up, he whistled. "Now, this is what I call something. It's amazing."

Once inside, as he gazed around in awe, John said, "Incredible;" "I've never seen anything like this before."

After wandering around with John, fascinated by the different designs, they left. Outside, John could not help but again stare up at the sight of such an unbelievable looking cathedral. He turned to Mia. "So, what next have you in mind?"

She hooked her arm back into his. "I suggest a hop on hop off bus tour of the city."

"Yes, I've taken such tours in other countries. I found it's a perfect way to see what's what."

A ten-minute walk brought them to a parked city tour bus. John bought their tickets, then they went upstairs and sat down.

With Mia sitting close beside him, he found the scent of her perfume so alluring, he leaned towards her and sniffed.

With a start, Mia sat bolt upright. A worried expression marred her face as she asked, "What is the matter? Do I smell?"

John squeezed her hand. "Only in the nicest way."

A relieved look crossed Mia's face. "Oh, thank heavens, you had me worried for a minute."

He shook his head. "Don't be silly. You smell divine."

With John's arm draped around her shoulder, Mia relaxed with a satisfied smile on her face.

When they later stopped at one stop, Mia said, "This is Park Guell. We will get off here." She tilted her head. "I feel sure you will find it interesting." As they got off the bus, she said, "Apart from the park, if we go up Caramel Hill, we will have a fabulous view over the city."

He chuckled as he glanced Mia over. "I don't know about the view from up there, but the view from where I'm standing looks pretty good to me."

She pressed a hand to her mouth to stifle a giggle. "Do you always give out compliments like this?" she tittered.

"Why? You're not complaining, are you?"

"No, but I'm not in the habit of receiving compliments like yours."

John's eyebrows shot up. "Oh, why is that? Do Spanish men have problems with their eyesight?" He shrugged. "They must have if you don't receive remarks like mine."

The next minute, he noticed Mia looked on the verge of crying. He squeezed her hand. "I'm sorry if I upset you."

"No, you did not, but it made me wonder how I'll manage after you have gone." On noticing his puzzlement, she said, "No man has ever said such nice things to me as you have."

John folded his hand in hers. "That's hard to believe," he said.

Mia felt the heat of a blush on her cheek as she said, "It's true, but never mind." A flicker of a smile crossed her lips. "Now, let's take a walk up the hill."

John was delighted to see decorative benches, colourful mosaics, and small fountains.

Once at the top, as Mia had said, the view over the city looked fantastic. The cathedral being the prominent building.

Upon their descent, Mia proposed, "Shall we visit the 'House Museum' where Gaudi lived who designed the cathedral. Inside is a collection of furniture and other decorations he designed."

John shrugged. "Thanks, but no thanks, I'm interested in buildings, not what's inside them."

"No problem. Still, as you like the cathedral's design, I will take you to see some of Guellio's other designs.

Chapter 5

A short taxi ride took them to what Mia said was Casa Ballo. As they climbed out, John shook his head in amazement at the sight in front of them.

"Wow, what an amazing building."

"Yes, it is." Mia cocked an eyebrow. "Would you believe if I said it's an apartment block?"

He shook his head. "It's the strangest designed apartment I've ever seen."

"Yes, no doubt. Also, although you cannot see from here, the roof tiles are in the shape of dragon scale"."

John let out a joyful chuckle. "Well, all I can say is I wouldn't say no to living there."

A smile quirked Mia's lip. "Nor I," She then continued saying, "There was talk of pulling it down a few years ago. There was such an outcry from the public; the authorities changed their minds."

"Well, I'm pleased they did. It's a massive change from the usual brand of soulless apartment blocks one sees these days."

"I couldn't agree more." Mia cocked an inquisitive eyebrow. "If you like, we can visit more places that Guellio designed." She glanced at her watch. "I know the perfect place to go." An impish smile made her mouth twitch. "While there, we can get a drink, and if you are hungry, something tasty to eat."

John's lips turned into a grin. "If it's that good, why are we waiting? Let's go."

After finding an empty taxi, they set off for what Mia had told the driver was the Colonia Guell.

As they drove along, she said, "It used to be an industrial area." John shook his head in puzzlement and wondered what sort of place they were going to.

On their arrival and going inside, he gasped. "Wow, now this looks fabulous." The columns supporting the ceiling were most unusual. Instead of being straight, they were in a variety of strange shapes. As for the ceiling, with curved ribs forming several circular shallow domes, it looked a work of wonder.

John shook his head in amazement. "The whole scene is nothing short of incredible." With a wide smile stretched across his face, he turned to Mia. "Thanks for bringing me here. It's just the kind of place I like. Still, I have never seen buildings like those you have shown me."

Mia's eyes twinkled with delight as she squeezed his arm. "I thought you would like this place. It's what's known as an Old Industrial Colony." To John's further surprise, she said, "There's even a church here, which is another of Guellio's designs." She arched a questioning eyebrow. "If you fancy a drink and a snack, there is also a boutique winery, where apart from wine, they also serve a selection of Tapas."

"What an excellent idea, lead on."

After a short walk, they sat inside with a carafe of red wine and a plate of tapas. John took a bite, then nodded in satisfaction. "Delicious, as is the wine." A ghost of a smile crossed his lips. "Do you know something? Apart from selling real estate, you would make a first-class tour guide."

Mia beamed with delight. "Thank you. I must admit I get pleasure when I visit these places." She flashed a smile, "Especially when I am with someone like you."

As she spoke, John thought, "I came to Spain to find a place to live, but now I have an added attraction. Mia is a lovely woman, both in looks and temperament. If I decide to move here, she would make a perfect .... wife. As she's no doubt Catholic, she would not expect anything else." He shook his head. "I can't believe I'm thinking like this, but I am."

John's thoughts then turned to Jasmin. "If you can see me, I hope you are not angry." His lips then turned into a grin as he wondered what Wendy and Gilbert would say when he told them about Mia. He shrugged. "Still, it was Wendy who suggested I come to Spain."

From the look in John's eyes and his faraway expression, Mia knew what was on his mind. Or at least, she thought so.

As they left, he said, "That was certainly different, and I loved the taste of the tapas." He chuckled. "So, what next have you got in mind?"

She threw him a sideways glance. "Well, as we are both well dressed, how about a walk down at the seafront? There are several miles of boardwalks along a golden sandy beach." She sighed. "In the summer, it gets packed, but it's usually pretty empty at this time of year."

John cocked an eyebrow. "I never knew Barcelona had any beaches, but some fresh sea air would make a nice change." He shrugged. "There are some excellent beaches in England, but they also get packed during the summer months."

After a short taxi ride, they were walking along the boardwalk that stretched away in the distance.

With a soft breeze blowing, the waves were light as they rolled up the sandy beach.

John turned to Mia. "It was a great idea of yours to come here."

"I thought you would approve," Mia said, then with her forehead creased in puzzlement, she squeezed his hand.

"John, you said you live in Dorset, but I don't know where it is?"

"If you look at the map of England and go down from London to the English Channel, you will see Weymouth on the left-hand side. I live in the country, which is about twenty-five miles from Weymouth."

A satisfied smile raced across her face. "So, you don't live in a city?"

"No, but Bournemouth, which is not that far away, is." He gave a whisk of a smile, then continued. "Although I can get to London on the train in a couple of hours, it's a world of difference from here in Barcelona."

Mia tilted her head. "Do you have any photos of your house?"

"Yes." From his wallet, John took out three photos. As he gave her the first one, he said, "This is what's called in England, a barn conversion." He grinned. "Not that it looks anything like a barn now." He then handed her the other two photos. "This is the lounge, and the other is the main bedroom."

Mia's eyes lit up as she examined the photos. "It looks much different from a normal house."

He shrugged. "That's because it's not."

She raised a questioning eyebrow. "I suppose you want to sell because of the death of your wife?"

John's smile changed to a frown. "Yes, and why I decided to leave England."

Mia looked nervous as she said, "Would you mind if I ask you a personal question?" On seeing his puzzled expression, she added, "No problem if you don't want to answer."

"No," he said, his breath tickling her ear, "What is it you want to know?"

She hesitated, then said, "If you left England, where you live in the country, do you think you could live in a city?"

"You mean like here in Barcelona?" Not wishing to prolong Mia's suspense, he said, "Yes, I could manage it okay." His smile widened as he caught hold and squeezed her hand. "Look, when I came to Spain, my only thought was to buy a house or an apartment. Anything else, like romance, never crossed my mind." As Mia went to speak, he put a finger to her lips. "Please let me finish. I did not know I would meet such a wonderful person like you, but I did. When you came out of your office to talk to me, I felt an immediate attraction to you." He shook his head. "At present, I can't promise you anything more than friendship." When he noticed her eyes mist, he kissed them. "Still, who knows, it could lead to much more." He lifted her head and gazed into her eyes. "What do you say to that?"

Mia closed her eyes and summoned a deep breath. "I cannot believe it, but for me, it was love at first sight." A sigh eluded her lips. "Therefore, I would like us to continue our friendship." She giggled. "If I told my friends I fell in love with an Englishman after only two days, they would not believe me."

John nodded. "Yes, I know what you mean." He cast a look upwards. "I wonder what my friends would say if I were to tell them about you."

Mia cocked an eyebrow. "So, can I ask what they might say?"

He let out a joyful chuckle. "Although shocked, they'd be happy for me."

Mia took hold of John's hands and gazed into his eyes. "There is one thing, though."

John's eyebrows pulled together in question. "Oh, what?"

"I'm a Catholic, and I presume you're a Christian."

"Yes, but I'm not religious. What about you?"

"Like you, I am also not religious, but I go to church on major occasions."

He shrugged. "So, in which case, we have no problems."

Mia sighed. "I'm glad of that. If we decide to carry on together, I wouldn't like a difference of religion to cause us a problem."

"Yes, it would not have been good for either of us." He folded his hand over hers. "Anyway, how about a drink?"

"Yes, a good idea." Hand in hand, they then walked off to find a bar. Once sat with each holding a glass of white wine, Mia said, "I'm glad we had our little talk." A smile quirked her lips as she added, "We both now know where we stand." She gave a subtle wink. "At least for now."

"You're right." John's smile fell away as he added, "Look, I don't want you to think we now have to sleep together."

She pressed a hand to her mouth to stifle a giggle. "Thank you, John." A smile crossed her lips as she said, "Still, I wonder if you would like to extend your stay? If so, I have two bedrooms. You could move out of the hotel and stay with me." She giggled. "After all, should you forget which bedroom is yours, I have Aza to protect me."

A wide smile stretched across John's face. "Well, as I have already extended my stay for three more days, then thank you?" He grinned. "As for Aza, I'm sure he and I will get on well."

Mia's eyes opened wide in delight. "You devil, why did you not tell me about your staying longer." She shook her head. "I'll have to tell Aza to keep an eye on you." She winked. "Still, he can't see through walls, if you know what I mean."

John gave an inward sigh. He had no objections about staying at Mia's apartment. Who would? As for them not making love, just to lie with Mia in his arms would be enough.

As they left the bar, Mia squeezed his hand. "Look, if you are sure about staying with me, why don't we go to your hotel. You can check out and then go to my place." With a smile, she said, "Once you have sorted yourself out, we can go out again."

As it made sense, they took a taxi to John's hotel. While he went inside to check out, Mia sat outside in the cab.

Ten minutes later, as Mia opened her apartment door, she called out, "Aza. The next minute, he appeared beside her, jumping up and down in delight.

When John slowly put his hand out, Aza came and licked it. He grinned. "See, I knew he would not be a problem."

Mia put a hand to her mouth to stifle a giggle, then said, "Aza eight." A split second later, John reared back in alarm. Aza had changed from a docile dog into a frightening spectacle. With his mouth opened wide, showing his gleaming teeth, he snarled from deep in his throat.

Mia laughed at seeing John's frightened expression. "Okay, Aza." In an instant, he changed back to a big, friendly dog.

With his face white, and still trembling, John said, "Christ, what a transformation. I can't believe he could change so fast." He shook his head. "Okay, I get the message; I'll be good."

Mia laughed. "Don't worry, Aza will not attack you. He knows you are my friend."

A relieved look washed over John's face. "Yes, but I'll have to remember never to upset you. I wouldn't like his jaws clamped on me."

Mia gave a wry smile. "Yes, I must admit he did look rather fearsome."

He cocked an eyebrow. "You said, number eight. So, I take it he's been trained to respond to whatever number you say?"

Mia flashed a mischievous smile. "You don't need to know anymore."

"Okay, but what if I wanted to leave? Could you get him to prevent me from doing so?"

She pressed a hand to her mouth to stifle a giggle. "No, so don't worry. I trained Aza to get people out of the house, not keep them inside."

He grinned. "When Aza looks like he did a few minutes ago, anyone with any sense would jump out of the window to get away."

Mia giggled. "Well, I've never had it happen yet." From John's expression, she could see he looked concerned about staying in the apartment with Aza. She took hold of his hand. "If it would make you more relaxed, when we go to bed, I'll shut Aza in the kitchen?"

John shook his head. "No, I know I'll be safe as long as I don't try anything on with you."

"Oh," Mia tittered, "does it mean you won't try? I'd rather hoped you might," she said laughingly.

Chapter 6

After sitting and talking for a while, they decided it was time for sleep. John kissed Mia goodnight, went into his bedroom, and closed the door.

As he lay there, he could not believe how strong his feelings for Mia were. After all, they had only met three days ago. He wondered what Jasmin would think of him being with Mia, then thrust the thoughts aside. In his heart, he knew she would want him to be happy. His thoughts then returned to Mia, so near and yet so far away, made him sigh. With thoughts of her wrapped in his arms, John fell into a restless sleep.

Later, when the creak of his door woke him, John tensed. He thought it could be Aza. However, as he sat up, to his surprise and delight, it was not Aza at the door, but Mia. Although wearing a long nightdress, it did nothing to hide her shapely figure as she came over to him.

As she pulled back the covers and went to climb in beside him, she hesitated. "You don't mind, do you?" she murmured.

John reached up, pulled her down. As they kissed, Mia cuddled into him. "What kind of man would I be to turn down the chance of sleeping with such a sexy woman as you?" He shook his head. "I'd have to be mad to send you away."

After they kissed again, Mia caught hold and squeezed his hand. I would like to sleep with you, but I don't want us to make love. Well," she tittered, "I mean, not go all the way."

John kissed her cheek. "We will only make love if you say. I'm happy to have you in bed with me. Anything else is not a problem."

He gave a short laugh. "Still, don't think I won't jump at the chance if you were to say yes."

They continued to kiss and caress before falling asleep. Despite not making love, John was content with Mia cuddled against him. He had no intention of spoiling things by trying to make love to her.

When he woke the following day, Mia lying beside him murmured, "Good morning, John, are you hungry""

As he nuzzled her neck, he said, "What a thing to ask a man when he's in bed with such a gorgeous woman."

With a twinkle in her eyes, she said, "You know what I meant."

He grinned. "Of course, but what else should a man say if in my position?"

She kissed him again, then slid out of bed. As Mia opened the door to leave, she turned, "I'll see you in a minute."

As the door closed behind her, John sighed on thinking about Mia getting into bed with him. He let out a joyful chuckle and got up. Once washed and dressed, he went into the kitchen. Here he found Mia dressed, her hair brushed and gleaming, as she prepared breakfast.

He crept up behind her and kissed her neck. "Now this is what I like."

She turned and flashed him a smile. "Oh, and what's that?"

With his breath nuzzling her ear, he murmured, "A cracker of a woman getting me breakfast."

Mia's cheeks flushed. "Thank you, John, you say the nicest things." He brushed a hand across her cheek. "What can I say? The words are true."

With breakfast over, they put on their outdoor clothing. Then with John holding Aza's lead, they went out for a walk. With both smiling and Aza beside them, several people stopped to stare as they passed them by.

Mia, who noticed, said, "We seem to attract some attention?"

"I'm not surprised. With you looking like the cat which got the cream. Plus, with Aza and a handsome man beside you, what else would you expect?"

A smile quirked Mia's lip. "Oh, so, you're handsome, are you?" She laughed and squeezed his arm. "Yes, you are, and I'm as happy as I look."

Once home, before going out again, Mia made sure Aza had enough food and water. As they went to leave, Mia's cell phone rang. She answered, spoke for a few minutes, then turned. "Sorry, John, but I have to go to the office." Cocking an eyebrow, she asked, "Would you like to come with me? If not, you can stay here."

"No, I'll come with you, as long as that's alright? I mean, what about your staff, will they say anything if I do?"

She giggled. "I expect so. After all, I've not been back since we went to check out those apartments. Still, it's not a problem for me. What about you?"

"No problem for me either." He shrugged. "You never know; you might have more apartments come in I could look at. That's, of course, if you would like me to stay in Barcelona?"

"What," she gasped, "Of course, I want you to stay."

He flashed a smile as he squeezed her hand. "I only joked."

She looked at him and raised her eyebrows. "You devil, I never know when you are saying things to wind me up."

XXX

As they neared Mia's office, they released their hands. Once inside, Carlos rattled off something which Mia responded to before turning to John.

"Please sit, Mr Philips. I'll be with you in a minute."

John sat as Mia disappeared into her office. On her return, she said, "While we were out looking around, we had two more properties come in that Carlos thinks may interest you."

John turned to Carlos. Two of the properties I've seen look promising. But before I return to England, I'll be happy to look at anything else you think might prove suitable."

Once Mia had dealt with what she had to, she said, "Right, Mr Philips. I have spoken with one owner who says we can visit now if you like?" She gave a subtle wink, which he took to mean, let's go.

"Now would be good, if you can spare the time?"

"Mia flashed him a dazzling smile. "Of course, it's our customers we are here for."

Once outside and away from the office, Mia caught hold and squeezed John's hand. "I said what I did so we could spend more time together. We can look at the property now or later, whichever you prefer."

"I think it's best we take a look now." He grinned and threw his hands up. "After all, it's your business, not mine."

As they climbed into a taxi, Mia pointed upwards. "The apartment is on the fourth floor. The lady it belongs to is moving out shortly, but has agreed we can look at it now."

On entering the hallway, Mia said, "It's a two-bedroom apartment with a lounge, a separate kitchen, plus a bathroom, of course."

Unlike some apartments they had looked at, this one had an elevator. Upstairs, Mia knocked on the door. It opened on a safety-chain, and a woman's face appeared. After she said something, to which Mia replied, the door opened, and the woman gestured for them to enter.

As they did, Mia said, "I've explained you don't speak Spanish, so I will translate anything either you or she wants to know."

He nodded. "Please thank her for allowing me to take a look around."

Mia spoke to the lady, who then smiled at John.

"She says you are welcome."

A look around showed the apartment was large, but when he heard Mia mention, "Dogs," the woman shook her head.

Mia turned. "I am sorry, John, but animals are not allowed in this apartment block. Some accept them, but others don't." After she spoke to the lady, Mia shook her hand. John did the same, and they left and went back down to the street.

"I will speak to Carlos about this," Mia said. "He knows you intend bringing your dog, so should have asked about animals."

A ghost of a smile crossed John's face. "Never mind, what is next on the list?"

"There is another apartment a bit further along, we can walk there." As they strolled along, Mia said, "It's an empty two-bedroom apartment. But as I have a key, we can look at our leisure."

Once inside, after a look around, John shook his head. "This would have been alright if I were on my own, but there is not enough room for Lucky."

"Yes, I agree," Mia said. After locking up, she asked, "Shall we go and have a coffee? Or would you like to take a walk around?" She shrugged. "I'm sorry John, but this has been a waste of time."

He shook his head. "No, we have been together, so it's not been a problem."

Mia flashed him a wide smile. "Nor for me." They found a nearby café where, after they each had a Latte, they continued to stroll around. When they found themselves passing a park, Mia stopped. "Let's go in and sit for a while."

"Sounds good to me. With the sun out and an attractive woman sitting beside me' I'll be more than happy."

She squeezed his hand and murmured. "Thank you for your kind words, but don't get carried away while we are sitting there. The Spanish police are strict about couples' behaviour in public."

"Oh, that's a shame." He winked. "It means I'll have to wait until we are back in your apartment before I can kiss you?"

"Yes, so remember what I said."

On coming to an empty bench, they sat and held hands. Flashing an innocent smile, John asked, "Is this acceptable?"

To his surprise, Mia leaned over and kissed his cheek. "Yes, it is." As they talked, she glanced at him, he looked happy and relaxed.

She gave a half smile. "John, can I ask you something?"

"Of course, ask away."

"It's just that I get the impression you are as happy as I am about our being together?"

He nodded. "Without a doubt. It's been a long time since I've felt this way, and it's all down to you."

Mia, sighed. "You are so different from Spanish men, or at least, the ones I have met."

He folded his hand in hers. "All I can say is what you see is what you get." He shrugged. "I never pretend to be something I am not. Also, my parents brought me up not to tell lies. So, I don't, and don't trust those who do."

Mia flashed him a huge smile. "That's good, as I feel the same."

Chapter 7

After sitting, talking, and enjoying each other's company, Mia asked, "What would you like to do? I mean, are you hungry?"

"I could eat something." He winked. "Still, as you are not on the menu, I guess I'll have to make do with something else."

Mia's eyebrows shot up and her cheeks coloured, replied, "You devil John. What am I going to do with you?"

He gave a dirty laugh. "Whatever you like, but first, let's eat."

She giggled, then said, "I noticed a restaurant near where we entered the park."

"Great, let's go there."

A few minutes later, they were seated and awaiting a large spicy chicken pizza Mia had ordered.

John chuckled. "With Spain noted for its pizzas, this should good."

When the waiter later placed it on the table, John's eyebrows rose. "This looks great."

Once he had finished eating, he licked his lips. "Well, that tasted as good as it looked."

A smile quirked Mia's lip. "So, you liked it did you?"

He gave a short, dirty laugh. "The only thing to taste better would be you," he muttered.

"Behave yourself John, at least until we are alone."

He threw up his hands. "How can I, with you looking so desirable."

Mia shook his head. "You are impossible." After she gave him a quick peck on the cheek, she murmured, "But I love you." She then thrust a hand thrust to her mouth. "Oh, sorry, it slipped out."

As John gazed into her eyes, he said, "It's not a problem, I love you."

Mia arched a questioning eyebrow. "Are you sure? Because I know I am."

"Yes, I can't believe it, but yes." After a quick look to see if any police were around, he kissed her cheek. "Now, what shall we do?"

Mia shook her head. "Well, after what we have both said, I would prefer to stay out with you than return to the office."

"I should hope so," he reported. "A glance up at the sky showed blue skies lined with a few fluffy clouds.

"As it's a nice day. How about we take a walk along the seafront?"

Mia hooked her arm in his. "Yes, as we both have coats, some fresh sea air would be nice."

After a taxi dropped them off, once on the boardwalk, like the lovers they were, arm in arm, they strolled along. They later paused for a break on a bench, where Mia sat cuddled up against him.

"This is so good," she murmured. "It was an excellent idea of yours to come here."

Flashing an innocent smile, John said, "You mean like me coming to Spain to look for somewhere to live?"

Mia gave him a quick kiss on the cheek. "Yes, and making me a happy woman." She looked at him and raised her eyebrows. "I cannot believe the effect you have had on me," she said, her voice a bare whisper. "I only hope I will not wake up to find you were only a dream."

"Not a chance," John exclaimed. With his breath tickling her ear, he whispered, "I am here now, and here I will stay." He shrugged. "Well, I will once my house gets sold."

"I sincerely hope so," Mia replied, then she sighed. "Well, we should go back to the office, even if only for a short time."

John grinned. "Yes, otherwise, someone may think you are up to something with your English client," he said.

As they walked into the office, Carlos and one of the office assistants looked up. Mia turned and said, "Take a seat, Mr Philips, I won't be long." She then went and spoke to Carlos. From his change of expression, John could see Mia had told him about the no animals allowed in the apartment. Carlos said something in reply, to which Mia nodded, before speaking some more.

While he waited, John looked at the various apartments for rent and sale. Five minutes later, Mia came and flashed him a smile. In a louder voice than usual, she said, "I've told Carlos he must ensure animals are allowed before we look at any other properties."

As they talked, he came and joined them. With eyes downcast, Carlos said, "I'm sorry, Mr Philips. I should have checked before you went to that apartment."

John patted him on the shoulder. "It's not a problem. It made a trip to another part of the city I've not seen before."

"Thank you, but in future, I will check that animals are allowed."

Once he had left, in a quiet voice, Mia said, "There is a café a short distance further along on the left. If you go there, I will join you a bit later." She gave him a subtle wink. "That way, no one will know we are together."

He nodded, then said, "Well, thank you for today, Mia, and it was not a problem about the apartment. Please call if you find any other properties which might suit me." He shook her hand and then left the office.

On coming to the café Mia had mentioned, he went in and ordered a Cappuccino. He had just finished, when the door opened and Mia came in. A smile quirked her lips as she sat down opposite him. "Sorry about that."

"No problem. May I get you a drink?"

"No, thank you." In a muted voice, she murmured, "We can have a glass of wine at my place before taking Aza out for a walk."

Once in her apartment, John took Mia in his arms and gave her a passionate kiss. "That's for saying you love me."

Mia, her eyes wide and bright, kissed him back. She squeezed his hand.

"You don't know how much those three words mean to me, or how happy they make me feel.

Mia poured them a glass of Merlot, which after touching glasses, they drank. Later, on their return from taking Aza out, Mia asked, "Do you like the theatre? John" She cocked an eyebrow. "Or is it not your scene?"

"It depends on what type of show it is?" He shrugged. "There is not much in that line around where I live, so I don't see many shows." With a smile, he enquired, "Anyway, what did you have in mind?" Before she could answer, he gave a short, dirty laugh. "Mind, if we go to a show, with you sitting beside me in the dark, how could I resist kissing you?"

Mia giggled. "Well, although it would be nice, not in the theatre. We can do so here without being interrupted." Then she pulled him close and kissed him. As they lay sprawled on the sofa, locked in each other's arms, John felt his passion rise. He sighed and eased Mia aside. "We had best stop. If we keep on like this, you know there will only be one ending?"

Mia, her breasts heaving with excitement, swept her hair back over her shoulders. She licked her lips.

"You are right. Your kisses set me on fire, and with your hands caressing me, I only want more."

With his eyes burning with passion, John said, "Look, nothing would give me more pleasure than to make love to you." He shook his head. "Before doing so, I want you to be sure it's what you want." As Mia went to speak, he put a finger to her mouth. "If we made love, and you later regretted doing so, I would feel terrible. I don't want to spoil what we have."

Mia's eyes opened wide in surprise. "John, you are incredible. I don't think many men would say what you did if given a chance to make love with a woman. Still, I thank you for saying so." She flashed her long eyelashes. "I may not have wanted us to make love before, but now I can't wait."

Chapter 8

John let out a sigh of relief. "That's good, as it's taken a lot not to rip your clothes off and get inside you. I would love to do so right now, but not without wearing a condom." He shook his head. "I wouldn't like you to get pregnant." His lips brushed her ear, raising goosebumps on her flesh as he murmured, "Of course, if we were to get married." He gazed into Mia's eyes, which were wide in excitement. "Would you want children?"

Mia gripped John's hands tight. "Do you mean what you said, about marriage." Before he could answer she continued. "You may be right about wearing a condom, but don't forget I am a Catholic. So, if you don't use one, it would not be a problem for me." She giggled. "Still, my parents wouldn't be too happy if I became pregnant." With her eyes sparkling in anticipation, she said, "If we were to be married, I would like us to have a baby." She tossed her hair and muttered, "When we go out, as I want you to make love to me, we'll get some condoms."

With his eyes burning with desire, John nodded. "Now that sounds like a great idea. I mean, what kind of man would I be to turn down the chance to make love to you?" He then pulled her close and they enjoyed a hot, steamy kiss.

"Wow, your kisses are something special," Mia gasped, on breaking it off. She shook her head. "Now, I seem to remember we talked about the theatre. If you like, we could watch a Flamenco Show?"

"Yes. I've always loved watching Flamenco dancers on the television."

Mia nodded. "Right, I'll phone and make a booking. If we are lucky, we could go this evening."

John then noticed a sudden change in Mia's expression. From a smile, a crease had appeared in her forehead, and her lips trembled. He caught hold and pulled her close. "What's with this face? You look almost in tears."

Mia wiped a hand across her eyes. "Sorry, but I've just realised you won't be with me for much longer." With a sigh, she got up and left the room. On her return, a relieved look washed across John's face, Mia now wore a broad smile.

"I booked us for tonight's performance. As the show starts at eight o'clock, we can either go out and eat now, or after the show?"

John glanced at his watch. "It's six o'clock, so if you have something to make up a sandwich? I could manage until after the show." A ghost of a smile crossed his face. "Mind you; I'll be starving by then, so be warned."

Mia, flashed him a smile. "I'll make you a sandwich. I am sure I have something you would like."

John gave a short, dirty laugh. "Are you winding me up? You know what I fancy, and it's not in the kitchen."

Mia cheeks flushed. "I didn't mean me, but I'll remind you what you said after the show." She tossed her hair. "Still, while we are out, we will do some shopping. I don't want any excuses about our not making love tonight."

John let out a joyful chuckle. "Not a chance." With his eyes burning with desire, he said, "You look good enough to eat, so tonight, I'm going to enjoy eating you."

Mia's smile came soft and dreamy as she murmured, "In that case, after we return here from the show and shower, I'll put on something nice."

John chuckled. "You can, but believe me, it won't be on for long."
Flashing an innocent smile, he asked, "Now, before we start again,
where is my sandwich?"

She pursed her lips and posed. "Now, which would you prefer,
me or a sandwich?" Before John could react, she turned, and ran into
the kitchen.

He called out after her. "I can imagine tonight already, so I hope
you won't be too tired?"

Mia felt a warm glow between her thighs at the thought of what
John meant. She might be tired later, but not until after they had
made love.

After eating a sandwich consisting of cold meat, cheese, and
some salad, John licked his lips. "Now that's what I call a real
sandwich."

Mia flashed him a smile. "So, are you satisfied?"

He caught hold and pulled her close. "It will keep me going until
tonight, but I'll be hungry again by then."

She winked. "Well, even if you're not, I will be, so be warned."

THE SHOW TURNED OUT great; The dancers put on a
fabulous show, and with Mia sat next to him, John was more than
pleased.

On their way to the theatre, he had noticed a pharmacy, so as
they left, he stopped. "Wait a minute, I have to get some toothpaste."

When he noticed Mia's look of puzzlement, he said. "You might
have forgotten what I need, but I haven't."

She put a hand to her mouth to stifle a giggle. "Had you not
remembered, I would have sent you out again. Anyway, I'm hungry,
so, I hope you will satisfy me?"

As John's lips brushed her ear, raising goosebumps on her flesh, he whispered, "Have no fear; I know how to satisfy your desires?" He grinned. "If not yours, for sure it will be mine. Now, let me go and buy what I need."

On his return, when Mia noticed the size bag John held, her eyes lit up. "Wow, are they all for tonight?"

"No, but I thought it best to have a few extras. Who knows, we might need them later."

Mia winked. "I am sure we will. Now, as it could be a long, tiring night, we had best eat out. It should give us enough energy for once we are back in my apartment."

"In that case, I'd best have a steak. I'm going to need all the energy I can get."

Once inside a restaurant. John's eyes lit when he noticed various steak dishes on the menu. "Oh yes," he said, "this looks great."

He chose a Sirloin steak with all the trimmings while Mia settled on a seafood paella. So not to cause a lack of performance, instead of wine, John requested a bottle of mineral water.

Mia realised why, so said, "Make it two, please."

With their meals finished, they lost no time in returning to Mia's apartment. After she showered, John followed.

On entering her bedroom, he found Mia in bed. The covers were pulled up to her neck, and the bedside lights turned down low. She flashed a smile as he moved towards her. Then in one swift movement, threw back the covers.

John gulped as he gazed at Mia's naked breasts. With her nipples standing out, he knew she was as horny as him.

When he dropped the towel from around his waist, the sight of his throbbing erection made Mia's eyes light. She sat up, reached out and caught hold of it.

"Oh, yes, this is what I want."

John grinned. "Good, as it's what you're going to get." When he pulled back the cover to climb in beside her, his eyebrows shot up and he licked his lips, Mia was naked.

As he climbed in beside her and ran his fingers through her mound, she sighed and spread her thighs. After easing a finger into her wetness, John slipped in another one. Then, while his fingers pleasured her, he took a mouthful of her breast.

Mia gasped, caught hold of his throbbing erection and ran her fingers up and down its length. In no time, both were panting in anticipation of what would come next.

John stopped and gazed into Mia's eyes. "I said I was going to eat you, but say if you'd rather I didn't?"

Trembling with excitement, she muttered, "I've never had oral sex before." Before John could comment, she continued. "A few of my friends have said how much pleasure they received while doing it; so; I'm willing to try it myself."

Chapter 9

After they kissed with tongues entangled, John moved down the bed, nibbling and kissing his way lower down Mia's trembling body. As he kissed her inner thighs and his tongue went to enter her wetness, she stiffened.

John stopped and looked up. "Do you want me to stop?" Mia closed her eyes and took a deep breath. "No," then spread her thighs.

"Are you sure? As you have not had oral sex before, I want you to enjoy the experience

Mia, wide-eyed and eager, muttered, "Your tongue and lips felt so good; carry on and don't stop."

"Good," he murmured as he resumed licking her wetness. As he sucked on her clit, she cried out, "Oh." With his hands squeezing her breasts and his mouth buried into her pussy, Mia could not keep still. As she writhed around, her squeals of delight grew louder until she cried out, "Oh, yes," as a climax burst inside her.

"Oh, my god, "she gasped, "Now I know what my friends meant about oral sex," She sighed, then spread her thighs in anticipation of John's next move. As she spoke, he moved up the bed, took a condom from under the pillows and slipped it on. Through half-closed eyes, Mia murmured, "There is no need, but if it makes you feel more relaxed, it's not a problem."

He nodded, straddled her, and eased the tip of his cock into her wetness. She drew in a sharp breath as it entered and he thrust deep inside. As he went to withdraw, Mia clasped him tight. "No, don't stop," she gasped. Then, as the heat built up again inside her, she said, "Oh, this feels so good. Why didn't I let you make love to me before."

"Never mind," John panted, as with her legs locked behind his back, and her fingers playing with his balls, they rocked up and down. A few minutes later, John shuddered as he came.

"Wow, that was fantastic," he gasped.

As they lay joined together, with Mia still trembling with excitement, she murmured, "I have never received so much pleasure when making love as what you gave me."

John grinned and said, "That's good, I'm happy to hear you enjoyed it as much as I did."

Mia gave a short giggle. "When you went down on me, I was nervous, but, what an incredible experience." She sighed. "Do you know something; you are such a wonderful lover. You made sure to satisfy me before you were." An impish smile made her mouth twitch as she continued. "From what I've heard from various of my friends, their boyfriends, and husbands are only interested in satisfaction for themselves. They don't seem to care if their partner gets satisfied or not."

John nodded. "Yes, I'm sure many men are like that. Still, for myself, the woman should get the same pleasure as the man."

Mia sighed. "I'm glad you think like that."

With both satisfied, once they had sorted themselves out, with Mia wrapped in John's arms, they fell asleep.

WHILE EATING BREAKFAST the following morning, John noticed Mia seemed far away.

"Is there anything wrong?"

She shook her head and kissed his cheek. Then, with her eyes caressing him, she said, "Can I ask you something?"

John's eyebrows pulled together in question. "Of course. We can ask each other whatever we like." He caught hold of her hands and pulled her down on his lap. "Now, what is it that's bothering you?"

Mia hesitated. "I know you will leave me shortly.... But... will I see you again?"

John's eyebrows shot up to his forehead and his smile fell away.

"What! Are you serious? Look, although I had no thoughts of romance when I came to Spain, I am glad I met you." Before Mia could comment, he went on to say, "and I don't only say it because we made love last night." He shrugged. "If I did not have to go, believe you me, I would stay here with you. But as it is, I have to go."

Mia brushed away the tears in her eyes. "Thank you, John. I know our making love did not influence what you said." She pulled him close, and gazing into his eyes said, "So, does it mean we will see each other again?"

With a wide smile stretched across his face, he said, "Of course, you can take that as guaranteed."

Mia took a deep breath. "What if I said I wanted to visit you in England?"

John's eyes lit up in unexpected pleasure. "Fabulous." With his eyebrows pulled together in question, he asked, "But what about your parents? I mean, what would they say about you going to England to see a man you have only known for a few days?"

Mia bobbed her head in agreement. "After I tell them what a wonderful and caring person you are, I am sure they won't object." A flicker of a smile crossed her lips. "Besides, I am not a child."

"That's for sure. You are an attractive and clever woman." He grinned. "I mean you picked me."

With her eyes shining bright, Mia said, "Yes, I did, and it's why I asked if I would see you again."

"Well, if you can sort things out with your parents and work, I'd welcome you with open arms." As John skimmed his lips along the sweep of her neck, he stopped. "If you remember, I said that I wondered what my friends would say if I told them about you. Therefore, it should prove interesting when they see you in the flesh."

On the day Mia went to the airport with John, although they had agreed to meet in England, she still had doubts. With an effort, she pushed these thoughts aside and tried hard not to break down and cry. John sensed her discomfort, as he held her close. However, he had already been away longer than planned. From some emails he had received, several people wanted his comments about him designing them a house. He shrugged. His architectural business was his main concern about going to live abroad.

As for Mia, she wondered how she would cope with John back in England. None of her previous boyfriends had ever made her feel like she did now. She shook her head. John was different. He never asked or demanded anything from her, especially on the matter of sex. The thought of which brought a smile to her face.

Still, she wondered what her parents might say when she told them about her plan of going to England. Although they could not prevent her, she did not want any problems between them. The fact John was English, not Spanish, was a minor issue. Mia put on a brave face as she kissed John goodbye at the customs section. With his head bent and shoulders slumped, John walked away. Before going inside, he turned and gave Mia a final wave, who blew him a kiss before he disappeared from view.

ON MIA'S RETURN TO her office, as she walked inside, Carlos noticed her downcast expression. He thought it due to their client Mr Philip's return to England. Until he arrived on the scene, his boss had seemed happy with her life. Also, when they came into the office two days ago, Mia looked a picture of happiness. Still, it was none of his business what his boss did in her private life.

Come to the end of the day, on Mia's return home alone to her apartment, she cheered up when Aza came to meet her.

"Hi Aza, you don't know how happy I am you are here. If you weren't, I would be all alone." She rubbed his head. "Anyway, first things first. Let's see if you need any food or water." After she filled

his dishes, the sound of him slurping his water brought a smile to
Mia's face.

After she prepared a salad for her dinner, she switched on the
television and then nibbled at what she had made. When her phone
rang and she opened it, her eyes lit with delight to see John's smiling
face.

"Hi Mia, I hope I didn't disturb you?"

"No, of course not. I have been waiting for your call to say you'd
arrived home safely."

"I did, but I can't say I'm happy to be here." She saw him shrug.
"I would much rather be with you in Spain."

Mia choked back a sob. "I wish you were too. I cannot believe I
feel as I do. You have only just gone."

"Yes, I know. It's the same with me." As they talked, John realised
Mia was concerned about speaking with her parents. However, it was
something she had to do alone.

While talking and seeing John's face, Mia felt calmer. It seemed
to make the distance between them unimportant. Given her
determination to go to England, she decided to speak to her parents
and explain all about John.

She gave a silent giggle. "Well, not everything. Their lovemaking
was something she would not mention to anyone, least of all her
parents." Then a thought struck her. "John, when you have Lucky
back, show him to me on your phone. I would like to see him., and I
will show his picture to Aza."

"Hey, that's a great idea. The next time we talk, if you do the same
with Aza, they will have seen each other.... Oh, there is one thing we
never talked about."

"What is it?"

"Well, I wonder how the two of them will get on when I bring
Lucky over?"

Mia raised her eyebrows. "As a dog lover, I never thought you would come without him."

"We...ll it might mean a larger apartment or even a house."

Mia's eyes lit up at the thought of them all in one place. But, of course, it would all depend on her parent's reaction when she told them about John.

After a long chat in which they repeatedly said how much they missed each other, they exchanged kisses and said goodbye.

Chapter 10

Although it had been good to talk with Mia, it made John feel sad. He would only look for a property in Barcelona, but would discuss this with Mia. She might have some suggestions about this.

For her part, Mia decided she would talk with her parents as soon as possible. Although it would be easier to tell them during a phone call, she would tell them in person.

Later, ongoing to bed and cuddling her pillow, Mia thought of how she and John had made love. He had been so gentle and gave her such a fantastic climax. The thought of which gave her a warm feeling between her thighs. She sighed and before falling asleep, wondered when they would next make love.

ALTHOUGH ONLY THIRTY-eight, John had qualified early and soon built a reputation for his outstanding house designs. Given this, he contacted the three people who had expressed a wish for him to design them a house.

When he explained about his move to Spain, two thanked him and wished him well. The third, a Mr Dawes, said, "If you can design me a house as I want and recommend a reliable builder that would be fine." To John's surprise, he added, "I would cover your expenses if you come over once or twice to check on the ongoing works."

This sounded a good deal, but John said, "First, let us meet. After you tell/show me what kind of house you would like, I'll be able to say yes or no to your offer."

Mr Dawe chuckled. "You let me know when you can come up to London, at my expense, of course, and we can discuss this further."

"Many thanks, Mr Dawe. Once I check out my schedule, I'll be in touch."

"Good, I'll await your call."

Meanwhile, Mia lacked the courage to call and arrange to visit her parents. She and John talked most evenings, and she looked forward to when they did. The sound of his voice was like music to her ears.

John sighed when Mia let slip her concern about what her parents might say.

"I'm sorry, but it's something only you can tell them." He paused. Mia thought their connection had broken, then John said, "That's if you are sure, you still want to come and see me?"

"Of course, I am going to come. Wild horses wouldn't prevent me from not.... unless it's you that has changed your mind about my coming?"

John laughed. "There's no chance of that happening from my side," he said. "There is more chance of getting blood from a stone."

Mia sighed with relief at his words. She had not expected John to change his mind, but was happy to hear him say so. After they said goodnight, Mia vowed to call her parents the next day.

In the meantime, John had gone to London to meet Mr Dawe. On his arrival, when shown into his office, apart from Mr Dawe, he found a striking young blonde woman sitting there.

Mr Dawe rose from behind his desk and held out a hand. "Welcome, Mr Phillips, and thank you for coming." A slight cough made him turn towards the blonde. "Sorry, this is my daughter

Sylvia. Darling, this is Mr Phillips, who I hope will design our new house."

A glance showed John, with a trim figure and long curling hair; Sylvia looked like a model.

She flashed him a dazzling smile and held out her hand. As he took hold of it, John noticed her beautifully manicured nails.

"Nice to meet you." On her releasing his hand that he thought she held longer than necessary, he turned back to Mr Dawe.

He was grinning after watching his daughter and John's reaction. "Right, now let's get down to business." He then explained what he had in mind regarding the design of his proposed house. As John listened, he could sense Sylvia's eyes locked on him. He gave an inward chuckle. Although she seemed interested in him, as far as he was concerned, she was wasting her time if she thought differently.

Mr Dawe, however, was another matter. John found him amiable and also one who knew what he wanted. After a long discussion how the exterior should look, they agreed on costs.

John would provide detailed drawings of both the outside and the interior of the house. As for his move to Spain, John told him this was definite. He did, however, agree that unless something unforeseen happened, he would check on things during the house construction. After they shook hands on the deal, John shook hands with Sylvia and then left. As the door closed behind him, John was glad Mia had not been with him. She would not have been unhappy about Sylvia's apparent interest in him.

On his way back home, John's mind was on preparing preliminary sketches for Mr Dawe's comments. He also decided not to mention his daughter Sylvia when he later spoke and told Mia of his new project.

During their next talk on the phone, Mia's heart sank when John told her his news. "Oh, does it mean you won't be coming to live in Spain?"

"WHAT! DON'T BE SILLY. Nothing is going to change my mind about that. Anyway, have you spoken to your parents yet?"

"Not in person, but I've arranged to see them this weekend. ... Wish me luck."

On noticing her look of concern, John said, "I am sure they won't raise too many objections. After all, you are only going to visit me."

"Yes, I know, but I hope I'll feel better after we have talked."

"So, which day will that be?"

"Sunday. I'm going to lunch. I said I wanted to talk to them, so they will be wondering what I have to say."

"Now don't worry. Oh, and once you have told them, call me. I'll want to know what your parents say."

"Of course. I only hope it will be good news I'll have for you."

COME SUNDAY, MIA FELT nervous when she knocked on her parents' door. It opened wide to reveal her mother, who embraced her.

"Oh, it is so good to see you." She held Mia at arm's length and looked her over.

"You look well, but your eyes show you have a problem. Still, never mind, come inside, and let us talk. Your father's washing his hands, he has been out in the garden."

No sooner than the two women sat in the lounge than her father came in to join them. As Mia stood, he took her in his arms and kissed her cheeks. His lips then turned into a grin. "Well, as you've come to tell us something in person, it must be important." With his eyebrows raised in concern, he asked, "Are you alright? You're not sick, are you?"

To his and her mother's relief, Mia shook her head. "No, I'm fine."

Once her father had poured them all a glass of wine, he sat down. "So, what is so special you could not tell us on the phone."

After taking a deep breath, Mia explained about John. To her relief, with a wide smile stretched across his face, her father said, "Thank you, my daughter. You are a grown woman and don't need our permission to go to England. However, it was good you thought of us before going." He chuckled. "So, tell us about this John? How old is he? What is his job, and last, is he a Catholic or a Christian?"

A satisfied smile raced across Mia's face. "John is thirty-eight and an architect." She gave a nervous glance at her mother and father. "He is a Christian." Before either could comment, she went on to say, "John's wife died two years ago in a traffic accident, and he came to Spain to make a new start." Then unsure of what they would say, she looked from her mother to her father.

Her father shook his head. "His not being of the same religion as you, is not a problem for us." His eyebrows then pulled together in question. "I only hope this John is better than Manuel, your last boyfriend. I am sorry to say I did not like him."

"Nor I," her mother added.

Mia sighed with relief at her father's words. "No, John is much different. He never asks or demands anything from me."

Her father cocked an eyebrow. "Well, I am pleased to hear that. Manuel always acted as though he was the boss, and what you said did not matter."

A relieved look flashed across Mia's face. "I'm sorry, father, you are right, but at the time, I never realised." She shrugged. "It's the reason we split up. My friends told me the same thing."

Her mother spoke. "If you are going to England to see this John, you must think a great deal of him?" As Mia went to speak, she put a hand up. "Please let me finish. What do you expect from this relationship? Are you thinking long-term?"

Mia glanced from her mother to her father, who sat grinning. "Yes, my daughter, I too await your answer?"

Mia sighed. "I can't explain it, but I felt attracted to John the moment I saw him in my office."

Her father nodded. "I know what you mean. The moment I saw your mother, I knew I wanted to marry her. Now, what? Thirty-four years later, here we are still happily married." He glanced at his wife. "So, what have you got to say to your daughter? I've said my piece."

"As long as you are sure of what you are doing? I wish you well. You are our beloved daughter, and we only want what is best for you." Then she turned to her husband. "I'm sure I speak for both of us when I say I would like to meet your John."

"Yes, it would be good." He grinned. "There, did you think we would not give our blessings about you going to see a man you are in love with?"

Mia embraced her mother and father. "I wasn't sure what you would say, but I hoped to have your blessing."

Her father cocked an eyebrow. "Now you have heard what we have said, but would you have still gone if we had objected?" Mia cast her eyes down. "Yes, but I would rather have had your blessings."

Her father pulled her close and kissed her cheeks. "Good, it means you are serious about this John. Now, let us sit and enjoy the lunch your mother has prepared." As he moved towards the dining table, he stopped. "Would you like to call and inform John you have our blessing about going to see him?"

Mia's eyes lit up. "Yes, he is waiting to know what you would say when I told you about him." She took out her phone and called him.

As John answered, he said, "I've been waiting for your call. So, is it good news or bad?"

"It's good. My parents have no problems with my going to see you. In fact, they are looking forward to meeting you on your return to Barcelona." She giggled and then turned the phone towards her parents. "You can say hello to them if you like?"

John waved. "Hello, Mr & Mrs Alvarez. Thank you for your agreement. I promise to take great care of your daughter and look forward to meeting you."

After her parents waved back to John, Mia gave him a subtle wink. "I will call you later." After enjoying a delicious lunch, they sat by the fire, where they had a good chat. When Mia mentioned John designed houses, her father's eyebrows rose. 'Now this could prove of interest,' he said to himself.

By the time she left her parents, it was a far happier Mia who returned home to be welcomed by Aza.

Chapter 11

WHEN MIA NEXT TALKED to John, from the sound of her voice, he knew something good had happened.

"Okay, what's happened? You sound as though you have won the lottery?"

She giggled. "Not the lottery, but my father called me this morning."

John gave a whisk of a smile. "Well, whatever he said, it must have good news? So, what did he say?"

Mia's smile widened. "He asked if I was sure how I felt about you. I told him I could not wish for a better man. I said you were loving, caring, generous and treated me with respect. He was happy to hear this and gave us his blessings." She paused, "He also said I should be careful and make sure nothing happens to change things." Mia giggled. "Although he never said that, he meant for me not to get pregnant."

"Yes, and that's why I wanted to wear a condom when we made love. It's also why I will next time."

"Well," she muttered, "you'd best make sure you have some when I come over in September."

John laughed. "Have no fear; I will. Anyway, I am delighted at what your father said, and understand why you sound so happy."

"Yes, it made me want to jump for joy." She paused, and then John saw her shake her head. "Oh, I almost forgot, my father said when you are next here, he wants to talk with you."

When she noticed a crease appear on John's forehead and his eyebrows rose, she shook her head. "There is no need to look worried. He said to tell you he will not have his shotgun with him when you talk."

John gave a short laugh. "There is no need for him to be concerned about our relationship, so he won't need his shotgun

At his words, Mia's eyes opened wide and her face broke out in a broad smile.

"Oh, really? No, you don't have to answer that," she tittered. "I know and am happy to hear what you have not said." She gave him a subtle wink. "I guess it might sound funny, but I know what you mean."

With a wide smile stretched across his face, John said, "Well, that's another week gone until we are together again." With his eyebrows pulled together in question, he asked, "So what your father wants to talk about? If it is not about us, what is it?"

She pressed a hand to her mouth to stifle a giggle. "I do not know. You will have to wait until you are here to find out."

He gave a nod of acknowledgement. "Anyway, if possible, I will return to Barcelona with you after your visit. Oh, that reminds me. How long do you intend to stay? You never said?"

He heard Mia sigh. "Wel...l, I thought two weeks? I am sorry, but I can't stay away from the office any longer."

"I understand, so no problem. Look, although I am sure you will enjoy your time over here, remember, where I live is nothing like where you do. From a large city, this will be a huge difference.... A look of concern crossed his face as he said, "I only hope you don't get homesick?"

Mia pressed a hand to her mouth to stifle a giggle. "Don't worry, John. As long as I am with you, I'll be happy."

"I know, but I don't want you to feel disappointed when you are here?"

"John, please, I know what you are saying, but I'll be fine. I mean, we will be happy together."

"Yes, that is one thing I am sure of. Still, reference your father, I will have to wait until we meet before finding out what he wants to talk about. Still, it cannot be anything serious."

Mia's smile widened. "When I arrive at Gatwick, I take it you will be there to meet me?"

"Of course. I will be waiting in the arrival's hall with open arms, and a bouquet of flowers."

Mia, her eyes bright with excitement, said, "Never mind the flowers. As long as you will be there, I'll be happy."

Love shone in John's eyes as he said, "Yes, and all I want is you. Now, although I'll leave home early, if traffic is bad and I get held up, call me or my secretary Joan. You have my business card."

As they said goodnight, John did not know what was in store for him.

Although time seemed to pass slowly, it came to the day when Mia would fly over to England. Wearing a broad smile and looking a picture of happiness, she boarded the flight to Gatwick. Within the short space of three hours, she would be once again in John's arms. With this in mind, her feet tapped on the floor as her excitement rose.

Meanwhile, in England, after a last check to see all was ready for Mia's arrival, John locked up, then climbed into his old but trusty Volvo.

On the way to Gatwick, John could not have been happier. His head was bobbing to the music coming from his favourite music channel. Soon he would have Mia back in his arms. Plus, he knew she would be pleased with the red roses he had for her.

As usual, traffic was heavy, but John was making good time. With it only thirty-five miles to the airport, he would soon be there. Suddenly, his smile turned to one of shock, when another vehicle smashed into his. As his car spun after being hit by a second one, his thoughts turned to Jasmin's accident.

Then, the last thing John thought of before he blacked out was Mia.

Not knowing this, having cleared the long customs queue at Gatwick and collected her case, Mia was excited as she walked into the arrival's hall.

However, her joy turned to disappointment when she found no sign of John. She shrugged. As he had mentioned, traffic must have been bad.

After sitting waiting for thirty minutes and still no sign of John, she wondered where he was. She waited another ten minutes, then opened her handbag. Taking out John's business card, she punched in his number on her cell phone. To her dismay, there was no answer, so she called Joan, his secretary. When she answered, Mia said who she was and John was not there.

"Oh, how strange," Joan said. "He left early to make sure he was there to meet you. Anyway, while I'll see what I can find out, you go and get yourself a coffee and relax."

> To avoid causing Mia extra concern, Joan did not mention her husband George. He was a police patrol driver on the M3, the route John would have taken to the airport.

She called him and explained about John not arriving at Gatwick. "Have there been any accidents on the motorway today?" she asked.

To her dismay, he said, "Yes, I am at one crash site now. About eight cars were involved in a pile-up. Look, I'll call you back after I've looked to see if John's Volvo is among them."

Five minutes later, George rang back. "John's car is here. From what I gather, along with some other people, an ambulance took them to Southampton General Hospital." On hearing her gasp of alarm, he said, "I don't think any of them were badly injured. Look, Gilbert,' office is near the airport, and it's about his time to leave. Call and ask him if he could pick up Mia."

"Great idea, and thanks." She rang off and then called Gilbert. When he heard of John's accident, he said, "No problem, I can be there in ten minutes." He chuckled. "Call Mia and tell her another handsome man will soon be there to take her to him."

She gave a short laugh, then said, "Okay, and many thanks, Gilbert." On calling Mia back, Joan explained what had happened.

"Oh my god," she gasped. "Is John alright?"

"Don't panic." Although not sure of John's injuries, Joan said, "He's not badly injured, and our friend Gilbert will be there soon to take you to him." As she closed her phone, Joan shook her head. 'Poor girl, what a way to start a holiday. Still, from what John has said about Mia, the sight of him will cheer her up.'

Frantic with worry over John, when a tall, well-dressed man in a suit and tie, entered the arrivals hall. Mia jumped to her feet. As he looked around, she guessed it must be John's friend Gilbert. He noticed Mia's worried expression, so came over and flashed her a smile. "Hi, are you Mia?"

She nodded and shook his hand. "Yes, but what has happened to John? His secretary said he was involved in an accident on his way here."

"So, I understand. Anyway, I will take you to him; it won't take long." He took the handle of her case and led Mia outside. Once in his car, he said, "I am sorry this has happened. John will be quite upset about not being here to meet you." He chuckled. "You certainly made an impression on him. He hasn't stopped talking about you since he arrived back from Spain." As he spoke, he thought, yes, and I'm not surprised; you are an attractive woman.

On arrival at the hospital and Gilbert enquiring, a receptionist told him where John was. They found him sitting up in bed in a recovery room. As soon as she saw John, Mia rushed towards him. Then, when she noticed the blood stains on his jacket, she cried out, "Oh, are you hurt?"

To her relief, he shook his head. "No, I'm fine." He shrugged. "The blood came from my nose after it hit the sun visor. Anyway, I'm sorry for not being there when you arrived. Oh, and the roses I bought are in my car."

"Never mind the roses," she gasped. "I am only sorry you had an accident on your way to meet me." Her lips trembled as she went on to say, "I've been worried sick ever since I heard what had happened. Still, thank heavens you are all right."

"Yes, never mind the flowers John," Gilbert said, cutting in. "How are you?" With tears running down her face, Mia said, "Yes, what does the doctor say?"

"He said, I am okay. It seems when another car hit mine, the sun visor came down. My head hit it and it knocked me unconscious. Because of this, they brought in to check if I had not suffered anything else. Anyway, all is well. I'm now waiting for the doctor to sign my release papers. Once done, I can then go."

Chapter 12

As they spoke, a doctor walked in, who, on seeing Mia and Gilbert, flashed a smile.

"Well, Mr Philips, you and your friends will be pleased to hear you can leave. A check revealed you had suffered no internal injuries." He gave a grim smile. "Unfortunately, several occupants of the other cars involved in your accident were not so lucky." After signing the papers, he said, "Take care," then left.

As John swung his legs off the bed and stood, Mia, not caring about Gilbert, embraced and kissed him.

He chuckled. "Alright, save that until you two are alone." John turned and said, "Many thanks Gilbert, I owe you one."

"No problem, I'm only too pleased to have met this delightful lady friend of yours."

Once in his car, as they set off, Gilbert asked, "So, what happened, John?" He sighed, squeezed Mia's hand, and then explained. "It seems after a car had a blowout, it slid and hit my car. It also hit a few more cars, with one sending me skidding sideways into the barrier. The next thing I knew was when I came to and found myself in the hospital." He kissed Mia's cheek. "I'm so sorry. Mia, I knew you would be worried about my not being there to meet you."

"I was, so I called Joan. She told me to relax with a cup of coffee." Mia shuddered when she remembered how Joan had called back to say John was in a hospital.

She leaned forward to Gilbert. "Thank you so much for coming to get me. As a way of thanks, John and I will take you and your wife out for dinner, at my expense." She flashed him a smile. "It's the least I can do."

"That's a great idea," John said, "Only I'll be the one paying, not you."

Gilbert laughed. "Okay, don't fight over this."

John kissed Mia on the cheek. "No problem, we won't."

On arrival at John's house, as she climbed out of the car, Mia's eyes lit up. "Oh, this looks even better than the photo you showed me."

Gilbert, who had taken her case from the boot, said, "Yes, and I'm sure you will like the interior even more so. Anyway, John, call us when it's good for Wendy and me to come over."

"Sure thing, and many thanks," John said.

As Gilbert went to leave, Mia kissed him on the cheek. "Yes, thank you, and I look forward to meeting your wife."

As Gilbert left and they entered the house, John thought back to when he and Jasmin had first moved into their newly built barn conversion. Those had been happy times. He shrugged and said to himself, 'I'm sorry, Jasmin, but I hope you don't mind Mia being here.'

After a glance around, with her eyes bright with excitement, Mia said, "Yes, I can see what Gilbert meant. This looks wonderful."

John swept her up in his arms. "Maybe, but not as good as you." They then collapsed onto the sofa and enjoyed a long and passionate kiss. As they broke it off, Mia sighed. "You don't know how happy I am to be here with you." She shuddered. "When I heard you were in hospital after being involved in a car crash, I almost died of shock. Still, thank heavens you were not badly injured. If you were, I don't know what I would have done." She paused. "I must thank your secretary, Joan. She was wonderful and helped me to relax."

John nodded. "Yes, after what she has done today, I'll have to give her a pay rise." After he helped Mia to her feet John held her at arm's length. As he gazed at her, it took him back to when Jasmin was alive. The moment passed, and instead, it was Mia standing there.

Mia, who had noticed John's expression change, realised that times like this must remind him of his late wife. However, before she could speak, John said, "You look like a dream come true." He waved a hand. "How I've managed without you since I've been back, I do not know."

Mia gave a short laugh. "In that case, I suggest you come with me when I return to Barcelona." Before John could respond, she added, "Of course, that's my idea, but you might not agree?"

John's smile changed to a frown. "I would love to, but first I must sell the house." He paused, then to Mia's surprise said, "Darling." As he gazed into Mia's eyes, he said, "I called you darling in Spain, but do you mind me calling you, darling?"

Mia's shriek of delight as she flung her arms around him, said she approved. Hugging him close, she said, "Mind! Of course not. I am only too happy for you to call me darling."

"In that case, what would you say if I said I love you?"

With her eyes opened wide, she said, "What can I say except I love you too." They then enjoyed a long and tender kiss. As they broke it off, Mia cast a mischievous smile.

"Right, that's all you get for now, but wait until later."

Her words made John's eyes light up. He put up his hands and said, "I might have suffered a knock on the head during the crash, but I've not gone crazy. I would have to be if I refused what sounds like an offer of what I have been missing."

Mia's eyebrows shot up. "Do you think you are the only one who has missed our making love?" As she spoke, the thought of when they had, caused a dampness to spread between her thighs.

When she noticed a sparkle appear in John's eyes, Mia shook her head. "If you can wait until tonight, we'll be able to enjoy ourselves much better." She winked. "I mean, after people hear of your accident, you may get some visitors?"

He nodded. "You're right." His lips then turned into a grin. "Oh, I forgot, Lucky is in the kitchen. I'll let him out."

As if he knew what John had said, Lucky barked. The next minute, as John opened the door, Lucky came in like a bullet from a gun. When he saw Mia, he jumped up and down wagging his tail in excitement.

"Oh, what big boy you are," Mia said, as she patted and stroked him. "I feel sure you and Aza will get on fine together."

John, who had followed Lucky over to Mia, nodded. "I hope so. Like us, I would like them to become friends."

Mia shot a hand to her mouth. "Yes, but one big difference, they are not liable to become lovers."

"That's true." As John gazed at Mia with love in his eyes, he asked, "Are you happy with us becoming lovers? I know I am."

"I'm more than happy." she exclaimed, then kissed John on the cheek. "Still, it's hard to believe we are in love after such a short time."

"Yes, but although it happened so fast, for sure, I love you."

Mia sighed. "When my friends heard, I intended going to England to see you, they said I was either mad or in love. So, when I, or I hope we return, I'll tell them it's love, not madness." She then looked down at Lucky. "Now, if you let me get up, you can show me around the rest of your house."

John spoke to Lucky, who got up off Mia and lay on the floor, shaking his tail.

"Oh, you are a good boy," Mia said.

John nodded. "So am I, but don't expect me to wag my tail like Lucky does." When Mia laughed, the sound was like music in John's ears. He caught hold of her hand and led her into the kitchen. When she noticed the size and all the fitted units, her eyes lit up.

"Wow. Now, this is what I call a real kitchen." She cocked an eyebrow. "Do you do much cooking? I mean," she said, waving a hand.

He shrugged. "I used to, but not for some time. Still, if you like, I can always cook you something."

Mia flashed her long eyelashes. "I'm sure you can give me something I like without going into the kitchen?"

John gave a dirty laugh. "I would like to think so." As he pulled her to him, she felt his tongue push between her lips and into her mouth. Her excitement rose even higher when she felt his hardness thrust between her legs.

"Later," she gasped as she pushed him away. "You haven't shown me upstairs yet. Nor where I'll be sleeping."

Chapter 13

J ohn shook his head. "I'm not sure if it's a good idea to go upstairs right now. I might not be able to control myself. Anyway, as for where you will sleep, I'll give you one guess." Before she could comment, he said," In bed with me." He cocked an eyebrow. "I think I'll turn the heating down, so you will want to cuddle into me to keep warm."

Mia pulled him close. "You will not need to adjust the heating. I'll be hot and passionate when I feel your body against mine."

"Oh no," he moaned. "You are making it even harder for me to show you upstairs." He grinned. "Still, I'm willing to take a chance if you are?"

As they climbed the stairs, Mia realised there was a walkway around the upstairs, it showed the lounge cathedral ceiling off to perfection.

She squeezed John's hand. "Even without going into the bedrooms, this is fabulous."

"Thank you. I'm pleased you approve."

Ongoing into what John said was his bedroom, Mia nodded. "This looks great." He opened a door set in one wall and beckoned to her. As she went to look, Mia gasped at the sight of a large jacuzzi bath that took up most of the room.

"Oh, yes," she exclaimed. "Now, this looks interesting." She fluttered her long eyelashes. "I think it's big enough for two?"

John angled a sideways glance at Mia. "I guess we could always try it out?" He shot her a look of anticipation. "That's if you would like too of course?"

Mia's cheeks coloured. "I've never showered with a man before, but... with you, I might."

"Well, I suppose I could be persuaded to join you if you do." As both laughed, John pulled her close and they embraced.

Once back in the lounge, Mia asked, "Shall we take Lucky out for a walk?" John laughed. "Well, as he's sat there looking at us, I guess the answer is yes."

She turned and patted Lucky's head. "Come on. You can show me where your master takes you."

With John holding his lead in one hand and Mia's hand in the other, they went out. As they walked along, the sun shining through the swaying branches of various trees, brought a smile to Mia's face. It reminded her of where her parents lived. John speaking brought her back to where they were as he said, "This is Gilbert and Wendy house. I'll call them when we get back. If it's alright, we'll visit them."

Mia squeezed his hand. "Yes, please do."

After a pleasant walk along narrow lanes with houses set back behind smart-looking lawns, they returned to John's house. Once he had wiped his feet and let Lucky off his lead, he disappeared into the kitchen.

As John and Mia sat down on the sofa, she said, "Our walk was much different from when I take out Aza for a walk."

"Well, as you live in a large city and this is a small town in the country, I guess it is."

Picking up his phone, Mia heard John say, "Hi Wendy, I'm calling to see if it's alright for Mia and me to come over? It is, great. We will be there in about twenty minutes."

Closing his phone, he said, "There you are, all set. Now come here; I want to feel you in my arms." He winked. "It will remind me what I have to look forward to tonight."

Mia's eyebrows rose. "Oh, and what have you planned?" She giggled. "Will I like it?"

He skimmed his lips along the nape of her neck. "I hope so, as I'm sure I will." They then enjoyed a long and passionate kiss.

"Do you know something? I'm so happy and content to be in your arms." She winked. "If you do not feel up to taking me out, I won't mind staying at home." When she noticed John's expression change, she said, "No, I don't mean now; I'm looking forward to seeing Gilbert's wife, Wendy."

John flashed an innocent smile. "After tonight, I'll be happy to stay at home in bed with you any time you like." He shook his head. "Whether we make love or not, I'll get great satisfaction just holding you close."

Mia bobbed her head in agreement. "Yes, it would be wonderful."

He shrugged. "Anyway, when you are ready, we will go." After checking Lucky was alright, they left him in the lounge, went out and locked up.

After a short and pleasant walk, John opened a gate and gestured for Mia to enter. As they walked up a pathway to the front door of a house, John kissed Mia on the cheek before he knocked on the door. It opened to reveal Gilbert, with a smiling woman standing behind him, who Mia guessed was Wendy.

Gilbert chuckled. "Ah, there you are. We wondered if you could tear yourselves away from your place." He then gasped as Wendy poked him in the back.

"Take no notice of him," she said. "Please come in." As Mia entered, Wendy shook her hand. "Welcome, Mia. I was sorry to hear your arrival did not go as planned. Still, thank heaven John was not injured."

"Yes, I would have been devastated had anything bad happened to him." When she heard what Mia had said, Wendy said to herself, 'So, things are more serious between them than what we'd thought.' Flashing a smile, she said, "As would Gilbert and me. We have known John for some years, and he is a dear friend." Her smile then widened. "I'm sure you will also become a good friend." She shook her head. "When John said he wanted to live abroad and I suggested Spain, I never expected him to find such a lovely woman like you."

Mia's cheeks reddened as she replied, "Thank you. When John and I talked on the phone about some properties he wanted to see, I did not know he would affect me the way he did." She sighed. "I owe you a big vote of thanks. John has made such a difference in my life, and to his as well, I hope?"

"That is a definite yes," John said, with a wide smile stretched across his face.

"So, what are you going to do about Lucky when you go to Spain?" Gilbert asked.

"I shall take him with me. After all, I could never go and leave him behind. Plus, Mia has a huge Doberman named Aza. We only hope they will get on well together?"

"Well, we do," Mia tittered, "so I'm sure they will."

Neither Gilbert nor Wendy asked questions about where John would be living. They had a good idea, but it was none of their business, so kept their thoughts to themselves. Instead, they were only too pleased to see John back to his old self.

Chapter 14

After a pleasant evening with Gilbert and Wendy, John, and Mia left and returned to John's house. Once inside and the door closed, John led Mia to the sofa, where cuddled together, they enjoyed a long and tender kiss.

"That's what I've been missing," Mia murmured on breaking it off. "It was nice to chat with Gilbert and Wendy, but I'm glad we left when we did."

"Yes. To cuddle you and feel your lips on mine is far better than talking," John said, "even with good friends."

Mia cuddled in closer to him. "Yes, without a doubt." She sighed and kissed his cheek. "I have missed you more than I thought possible." After kissing him again, she said, "Do you know something? I never thought I could be as happy as I am with you."

"That's good." John shook his head. "Had you seen me six months ago, you would never have given me a second look. Then, I was a mess, and so was the house." He shrugged. "I had no interest in anything." His face then lit up with a smile. "I have to thank Gilbert and Wendy for inviting me in for New Year's dinner. As I was going there, I shaved, something I'd not bothered to do for some months." He gave a wry smile. "Thinking back, I must have looked down and out. Anyway, while we talked, I said about moving abroad. I told them I had looked for a house in South Africa." His face broke into a wide smile. "I had even thought about having one built at a wild animal rehabilitation centre in Thailand." At Mia's look of puzzlement, he chuckled. "I once worked there as a volunteer."

She shook her head, pulled him towards her, and kissed him. "All I can say is thank heaven you didn't and looked in Spain."

"Well, as Wendy said, it was her suggestion I did."

"Yes, and it is something I will always be thankful for her doing." A flicker of a smile crossed her face. "So, what are we going to do for dinner?" When she noticed the sudden gleam in John's eyes, she giggled. "I mean like food on a plate, not me."

John licked his lips. "Well, I suppose I can wait." When Mia's eyes flashed, he added, "It's alright; I only joked."

She gave a short laugh. "Oh, that is a pity. I thought you would rather have me than a plate of food?" As John went to catch hold of her, she giggled and jumped to her feet. "I think we could both manage to wait until after we have eaten? Besides, Lucky is watching us."

John shook his head. "Okay, you win Lucky. We will have a short walk, and then this gorgeous lady and I will eat." He wagged a finger at Lucky. "What happens after that, you don't need to know."

Mia put a hand to her mouth to stifle a giggle. "Sorry, Lucky, but Aza is also a male, not a bitch."

With John holding Lucky's lead in one hand and Mia's hand in the other, they went out. Although the temperature had dropped from earlier, both were too happy to notice as they walked along.

Once back inside the house, John asked, "Now what would you prefer. I stocked up so you can have fish or a meat dish?"

"Whichever you fancy. I mean, what we don't have tonight, we can eat another time."

"That's a point. In the meantime, I have to find out how bad my car is. If it's too bad; I'll hire a car while it's being repaired. Still, never mind about the car. Would you like to watch television or listen to music while I'm in the kitchen?"

"Some music would be nice." Mia cocked an eyebrow. "What type do you have?"

John grinned, led her over to a wall cabinet and opened a door to reveal it full of CDs.

Waving a hand, he said, "You'll find a wide variety of music from country and western to rock-n-roll. Oh, and there is also quite a selection of jazz, which is my favourite. I like to relax and listen to jazz with a drink."

Mia's eyebrows shot up. "Oh, I also love jazz, and some classical music."

"So, that's something else we have a common interest in."

Mia turned towards him and flashed a warm smile. "Yes, and I'm sure we will find more things as we go along."

"No doubt." As he showed her how to operate the stereo, his thoughts again returned to Jasmin. They had spent many happy hours sitting listening to music. He shrugged. It was yet another reason to sell up and move away.

"Right, I'll be in the kitchen." As he went to leave, he stopped. "Would you like a glass of wine, or have one later."

"Later would be best. I don't want to end up drunk before dinner." Mia gave a mischievous smile. "I mean, you might try and take advantage of me?"

John gave a dirty laugh. "As if I would do a thing like that," he said, and still laughing, went into the kitchen.

While sitting relaxed on the sofa, Mia felt at home. She knew that her and John would have a wonderful time together. Then, on thinking about later and going to bed, Mia felt a wetness between her thighs. It made her look forward to this, and knew John was as well.

Chapter 15

After what seemed only a short time, John entered and announced with a flourish, "Dinner is ready." He helped Mia to her feet, then led her into the dining room. Her eyes lit with surprise and delight, to find candles burning in fancy holders on the table.

"Oh, this looks wonderful," she said, fluttering her eyelashes. "Are you expecting someone special to join us?"

He shook his head. "No, and I don't want anyone to come; this is for a special lady in my life." His lips brushed against her cheek as he gave her a gentle peck. "In case you don't know who, it's you."

Mia felt herself colour at his words. "Thank you for your kind words, John."

Once she had sat down, John brought in two plates. The aroma rising from what was on them made Mia's nose twitch. When he removed the covers, her eyes lit up to see chicken slices, mushrooms, and peas, covered with a delicious smelling sauce. In a separate dish, he said, is fluffy steamed rice.

"I am impressed," she exclaimed. "This looks wonderful."

John bowed. "Thank you. I only hope you enjoy eating it as much as you do, admiring the look?"

After she had finished, Mia rose and kissed John on the cheek. "Thank you, it was delicious." She gave him a subtle wink. "With you cooking meals like that, I can see we won't go hungry."

"Thank you, but if I remember, you cooked us a lovely meal at your place."

Once they had eaten and cleared away, on returning to the lounge, John called George.

"Hi, George, Sorry to trouble you, but do you know where my car is? I guess it's a bit of a mess?"

No problem, John, and yes, your car took a bit of a beating. Still, you were fortunate to have been in a Volvo. They are well-built, and no doubt saved you from serious injuries. Anyway, it's in our police pound, close to where the accident happened. I can take you there." George laughed, then said, "As you have your lady friend with you, maybe later would be better?"

"No, sooner would be best. I need to contact my insurance company, as I'll need another car."

"In that case, I suggest you inform them where the car is. They should be able to view it without you having to be there."

"Yes, good idea, and thanks, George. If you send me details of where it is, I'll pass it on to them. Still, if my car is too bad, they may write it off."

A few minutes after John had closed his phone, a ring told him George had sent the required details.

John turned to Mia. "My car is a mess, so tomorrow I'll inform my insurance company and get a hire car." He shrugged. "It's nice living here, but you need a car."

"Yes, that is one advantage of living in a city. If you don't have a car, you can use public transport or take a taxi."

"Maybe, but I've been used to having a car since I was old enough to drive."

Mia giggled. "Well, you may not have a car at present, but at least you have me."

He gave her a wolfish smile "Yes, and I know which I'd rather have," then pulled her close. As his tongue pushed inside her mouth and he kissed her, it sent Mia's emotions on fire.

Chapter 16

"Wait, she panted, "Let's go upstairs to yours or maybe it's our bedroom."

John couldn't help but chuckle. "It's ours, and that's a great idea." They were soon in bed and wrapped tight in each other's arms. With lips kissing and tongues in each other's mouths, both were getting horny.

While John caressed and nibbled on her breasts, his fingers stroked her pussy, driving Mia mad with desire.

"I hope you have a condom at hand, she muttered, "or I will take you inside me without one?"

John reached under his pillow, took one out, and slipped it on. The next minute, Mia gasped as he pushed himself inside her wet and eagerly waiting pussy.

"Oh yes. I've missed this."

"That makes two of us." He shook his head. "Since we made love in your apartment, I've longed to do it again."

"Me too," she muttered.

With both desperate to make love, although short-lived, it left both happy and content.

On their return to the lounge, anyone who came to visit, would know at a glance they had just made love. The radiance on Mia's face and her eyes gleaming bright was an unmistakable giveaway.

As for John, his cheeks were red, with a broad smile spread across his face. "That was great," he murmured as he nibbled her neck.

"Yes, wonderful," she sighed.

After John poured them a glass of wine, while sitting on the sofa cuddled together, they looked as happy as a pair of Lovebirds.

Mia sat up and turned to face him. She bit her lip, then said, "As you have not said, I guess you won't be coming back to Spain with me?"

John shook his head. "It does not look as though it will be possible. I'd hoped I could, but I'm still waiting on a definite offer on the house. Although several people have viewed it and said they liked it, none have put in an offer." He leaned over and kissed her cheek. "Still, with you here; who knows, someone may. Anyway, since you mentioned the house, what should I send out to Spain? Once we've decided, I'll get a removal company to give me a price and how long it would take to get there. Oh, and if I do, where am I going to put it once it arrives?"

Mia gave a subtle wink. "Yes, well, I've given that some thought."

"Ah, you have, have you. So, what have you come up with?"

"I would like us to live together." She gazed into John's eyes, waiting for his answer. "But, although I don't think my father would object, I'm not so sure about my mother. Anyway, I've found a storage company where you could store anything you send over."

"My, you have been a busy bee."

"Of course, I am trying to prevent any delay in your moving to Spain." She sighed. "The sooner you are there with me, the better."

"Yes, that's for sure. Still, with the storage problem solved, it's one less job for me to do, so many thanks." He grinned. "Right, now that's sorted out, do I move in with you or get myself an apartment?"

Mia gave a mischievous smile. "I don't want to push you into anything you might regret, but there is a third option." She caught hold and squeezed his hand. With her eyes rapt on his she said, "We could always buy a house between us?"

Although taken aback by her statement, John nodded in agreement. "It's an ideal, but it would be no different from living together." When he noticed Mia's smile fade, he said, "Please, don't look like that. I am not saying it's not an idea." With a broad smile stretched across his face, he said, "Look, unless you have already found somewhere you fancy, we could look for somewhere when I come over?" It pleased him when Mia's face broke into a beaming smile.

"I've not, but I have a few ideas. Anyway, we don't have to live in the centre of Barcelona. Although my parents live out of town, it does not take too long to get to my office."

"Well, as we will have two big dogs, that could prove a better idea." John looked thoughtful for a minute. "Your office, do you have any spare room?"

Mia cocked an eyebrow in puzzlement. "No. Why, what are you thinking?"

"When I'm there, I'll need an office where I can do my business." He shrugged. "After all, I'll have to work."

"Ah, yes, I see what you mean. Well, I'm sure we could sort something out." She giggled. "Still, if you were in my office, I could keep an eye on you."

John shook his head. "I have one woman who gives me all I could ever wish for. I don't need another one."

Mia bent, took his face in her hands, and kissed him. "Thank you, John, but I don't have any doubts about you."

"Good. So, we have most things sorted out between us. Anyway, tomorrow, I will talk with my insurance company. I'll know then about the situation of getting a hire car. Still, the main thing is to sell the house. The sooner I have a definite offer, the better."

"Yes, and the happier I will be," Mia murmured as she kissed his cheek.

Chapter 17

When Mia later went to climb into bed beside John, she was bubbling with excitement. He chuckled as he pulled back the covers. "Come here, gorgeous. I've been waiting for this."

She cocked an eyebrow. "Oh, and why is that, any special reason?"

"Yes, because not only do you look fabulous, but to feel your body next to mine is nothing short of fantastic."

Mia squealed with delight and flung herself into John's arms. With hot, passionate kisses and bodies pressed together, both could not have been happier. Even without making love, they were only too happy to be together.

WHEN MIA WOKE THE NEXT morning, she found John looking at her. She sighed. "Good morning. Did you sleep well?"

He chuckled. I thought I was dreaming when I woke up and saw you next to me. Then, when I realised, I was not, it was as though I had won the lottery. Anyway, what about you? How did you sleep?"

Mia laid a delicate hand on his cheek. "With you cuddled up against me, it made me feel in heaven. I want it to be like this forever."

John hugged and kissed her. "Me too." He shook his head. "I can't believe I've fallen in love with you?"

Mia sat up and gave a mischievous smile. "You're not sorry, are you, John?"

"What! No, but I can't get over how fast it happened. When I went to Spain, romance was not even a thought in the back of my mind. Now, here we are talking about buying a house together."

"I know it's amazing." She sighed. "Like you, I find it hard to believe, but I'm so happy it happened."

After another session of kissing, they dressed and went downstairs. Lucky barked, and stood wagging his tail.

"Yes, I know, you want to go out," John said. As he picked up Lucky's lead, he asked, "Do you fancy a walk, darling?"

Mia giggled and clutched his arm. "As you called me darling, what can I say but yes?"

"You are a darling, my darling," he said, kissing her cheek. "Right, let's take this boy out for a walk."

With John calling her darling, Mia felt as though floating on the soft breeze as they walked along. It made her heart full of joy and her eyes shine bright. After Lucky had performed and John cleaned up, they returned to his house.

Mia pushed John onto the sofa. "Now, you sit while I'll get breakfast. I'll soon find where everything is."

John cocked an eyebrow. "Are you sure?"

"Yes, of course."

"In that case, I'll phone my insurance company about the car." While he talked on the phone, he could hear Mia softly singing. She sounded as happy as he was.

On hearing about his accident, the line went quiet, then the agent said, "I'm sorry Mr Williams, but you have no insurance."

John's gasp of astonishment made Mia turn towards John. Before either John or Mia could speak, the agent said, "You never renewed your policy. We sent you reminders, but when you never answered, we cancelled your policy."

John shook his head in disbelief. "It must have been when my wife died," he said. "I couldn't think of anything else at that time."

"I'm sorry to hear that Mr Phillips, but we can do nothing about your car."

"Thanks," John mumbled, then closed his phone.

"What's up John," Mia asked, her face twisted in puzzlement.

"I forgot to renew my car's insurance policy. It must have come up when my wife died."

Mia came and caught hold of his hand. "I'm so sorry John. At that time, your car's insurance was the last thing on your mind."

"Yes, it was." He paused, then said, "Still, it was an old car and with my wife's life insurance money, I'll buy another car." He shook his head. "I think it's best I wait until we are in Spain." At her look of puzzlement, he said, "They drive on the other side of the road here in England. Nevertheless, I'll phone the car-hire company I use, they will bring us one.

Mia kissed John's cheek, then returned to the kitchen. She only asked if John would prefer tea or coffee with his breakfast. After he said tea, a short time later, she came into the lounge and flashed him a smile.

"Breakfast is ready."

Once both had finished, John caught hold and squeezed Mia's hand. "Darling, would you mind if I did a bit of work? I have to complete Mr Dawe's new project." He paused. "Now there's a thought. When I go to London to show him my latest drawings, I'll take you with me."

Although not amused when John said about doing some work, her eyes lit

when he said he would take her to London.

"Oh, yes please, it would be wonderful."

"Right, so, how do you feel about seeing a show while we are there?" Her shrieks of delight gave him his answer.

After she picked out a book from John's bookcase and made herself comfortable on the sofa, John set to work.

What he wanted to do did not take long, and once finished, he nodded in satisfaction. He felt sure it would please Mr Dawes when he showed him his sketches. Only one thing bothered him, Mr Dawe's daughter Sylvia. He had not paid her any attention except to shake her hand. But, from the sly glances, she kept giving him; she seemed to have fancied him. Given this, John hoped she would not be present when he had Mia with him. He shrugged. His conscience was clear. Mia was the only woman he cared about. Pushing these thoughts to one side, he called Mr Dawes.

After pleasantries, John said, "I have the sketches ready. When would it be convenient to bring them to you?"

"One minute, let me check?" After a pause, he said, "How does Wednesday suit you?"

"Perfect. Would the same time as before be, okay?"

"Yes, two pm would be good,"

"Right, I will see you then." John closed his phone, then went and informed Mia he had finished his work.

"Now, what type of show would you prefer to see?" He shrugged. "Of course, it will depend on if we can get tickets."

After Mia said a musical, a check revealed they had a choice of two. Bohemian Rhapsody and Pretty Woman. When Mia said she preferred Pretty Woman, John phoned a ticket agency. They were fortunate, and he booked tickets for the late show on Wednesday afternoon.

He turned to Mia. "Right, that's us all set. After I've dealt with Mr Dawes, we can get a tube to Piccadilly. The theatre is only a short distance from the station."

Mia's eyes lit with delight. "Oh, thank you, John. I am so looking forward to going to London. Although I went there once for a

real-estate conference, this will be much better. I will be with you."
She kissed him on the cheek. "You are a darling."

Chuckling, he responded. "So, I'm your darling, am I?"

"Yes, you are, and I'm so happy to say so."

"Right, now the theatre is sorted out, let me arrange for a hire car. It should not take them long to get it here. They delivered one here before."

Sure enough, about an hour after John called, they heard a car's horn. A glance outside revealed two cars, so John went out.

On his return, he waved a set of keys. "It's only a Ford Focus, but it will be fine for us to get out and about."

Chapter 18

John thought for a minute. "If you like, we could take a ferry over to the Isle of Wight, or anywhere else you fancy. The choice is yours."

A flicker of a smile crossed Mia's lips. "I have never been to the Isle of Wight, so let's go there."

After John had made sure Lucky was okay, they set off. On arrival at Lymington, the ferry port, they were on board a ferry after half an hour's wait. Ongoing up to the top deck, while holding hands, the ferry set off. They then watched as several ships and yachts passed by.

On arrival at the Isle and disembarked, a glance showed the sky clear of clouds, with only a light breeze blowing.

John kissed Mia's cheek, then set off on a drive around the Island. "There are several interesting places, but we won't get to see them all," he said. "Still, there's an old steam railway that although it only runs for about five and a half miles, I think you would enjoy the ride."

Mia's eyes lit up. "Oh, yes please, I've never been on a steam train before."

John nodded. "In the season, when the island becomes packed with tourists, you can book an island tour with a guide." He grinned. "As it is, you will have to make do with me."

Mia leaned across and kissed his cheek. "I could not wish for a better guide than the one I have, thank you," she replied.

"When I kiss you, your lips are like the gossamer wings of a butterfly," he murmured. "I could not wish for a more attractive passenger."

At the train station, once John had purchased the tickets, they stood to wait for the train's arrival. A short time later, a loud toot let all those waiting know it was approaching.

Once the passengers onboard had disembarked, John helped Mia to board. Both smiled, when with another toot on its horn, the train pulled out of the station. Although only a short ride before they turned around, Mia said she enjoyed the experience.

At their next stop, Carisbrooke Castle, a crease appeared on John's forehead and he shook his head. "King Charles 1st was imprisoned here before his trial and beheaded."

Mia gasped and her eyebrows shot up in alarm, "Oh, how terrible."

John nodded. "King Henry 8th ordered the execution of numerous people, including several Queens."

After a trip through the castle and seeing an array of suits of armour and weapons, they called into the castle café for coffee.

As they sat and sipped their drink, John asked, "So, have you liked our little trip?"

Mia reached across and squeezed his hand. "Yes, and thank you for suggesting we come here."

He grinned. "Well, the day is not over yet. We still have a few more places to visit." They then went to the dinosaur museum, where apart from some fossilised skeletons and other bits and pieces, they watched a display of birds of prey.

Mia found it fascinating to watch them catch objects thrown up by their handlers. However, the sight of the huge curved claws of the Golden Eagles made her shudder. "I wouldn't like to think of those sinking into my flesh," she said.

John chuckled. "Don't worry; you're with me."

She cocked an eyebrow in his direction. "Sorry, John, but I don't think you could save me if one of them attacked me?"

He shrugged. "You could well be right, but at least I would do my best. Anyway, from here, we will go to the Amazon World Zoo. As an animal lover, I'm sure you will find it interesting?"

Inside the zoo, Mia's eyes lit up in amazement at the sight of animals usually found in the vast forests of the Amazon.

"Oh, this is wonderful," she trilled. "Fancy being able to see a scene recreated from the Amazon jungle." She shook her head. "I've never heard of something like this before."

John nodded. "Me neither. Now no visit to the Isle of Wight is complete without seeing the "Needles." At Mia's look of puzzlement, he explained.

"These are rocks out in the sea, that although not shaped like needles, we know them as the Needles. History says there used to be a fourth pillar named Lot's Wife. It collapsed into the sea during a storm in the 1700s." He shrugged. "Still, as they are made of chalk, it's a wonder the other three are still standing."

Ongoing and looking out at them, Mia said, "With the waves crashing against them, I can see what you mean. It's a miracle those three are still there."

"Yes, but who knows how many more years they will survive?"

ONCE BACK IN LYMINGTON, John asked, "Are you hungry?" Mia winked. "Yes, but only for you."

His eyes lit. "And me for you." He gave a dirty laugh. "Still, for now, a snack would be good. I know we can call in and have a Ploughman's Lunch." When he noticed Mia's look of puzzlement, he said, "It's a mixture of cheeses, pickles, cold meat, and a crusty bread basket. It's ideal to keep one going while waiting for dinner time."

"It sounds good to me, so lead on."

On finding a pub still serving ploughman's lunches, they went in and sat down. A few minutes after John had ordered, a waitress laid down what Mia thought a feast.

"Wow, after eating all this, I won't want much for dinner," she muttered.

John leaned over towards her. "I'm sure you will manage to eat a little something." As he spoke, a gleam appeared in his eyes.

Mia, who had noticed, nodded. "She glanced around and, with no one nearby, kissed his cheek.

When they later arrived back at John's house, after being greeted and stroking Lucky, they collapsed on the sofa, tired but happy.

Mia, purring with delight, said, "Thank you, darling. I enjoyed our trip over and around the Isle of Wight. I found it most interesting. Oh, and the ploughman's lunch tasted delicious,"

As they sat talking, John's phone rang. When he opened it, he saw it was Wendy.

"Hi John, I hope I'm not interrupting anything?"

"No, we have just got back from a trip over to the Isle of Wight."

"Oh, well, if you are not too tired, I'm inviting you and Mia for dinner. Still, as you've only just got in, if it's alright with you, say at 8 pm."

John held a hand over the phone. When he told Mia about dinner with

Wendy and Gilbert, her eyes lit with delight. "Yes, it would be nice."

"Thanks, we will see you at eight." As he closed his phone, John shook his head. "I had hoped to have you all to myself tonight. Still, we won't stay too late."

Mia tossed her hair. "Oh, why? May I ask if you had something in mind for us to do later?"

John grinned. "What a thing to say." He put a finger to his mouth and glanced her over. "Now, what could a man possibly do if alone with a gorgeous woman like you."

Mia giggled, pulled him close and kissed him.

Chapter 19

Once both had showered and dressed, John took a bottle of wine from a cabinet. At Mia's look of puzzlement, he explained. "In England, if a friend invites you around for the evening, you take a bottle of drink with you."

"Oh, that's something I'll have to remember. I never knew that."

When John knocked on Wendy's door, it opened to reveal Gilbert standing there.

"Hi John, Mia, come in." As they walked inside, he said, "So, Mia, you've been over to the Isle of Wight. What did you think of it?"

Her eyes lit up on remembering all she had seen. "It was wonderful, and I loved the ride on a steam train. It made a huge change from going on a high-speed electric train." She squeezed John's hand. "If John ever gives up being an architect, he would make an excellent tour guide."

At this, Wendy, who had just walked in, said, "There you are, John, that's another project you can think about doing." He and the others then laughed.

Wendy turned to Gilbert. "Have you not given our guests a drink yet?" When Mia noticed his eyebrows rise in annoyance, Wendy shook her head. "It's alright Mia; Gilbert knows I'm only joking."

She shook her head. "Your English joking is something I'm not used to."

John flashed her a smile. "Never mind, all being well, we will soon be back in Spain."

Wendy and Gilbert exchanged glances. Then Wendy said, "Is it my imagination, or have you two decided what you intend to do once you are there?"

John looked at Mia, who nodded, her eyes bright with anticipation at what he would say.

"Yes, we are going to get married." His lips turned into a grin. "I can't believe how fast things have gone for us, but I have no doubts about our future." He glanced at Mia. "Do you, darling?"

Mia, whose cheeks had coloured up in embarrassment at John calling her darling in front of his friends, nodded. "No, but I'm also surprised at how fast things developed between us." She reached and took hold of John's hand. "Still, I couldn't be happier."

Wendy shook her head. "I'm surprised by what you say, but happy for you."

Gilbert shook John's hand, then kissed Mia on the cheek. "Well, Wendy, it seems we are going over to Spain next year."

Mia and John exchanged loving glances. "Who knows, it might be sooner, but I doubt it," John said.

When John noticed Wendy's eyes locked on Mia, he shook his head. "No, it's nothing like that."

"No, it's not," Mia gasped. Although my father wants to talk with John when he comes over, it has nothing to do with our relationship." She glanced at John and shook her head. "As I have previously mentioned before, I do not know what he wants to talk to you about. You will have to wait until you are there to find out."

After a tasty meal and a good chat, John, and Mia said their goodbyes and returned to John's house.

Once they had gone, Gilbert turned to Wendy. "Well, that's a turn up for the book."

"Yes, but I'm delighted for them. John is lucky to have found such a nice woman like Mia. I'm sure they will be happy together."

"I think you're right," Gilbert added. "Anyway, we'll have to wait until they tell us when to be in Spain."

"Yes, but whenever, I shall be looking forward to it."

XXX

Once inside John's house, he took hold of Mia's hand. "I hope I didn't say anything to embarrass you?"

"Not in the least. I am happy with what you said."

He pulled her into his arms and gave her a long, lingering kiss. Then, holding her at arm's length, he asked, "Darling, what do you think? Should I ask your parents for their permission to get married?"

Mia giggled. "If you do, they will think I'm pregnant, but will be relieved when I say I'm not. Anyway, as for asking their permission, although it's not necessary, I'm sure they would be pleased if you did."

"Right, then I will. Now I'll have to let my parents know about our getting married." He gave a wry grin. "I'm sure they'll also be surprised, but will be happy for us."

When they went to bed, with John wearing a condom, their lovemaking was long, tender, and passionate. Like Mia, he did not want anything to spoil things between them. As for a baby, once married, they would decide if they wanted one or not.

Later, locked in each other's arms, they fell asleep, both happy about what they had agreed.

Chapter 20

Come the day John and Mia set off up to London to see Mr Dawe; John felt uncomfortable. He hoped his daughter Sylvia would not be present at their meeting. However, when Mr Dawe's secretary opened his office door to announce his arrival, John's smile changed to a frown. Sylvia, who stood by his desk, flashed him a big smile as he entered, with Mia right behind him.

My Dawe stood. "Good morning, John." He shook John's hand and then Mia's. Before he could continue, Sylvia held out her hand. "Nice to see you again, Mr Philips."

John took her hand. "Good morning, Miss Dawe." He chuckled inwardly to see her smile fade at his greeting. Taking a folder from his briefcase, he said, "Here are my ideas for your proposed new house."

Once Mr Dawe had cleared a space on his desk, John laid out a series of sketches. After scrutinising each one, Mr Dawe nodded. "Yes, these look just what I wanted." He looked up. "Right, now all we have to do is agree on the price for the architectural drawings." As John went to speak, Sylvia cut in. "If you would like to discuss this in private, your secretary could wait outside."

Mia gasped at her rudeness, but before John could set Sylvia straight, Mia looked at Mr Dawe and flashed him a smile.

"Yes. your secretary and I can talk outside while you two gentlemen discuss details."

Mr Dawe chuckled. "Sylvia, I don't think this lady is John's secretary."

"No, she is not," John reported. "This is Mia, my fiancée."

"I'm sorry, my dear," Mr Dawe said. "Please forgive my daughter's mistake." The look of surprise and disappointment on Sylvia's face brought a smile to Mia's face. "Oh, I'm sorry, I thought Sylvia was your secretary."

Mr Dawe grinned and shook his head. "Right now, perhaps we could finish our business." John, trying hard to cover his anger, forced a smile. "Of course," he replied.

Once they had agreed on John's costs, the two men shook hands. "I'll make a start on your plans shortly," John said. "Once completed, I'll get back to you."

Mr Dawe nodded. "Many thanks Mr Philips, I await your call."

As they left the building, John pulled Mia close. "I'm sorry about what happened there."

"It was not a problem." She cast a suspicious glance across at John. "I had the impression Sylvia fancies you."

"If so, she is wasting her time." he snorted. "You, my darling, are the only woman I'm interested in. Anyway, I thought you handled her very well." He glanced at his watch. "Now, as we have time for a snack before the show starts, I suggest we find somewhere here. Then we'll take the tube to Piccadilly."

Mia squeezed his hand. "Whatever you say, my darling."

After enjoying a drink and a sandwich in a pub, they made their way to the

theatre. Once inside, they sat holding hands, enthralled as they watched the show.

Come to the end, both were pleased with their decision to see Pretty Woman. It was fabulous. After a short chat, instead of eating out, they decided to return to John's house.

"If you like, once there, we could go out for an Indian or a Chinese?" John said.

Mia shook her head. "We will order in. I would like to relax with you and Lucky in the house."

XXX

Once home, after making a fuss of Lucky, and taking him out for a walk, John ordered Chinese. This they enjoyed while sitting in the lounge, with Lucky lying beside them. Both agreed Pretty Woman had proved an excellent choice. "Yes, and so was the Chinese," Mia said. "I thought it delicious."

John grinned. "You are right, but I'm sure you are tastier."

Mia blushed. "Behave yourself, John. Lucky is watching." He turned and said, "Sorry, Lucky, but what is to come, is for humans, not dogs."

A flicker of a smile crossed Mia's face. "Oh, and what do you have in mind, may I ask?"

John gave a wolfish smile. "Never mind, you will soon find out." Once both had showered and cuddled together in bed. "Mia asked, "Now, what is for humans, but not for dogs?"

The next minute, she gasped when John took a mouthful of her breast and sucked. He then slipped a hand down between her legs, with his fingers stroking her pussy.

"Oh, I see what you mean," she murmured. Then, as her fingers encased his throbbing cock, she asked, "How do you like this?"

"It feels nice, but I'm sure it will be much better when it's inside you."

Mia giggled. "Less talk and more action," she murmured.

As he climbed on top of her and she felt him enter her waiting pussy, she sighed, "Oh, yes, it feels wonderful."

After a hot and passionate session of love making, with both well satisfied, John said, "Darling, that was fantastic."

"Yes, I couldn't agree more," she muttered.

A short time later, with Mia lying contented in John's arms, they were fast asleep.

THE FOLLOWING DAY, upon waking, John nuzzled Mia's neck. She sighed, turned, and kissed him. "Good morning, darling. Did you sleep well?"

"Of course, after making love, what else would you expect?"

John pulled her close, with them enjoying a lingering kiss. Then, as Mia climbed out of bed, he said, "Darling, please put something on. With you looking so sexy. I have a job to control myself."

She laughed and tossed her hair. "If you want more of what you had last night, you will have to wait until tonight," she said, laughingly.

John's eyes lit up, "What can I say, but roll on tonight."

Once dressed, they took Lucky out for his usual morning walk. Later, with breakfast finished, John flashed Mia a smile. "I'll call my parents and give them our news."

Mia, her eyes bright with excitement, kissed his cheek. "Yes, I am sure they will want to know." She gave a nervous smile. "John, what do you think they will say? After all, we have not known each other for long?"

He shrugged. "They'll be surprised, but relieved to know I'm now back to being normal."

At her look of puzzlement, he said, "Before the night I went in for dinner with Gilbert and Wendy, I was drinking as though there was no tomorrow. I didn't shave and looked a mess." He kissed Mia on the cheek. "But since I met you, I've been a happy and contented person. Therefore, I'm sure they will be pleased to hear our news."

A smile warmed his lips. "Now, although I mentioned you to them on my return from Spain, I don't expect they took too much notice. No doubt it surprised them when I told them you were coming to visit me. Still, they must have realised you had made an impression on me." With a hint of amusement, he said, "I know; I'll call to ensure they will be at home when we visit, but I won't tell them you will be with me." He turned to Mia. "Oh, sorry, I should have asked. Is that alright with you?"

She pulled him close and wrapped her arms around him. "Of course, I would like to meet your parents." Her smile then changed to a frown. "John, you don't think they will mind my being Spanish and a catholic, do you?"

He laughed. "No, like me, my parents are not religious, so don't worry. I'm sure they will welcome you with open arms."

When John called them, he put the phone on speaker. On his mother's answer, he said, "Hi Mum, are you an' Dad both okay?" Mia heard her reply, "Yes, thanks, and how about you?"

John covered the phone. "As I thought, she must have forgotten you would be here." He then opened the phone. "I'm fine. I thought I would visit you this afternoon. Will you be home?"

"Yes. While the weather's good, we are working out in the garden."

"Well, don't tire yourself too much. Anyway, I'll see you around two-thirty. Love you."

As he closed the phone, grinning like a Cheshire Cat, John turned to Mia.

"They live in Guildford, which is a couple of hours' drive from here." When he noticed Mia's look of apprehension, he pulled her close.

"John, are you sure they won't mind when they see me?"

"No, they'll be surprised, but Mum should have remembered you were coming over." He hugged Mia tight and kissed her. "Now, don't worry; everything will be fine."

Chapter 21

When they arrived at John's parents' house, Mia gripped John's hand tight as he rang their doorbell. The lady who opened the door gasped when she saw Mia stood beside John.

"Oh, you must be Mia, John's Spanish lady friend?" She wagged a finger. "John, you devil, why didn't you remind me Mia was here when we spoke? You knew I had forgotten. Anyway, come in, my dear, it's good to see you."

As Mia stepped inside, his mother shook her hand. "Welcome, Mia." She led them into the lounge, where a man sat reading a newspaper. As he turned to welcome who he thought was only John, he dropped his paper and stood.

"I'm sorry, my dear, but my son never reminded us you were here. I guess it slipped his mind. Is that not so, John?"

"Yes, it must have done." The two men laughed, then his father held out his hand to Mia. "John said you were attractive, and I can see why. Anyway, welcome my dear, and please sit down."

Mia gave a silent sigh of relief. As she sat, John squeezed her hand. "See, I told you they wouldn't eat you," he whispered.

After greetings, John's mother disappeared, then returned with a tray of cups of tea.

"I hope you drink tea Mia, which is a custom in England. If not, I will make you a cup of coffee?"

"Tea will be fine, thank you."

"So, what do you think of where John lives in the middle of nowhere," John's father asked. He cocked an eyebrow. "John said you live in Barcelona, so it must be a considerable difference than there?"

"It is, but it's a lovely house. Plus, my parents live in the country, so it's not a problem for me to be there."

"Have you been to England before Mia?" John's mother asked.

"Yes, I went to London once for a business meeting."

After they had talked for a while, John gave a short cough. "I have something to say." He caught hold of Mia's hand, who had gone quiet.

"We are going to get married."

While John's mother gasped and thrust a hand to her mouth, his father grinning stood. "Thanks for coming to tell us, son, I am happy for you both."

His mother shook her head in disbelief, and then kissed Mia on the cheek. "Well, although shocked by your news, like my husband, I am happy for you." A hint of a smile crossed her face. "Some people may think you have only known each other for a short time and are jumping the gun. However, you are both adults, so I wish you every happiness." She raised a questioning eyebrow. "Perhaps I shouldn't ask, but is it a necessity?"

John shook his head. "No, it's not, but I don't blame you for asking." He then explained how when they first met. "There was an instant attraction between us. I can't explain it, but we fell in love."

John's father came and kissed Mia on the cheek. "Welcome to our family, my dear." He glanced from one to the other. "So, when are you planning to get married?"

"We haven't decided yet. When I return to Spain, I intend to ask Mia's father for her hand in marriage." On seeing his father's eyebrows rise, John said, "Over there, it's custom, but not in England, so I didn't ask you first."

"No problem, son." He shrugged. "You are a grown man and don't need our permission." His eyebrows then pulled together in a scowl. When he noticed the look of concern on John and Mia's faces, he burst out laughing. "Sorry, my dear, but you should have seen yours and John's faces."

Mia shook her head. "You had me worried for a minute. Still, I should have realised you were only playing an English joke on me."

"Well, this calls for a drink to celebrate," John's father said. "Mia, I have wine, whisky, or vodka."

"A glass of white wine, please, or else red."

"I have both, so you can have a white wine. What about you, John?" Before he could answer, his father shook his head. "As you are driving, you can only have a small glass of white wine."

"Thanks, Dad."

Once everyone had a drink, John's father raised his glass. "Here's to a happy couple." After all touched glasses, they sipped their drinks.

Later, after a pleasant chat and a delicious dinner, John, and Mia said goodnight to his parents. Mia kissed his mother on the cheek, and to his father's embarrassment, hugged him. As they went to leave, Mia said, "Thank you so much for making me welcome. It was good to meet you."

"And you," John's mother said, with his father echoing his agreement.

Once in the car, after a final wave out of the windows, John drove away. As they did, his mother turned to her husband. "Well, that came as a big surprise."

"It certainly was. Still, I'm glad to see John back to normal. I mean, the boy now looks human again."

"Yes. Mia is a lovely girl, and they seem happy together."

He grinned. "It means we will be going to Spain for a holiday."

"Yes, and Mia said she comes from Barcelona; We've not been there before."

XXX

While driving down the road, John said, "So, that wasn't so bad, was it?"

Mia leaned over and kissed his cheek. "No, they were friendly and made me welcome." She giggled. "Now, you will have to wait and see how my parents react when you ask my father for my hand in marriage." She paused. "You know you don't have to ask him?"

"Of course, should your father refuse, unless you said no, I'll still marry you?"

Mia's eyebrows shot up. "I should hope so," she exclaimed. "Still, I'm sure there won't be any problem."

John glanced across at her. "Are you sure you don't know what your father wants to talk to me about?"

"No. I do not know."

Chapter 22

Once home, after they put on coats, with Lucky on his lead, they went out. As there was a touch of rain in the air, once Lucky had performed, they quickly returned to the house. After John filled Lucky's dishes with food and water, he and Mia sat and cuddled together on the sofa. Mia turned her head towards him and looked in his eyes. "I love you," she murmured.

"And I love you." He squeezed her hand. "No regrets about my saying we are going to get married?"

Mia's eyebrows shot up. "No, not for a minute."

"Good, because I don't." As they embraced, Lucky came in and sat in front of them, wagging his tail.

Mia put a hand to her mouth. "Oh, that is something I meant to ask you. Is Lucky microchipped? If not, you had best get him done. Under Spanish law, all dogs must be microchipped."

"No problem, I had Lucky done when he was a puppy. I know about this law, as I went online to find out the laws about taking a dog to Spain." He cocked an eyebrow. "That reminds me. Dobermans are classed as dangerous and have to wear a muzzle when outdoors. So, what about Aza? He doesn't wear a muzzle?"

"No, there is no need for him to wear one." At John's look of puzzlement, she said, "He passed a special test to show he is not a danger to anyone."

John laughed. "Well, whoever tested him, has never seen Aza react like he did when you said Eight."

A smile crossed Mia's lip. "No, he did not. If he had, I could not take him out without a muzzle." She laughed and shook her head. "In which case, he wouldn't be able to protect me should anyone try to attack me."

John grinned. "That's a fact. If he wore a muzzle, you might as well have a toy poodle."

When he noticed Mia's smile change to a frown, he asked, "Are you alright? Or is something bothering you?"

She sighed. "No, but looking at Lucky; it reminds me Aza is not with me. I miss him when he is not."

On noticing a shadow flicker across Mia's face, John thought it a sign she was not looking forward to returning home without him. He put his hands around her waist and pulled her close. "I know what you are thinking, but I promise I'll do whatever I can, so I go back to Spain with you."

After brushing Mia's long hair away from her eyes, he said, "But, first I have to get a signed contract on the house." He lifted his shoulders and let them fall in a gesture of indifference. "Still, I feel sure I'll receive good news regarding the house soon." Although he had his fingers crossed as he spoke, John hoped what he said would happen.

That night, while fast asleep, Mia woke with a start and buried herself into John's arms. A loud bang, followed by a bright light had lit up the bedroom.

"It's only a storm," he said. "You are quite safe." He kissed her cheek. "There is a lightning conductor on the roof, so don't be worried about the house being struck by lightning."

"Thank heavens." Mia's voice trailed off as she continued. "Lightning hit my friends' house. Although not injured, her home suffered considerable damage."

After a while, the storm passed over, and the couple went back to sleep.

The following day, although the storm had passed, the skies threatened more rain. As a precaution, John checked the house, but as he expected, no water had entered.

After breakfast, the rain returned with a vengeance. It hammered against the windows as if to say, let me in. With this and the drop in temperature, John lit the fire. He put on some music, and with Mia curled up on the sofa beside him, they talked.

As they did, John's thoughts turned to Jasmin, his late wife. They had been happy together, and her tragic death had caused him to sink into depression. He knew he had been drinking too much, but then, it seemed the only thing that kept him going. Now, with Mia, he was no longer dependent on a drink to help him survive another day.

His mind then went to what Jasmin would think about his getting married again, but he believed she would not mind. For sure, Mia was the right type of person for him. Not only did she look fabulous, but was loving, caring, intelligent and thoughtful.

Unknown to him, Mia was also deep in thought. From what John had told her, he had loved his late wife. Still, she knew he loved her and she loved him. Money wise, she was not concerned. Her real-estate business was doing well, and her family were well off. Also, John had discovered he could lawfully conduct his business in Spain, so planned to do the same business. Plus, due to their shared love for animals and interest in old buildings and the environment, they were a good fit. They also shared a common interest in the same kind of music. Mia muffled her laughter. As for children, they would decide on this once they were married. Her lips parted and she licked her lips before turning to John and saying, "I love you."

He replied with a simple "likewise. Anyway, from your expression, I could see you were deep in thought. So, what were you thinking? Or is it a secret?"

"Nothing special. But if you must know, it was about us."

"Ah, so what about us, may I ask?"

"Well, I don't expect us to have any problems once we are married."

John's eyebrows shot up. "What, I should hope not."

"No, don't get me wrong. I didn't mean it that way." She flashed him a beaming smile. "I was thinking of money, not about our feelings for each other."

He gave a short laugh. "Thank heavens. Still, in that respect, don't worry. I have money, plus, once I sell my house, I will have more than enough to buy us a suitable one in Spain." His face broke out in a smile. "Who knows, I might design one for us and have it built. In which case, it would have to be on the city's outskirts."

Mia gave a whoop of joy, grabbed hold of John, and kissed him. "Oh, yes, that would be fantastic."

When he noticed Mia's happy expression, he nodded. "Well, it's something to consider. Yes, we will have to give it some thought."

The mere thought of living in a house with a garden and not in an apartment made Mia tremble with excitement. "If we could, it would be wonderful," she exclaimed.

"Well, keep it in mind, but first, I have to sell this place."

Mia, her thoughts on this, said, "It's a pity it's not in Spain, or I could sell it for you. Of course, as it's you, I wouldn't charge you the normal rate." She burst out laughing, then stopped. "John, it's just an idea, but I could put your house for sale on my company's website. I would also display it in my office window." On seeing John's eyes light with interest, she went on to say, "We have several wealthy clients. Who knows, one might be interested when they see photos of your house."

He nodded. "Well, we can but try. At least it will give us more of a chance of finding a buyer."

"Right, if you send me photos of both the outside and the interior to my phone, I'll pass them on to Carlos. He will put them on our website and in the local real estate papers. Plus, of course, in our office window."

Once John had done as Mia's suggested, she emailed all to Carlos. She then phoned and informed him of what to do. On closing her phone, she sighed.

"Well, that's it. Whoever checks out our website or looks in our office window, will see your house." She let out a small laugh. "I've told Carlos to expect a bonus if he manages to find a buyer before I return."

"Thank you, my darling. Although it may come to nothing, nothing ventured, nothing gained." He grinned, pulled Mia into his arms and gave her a long, passionate kiss.

"Chapter 23

AN HOUR LATER, JOHN said, "Look, as the weather is not good, I have an idea."

Mia cocked an eyebrow. "Oh, do tell, what?"

"If you remember, I said maybe I would design us a house. Well, if you tell me what style you like, I could make up some sketches for you to look at."

"Oh, what a great idea."

"I have a variety of house design books you can look through. I'm sure you will find something in them you fancy?" He shrugged. "At least, they might give you an idea of how you would like the house to look like."

Afte picking out several books, he placed them on the dining table, along with a pencil and a notebook.

"Now, while you look at the various designs, think of what kind of windows you would like." When he noticed Mia's eyebrows rise, he said, "For instance, due to the weather in England, we tend to have large windows. In hot countries like Spain, Italy, and France, windows are usually smaller."

Mia nodded. "I see what you mean." She then opened one book and started to look at the various house designs.

When he later checked, John nodded in satisfaction. Mia had jotted down several items.

"Great, that's it. If you see anything you like in the shape of a roof, make a note of that as well. Anything that catches your eye would be good. Now, while you do that, I'll do a final check on Mr Dawes" details. I don't want any delays in being able to finalise everything."

With Mia so engrossed in what she was doing, she merely nodded. John left and entered his part-time office. He took out the set of drawings he had prepared for Mr Dawes and started a final check.

On his later return to the dining room, John could see Mia had opened all the books he had left her.

"So, how are you doing?"

"Fine." Mia looked up, then leafed through a pile of pages on the notebook. "I did as you said and made-up lists of different roof shapes, windows, and doors." Still, I'm surprised at all the variations."

"Yes, there are countless ones. Anyway, I've finished my work, so let's call it a day. We can have a drink of coffee, or would you prefer something else?"

With her lips parted and fluttering her long eyelashes, she murmured, "Well, that's a leading question." She then flung open her arms. "I want you to kiss me."

John couldn't help but chuckle at the situation. "Now that I can manage with no problem," he said. The next minute, with tongues tangled, they devoured each other. As he thrust his leg between her thighs and she felt his hardness, Mia's passion rose.

"Wow," she gasped; you are getting me so hot."

"Me too. We should stop before we get carried away. I wouldn't like us to get caught out if Wendy or Gilbert call in."

"Oh, do you think they would?" Mia said as she sat up and swept her hair back over her shoulder.

He shrugged. "Although it's doubtful, I'd rather not take a chance."

"Nor I." She giggled. "To prevent any embarrassment, we'd best wait until later? What do you think? After all, they are your friends."

John sighed at having to wait. "You're right, they do call in sometimes unannounced."

With that, after tidying themselves up and sitting at the table, John glanced through Mia's notes. "Well, from this, I'm sure we can pick out a suitable design between us. At least, it will give me an idea on how I should proceed."

"Thank you. It means I haven't wasted my time."

"No, not in the least. Now, as I asked before we all got carried away, would you like a drink? or coffee?"

"Coffee might be best." She gave a subtle wink. "I wouldn't like you to take advantage of me."

Flashing an innocent smile, John said, "Well, with you looking so gorgeous, you never know." Then, wrapped in each other's arms, they enjoyed a long, and tender kiss.

Come ten pm and no knock on the door; John said, "Well, that's it. I don't think we'll be having visitors now. So, white, or red wine?"

"Red, please."

He poured out two glasses that they clinked while cuddled together on the sofa. Once they had finished their wine, John said. "Shall we go up? I think there was something we wanted to do earlier."

Mia raised one of her eyebrows in a quizzical manner. "Are you sure about that?"

John almost choked as he gasped, "Of course." He then shook his head as Mia burst out laughing.

"I knew what you meant, John, but you should have seen your face when I asked you."

"You devil, you had me going then." He pulled her close and kissed her. "There, that's to keep you going until I get you upstairs."

"Promises, promises," Mia muttered, then led him towards the stairs. As they went upstairs, she said, "Enough talk. Action speaks louder than words, or at least, so I've been told."

Once in bed, they caressed and kissed as though there would be no tomorrow.

XXX

When John awoke the next morning with Mia still lying fast asleep, he crept from the bed and went downstairs. He thought Mia might feel tired, so motioned Lucky to be quiet, put on his lead, and they went out for a walk.

The crisp fresh air felt good as they walked along, with hardly another person seen during their walk.

Once back indoors, as expected, he found Mia still asleep. After topping up Lucky's dishes, he then set to prepare breakfast. For a change with scrambled eggs, he cooked some slices of bacon and a few mushrooms.

The faint smell of his cooking woke Mia. She got out of bed, slipped on a shirt of Johns, then made her way downstairs. On entering the kitchen, she found John busy checking his cooking. On tiptoes, she crept behind him, put her hands over his eyes, and kissed his neck.

"Guess who?" Before he could answer, she said, "And don't you dare say, Sylvia."

John laughed and put his hands up. "Not a chance," he said.

XXX

While sat eating breakfast and discussing what they would do during the day, John's phone rang. When he opened it, Mia noticed a smile appear on his face.

"Yes, that would be fine; I look forward to seeing you later." After he closed the phone, he caught hold and kissed Mia.

"Oh, I think your phone call was good news?"

He nodded. "It could be, but we will have to wait and see."

"Well, don't keep me in suspense; what's going on?"

Holding back his excitement, he said, "Someone is interested in the house. They want to see it."

Mia's eyes lit up. "Oh, that's good."

"It could be. I've had several people come and look it over, but so far, no offers."

Mia caught hold and squeezed his hand. "Who knows, the people coming today might prove the ones to buy it."

He nodded. "You could be right. Anyway, we'd best have a tidy up. The house should look its best when they arrive."

Mia glanced around. "It looks good, but I'll pick up the notes I've made." Cocking an eyebrow, she asked, "What time are they coming?"

"Around noon."

"In that case, we have plenty of time." Collecting their breakfast things, Mia took them out and put the dirty dishes in the dishwasher. While she went upstairs to make their bed, John put away the design books she had been looking through. Her sketches and notes he placed in a folder and put them in a drawer. After a quick check around, he nodded in satisfaction.

When Mia came back down, she found John busy using a vacuum cleaner. She reached out and caught hold of his arm. "No, I'll do that. Why don't you give Lucky a brush? After all, you and I will look ready for our visitors, so why not him?"

"You're right, but there is no need for you to clean up. I mean, you are a guest."

She laughed. "Yes, but don't forget I want you to sell your house sooner than later." "Then you won't have a reason to stay here while I'm alone in Spain."

"That's a fact," he said, handing Mia the cleaner. When he called Lucky, who had been lying on the floor, he rose and followed John out onto the rear patio.

When he and Lucky returned to the lounge, they found Mia had finished and about to put the cleaner back in the cupboard.

After closing the door, she turned and nodded in satisfaction. Lucky's long hair looked sleek and tidy. She stroked his head. "Now, who's a pretty boy? You look ready as an entrant in a dog show."

JUST BEFORE MIDDAY, a car pulled up outside, followed by a knock on the door. When John opened it, he gasped in surprise? Along with Mary, the real-estate lady, was a familiar figure.

Chapter 24

The woman put a hand to her mouth. "Oh, John, I never knew this was your house?" Mary, taken by surprise, said, "Oh, do you know Mrs McCarthy, John?"

With Mia standing beside him, he merely nodded. "Yes, we are old friends. So, it's Mrs McCarthy, is it?"

The well-dressed woman tossed her head. "Yes, that was my late husband's name. Anyway, long time no see, John." She glanced at him, then nodded. "You are looking well." She then put out a hand to Mia. "Hi, I'm Susie. Nice to meet you....?

Mia reached out and took her hand. "Yes, and you. I am Mia, John's *girlfriend,*" she said, emphasising the word girlfriend.

Trying not to chuckle, John stood to one side and gestured, "Please come in." As Susie and Mary passed him, he squeezed Mia's hand. From the sudden change in her expression, she did not look happy.

Once inside, after a quick look around, Susie nodded. "This looks great, and I love the cathedral ceiling."

"Thank you. All those who have viewed the house said the same thing."

Susie, who got the message, flashed a smile. "I'm not surprised...." Mary cut in. "John, would it be alright if I showed Mrs Mc Carthy around?"

"Of course." He waved a hand. "You know where everything is. If there is anything you want to know, we will be in the lounge."

"Thank you," Susie said, then followed Mary, who led her out and into the dining room.

John turned to find Mia looking at him. She arched a questioning eyebrow. "Did you know it was your old friend Susie who wanted to look at the house?"

"No, as she mentioned, she has been married since we last spoke. I did not know who wanted to look over the house." He shrugged. "Why, don't tell me you are jealous?"

Mia felt her cheeks colour as she replied, "Of course not, but she is pretty."

John pulled her close and gave her a quick kiss. "No one, and I mean no one, is ever going to come between us, so don't worry." As he spoke, Mary and Susie came back into the room.

Susie flashed them a smile. "I like your dog John, who I think you have given a brush. I also like dogs and have a four-year-old Great Dane. Therefore, a house like this with a good-sized garden is a must. Anyway, so far, I've liked what I've seen. Mary is now going to show me upstairs."

When they came back down, Mary, who followed Susie, gave a thumbs up. Out of the side of his mouth, John said to Mia, standing beside him, "That seems promising."

As the two women approached them, Susie spoke. "Well, you have a lovely house, John." She cocked an inquisitive eyebrow. "Dare I ask why you are selling?"

John shrugged. "After losing my wife in a traffic accident, I decided to move abroad." He reached out and pulled Mia towards him. "While in Spain looking at properties, I met Mia. We hit it off, and she came over to see me." He took Mia's hand. "Since then, we fell in love and are going to get married."

A brief flicker of disappointment crossed Susie's face. Then flashing a broad smile, she stepped in close and kissed Mia's cheek.

"Congratulations. I wish you every happiness. Now, as for the house, I'm tempted. But I have a few more properties to check out before making a final decision."

John nodded. "I understand about the house, and thank you for your kind wishes about Mia and me."

Mary stepped forward. She beamed them a smile, then shook hands with John and Mia, "Like Mrs McCarthy, I wish you all the best."

Once they were gone, John picked up Mia and swung her around.

"Well, that's another possibility of someone buying the house."

Mia cocked an eyebrow. "Would you mind if your old girlfriend bought your house?"

John threw back his head and laughed. "Darling, even if the Devil wanted to buy the house, never mind Susie, I would have no objections. I would like to sell it, move to Spain, and be with you."

Mia reached up and kissed him. With her tongue exploring his mouth, John felt his emotions rise. He gasped and held her at arm's length.

"Do you have any idea what a kiss like that does to a man?"

"Of course," she murmured, "I feel the same."

John shook his head. "How in all of Spain did I manage to find such an incredible woman like you? To cuddle you gives me a thrill, but when you behave like that, I'm well and truly lost."

Mia put a hand on her hip. "You're not complaining, are you? If so, then you are not the man I thought you were?"

"Darling, if you ever hear me complain you are too sexy, take me to see a doctor. I would have lost my mind."

Mia responded by throwing her arms around him and giving him a long and passionate kiss. As she released him, she said, "That's what I wanted you to say."

"Yes well, I think you should take more notes on details you would like included in our new house."

Mia chuckled. "Coward. Now, where did you put my notes, etc?"

John turned, opened a drawer, and took out a file. "Here we are, my darling," He then took out the design books and placed them next to the folder.

A smile lit up Mia's face as she glanced at him. "Thank you, kind sir." She opened the book she had been looking through, then carried on where she had left off.

JOHN SHOOK HIS HEAD in wonder. "After all the years that had passed, Susie had appeared back in his life. They had been close, at one time, but she had left him for another man. From what he could remember, his surname was Wilson. It meant Susie had moved on to someone named McCarthy. He shrugged. It made no difference to his feelings for Mia. She, and only she, was who he was interested in. However, he did wonder if Susie would buy his house. If she did, it would be great for him and Mia.

After pottering around the house and sorting out a few things, he returned to find Mia, engrossed in making notes of various house plans.

His eyes lit. "Wow, I can see I'll have competition if you make up designs like these?"

She looked up. "You are too kind, John, but thank you for saying what you did."

He shook his head. "No, from a glance, I can see you have an eye for design. Anyway, from this, I'm sure I'll be able to design a house that we both like. Now, how about we take Lucky for a walk. We can then have dinner out?"

Mia gave a subtle wink. "That sounds good, but maybe we can have dessert back here?" The next minute she gasped, when John took her in his arms, and they exchanged a long and deep kiss.

When they broke it off, John gasped, "I thought it was the dessert we would have here, not the main course?"

Mia fluttered her long eyelashes. "We did; that's just a sample of what dessert will be like."

Chapter 25

"In that case, I'll need to be prepared for a feast. Now, there are three restaurants in town. Annie Jones, The Fez restaurant, which is Turkish, or La Pizzella. Which would you like to try?" Before she could answer, he said, "I think you would prefer Annie Jones. She is both owner and chef, and does a delicious Bouillabaisse loaded with seafood."

Mia licked her lips. "As you recommend it, let's go there."

He shrugged. "Well, I've never been disappointed after eating there."

After they took Lucky out for a walk, once showered and dressed, John drove them to the restaurant. On arrival, with only a few customers, they had a choice of tables. Once sat at a table, a waitress took their order of the Bouillabaisse and a bottle of white wine. When she later brought their meal, Mia exclaimed, "This looks great."

"Yes, but I hope you say that after you have eaten."

Once both had finished, he turned to Mia. "So, what did you think?"

"It was delicious thank you. How about you?"

"Like you said, it tasted delicious."

When the waitress came to ask if they would care for a dessert, John felt Mia's foot touch his leg. He looked across to see her give a subtle shake of her head.

"No, thanks, but could we have two coffees, please?"

"Certainly." She flashed them a smile. "I'm glad you enjoyed your meal." On her return, she placed down two steaming cups of coffee.

Later, before leaving the restaurant, John thanked the waitress, who noticed he had left a large tip.

Back at John's house, he said, "How about we take Lucky out? It will help walk off our meal."

"Oh, I see, it's just to get you fit for dessert, is that it?" Mia tittered.

John looked skyward. "What dessert is that?"

She gave a subtle wink. "Once we are back from taking Lucky out, you will find out. Anyway, you take Lucky while I sort myself out."

On his return, John went upstairs to find Mia in bed. She patted it and gave a mischievous smile. "I was beginning to think you had changed your mind about dessert?"

With his eyes burning with desire, John shook his head. "Are you kidding?" He then all but ripped off his clothes in his haste to join Mia.

After a heavy petting session, with John kissing and sucking her breasts while she stroked his throbbing erection, Mia said, "Enough."

She threw back the sheet and licked her lips. "Now, are you ready for dessert?"

"Yes. What do you fancy?"

Mia pointed. "I don't know about you, but that would do me nicely."

Sliding down the bed, her fingers caressed his body before moving lower to tease and play with his balls. After kissing the head of his cock, she opened her mouth and took it inside. The more her lips moved up and down his length, the more aroused John became. In the end, he could take no more.

"Darling, I can't hold on any longer. I want to get inside you."

Mia paused for a moment and lifted her gaze upwards. "No, I want to finish what I started." She winked. "Once I have, you can satisfy me." Before John could reply, her mouth closed over his cock, and after taking it deep inside, she felt his semen flood into her mouth.

He gasped and held her tight. A few minutes later, after Mia returned from the bathroom, he said, "Well, I've had my dessert. Now it's your turn." After they enjoyed a passionate kiss, breaking it off, she asked, "So, are you up to giving me dessert?"

As John went to put his head down between her thighs, he said, "I am, are you?" He then kissed the lips of her pussy before pushing his tongue inside. With long, deep strokes, flicking it faster, he was driving Mia crazy with desire. After an orgasm flooded through her, she lay back exhausted.

With her thighs still trembling, John moved up the bed. He took a condom from under the pillow, slipped it on and thrust his throbbing hardness into her wetness. Mia gasped, then ground her hips into his as he pushed in deeper. Finally, to her delight, as she climax again, with a last thrust, John came.

With both spent, they disentangled themselves, and in minutes, were fast asleep.

When John awoke and turned to kiss Mia, good morning, to his surprise, she was not there. He climbed from the bed and made his way downstairs. To his further puzzlement, neither Mia nor Lucky were to be seen. A glance at his watch showed it was almost ten am, much later than his usual time to get up. He padded into the kitchen and had started to prepare breakfast when he heard the front door open. The next minute, Lucky bounded in, wagging his tail as he ran up to him.

"Hi, Lucky, what's all this, going out without me?"

As he spoke, Mia walked in wearing a broad smile. "Oh, you're awake, are you?" She giggled. "What happened last night to make you so tired that you couldn't wake up this morning?"

He shook his head. "Whatever it was, I can't wait until it comes back again." Pulling Mia into his arms, he kissed her.

"So, you took Lucky out on your own. Did you have any problems? I mean, did you get lost at all?"

"No, after being out with you and Lucky, I knew which way to go. Oh, and don't worry, I also cleared up behind him."

Thank you, darling. In return, I have breakfast ready." As he spoke, they could hear Lucky getting stuck into the bowl of food John had put out.

THEY HAD EATEN AND cleared away, with Mia taking a shower when John's phone rang. He felt puzzled when he did not recognise the caller's number.

"Hello." He then heard a familiar voice say, "I hope you don't mind, but I got your number from Mary." It was Susie. "I told her I wanted to discuss the price of your house. As she knew we were old friends, she gave it to me, so please don't be cross with her."

John felt puzzled why she was calling him. "Oh, hi, Susie." He paused, awaiting her to speak. Her next words came as a shock. "I called to see if we could meet for a chat?"

His expression slid into a frown. "Sorry, but I don't think that's a good idea. Mia would not appreciate my talking with an old girlfriend without her being present."

He heard Susie sigh. "I'm sorry, John, you are right. I should not have called." She then went on to say, "Mia is lucky to have you. Most men would have said yes to an offer like mine. Still, forget, I asked. Now, regarding the house, once I've checked out the other places on my shortlist, I may get back to you. In the meantime, take care and look after Mia, she seems a nice woman."

"She is, and thank you, Susie." He chuckled inwardly as he said, "Should you decide to purchase my house, Mary will take care of all the details." Although he never said, he felt sure Susie understood what he meant.

After they said goodbye, John closed his phone. Susie looked great, and they would have had a good time together. But, there was no way he would see her without Mia. He also knew she would not be pleased to hear of Susie's phone call, so decided not to tell her.

When Mia came back down, John noticed she had brushed her hair and put on her make-up. She looked irresistibly beautiful.

"Wow, now there's a sight for sore eyes."

Mia's eyes lit up, and she twirled around, showing off her slim, curvaceous figure. "So, do I look as good as Susie?" She shrugged. "I must say she looked most attractive."

John couldn't help but chuckle at that. "Don't worry. I wouldn't push you out of bed to get to her." A ghost of a smile crossed his lips. "Look, as I have previously mentioned before, no one will tempt me away from you."

"Thank you, John." She shook her head. "Still, that's two women I wouldn't want to leave you alone with."

He cocked an eyebrow. "What about you?" Before she could answer, he put a finger to her lips. "I mean, you are an attractive woman with your own business. Now, what more would a man want?" Taking hold of her hands, John gazed into Mia's eyes.

"You told me that you had a steady boyfriend before I came along. So, how would you react if he came and asked for you two to get back together?"

"Not a chance," she snorted. "Nor any other man I've ever met." A satisfied smile crossed her lips. "No one has ever affected me the way you have. Some of my girlfriends have noticed how I've changed." She giggled. "They have asked if you have a friend like you." She wagged a finger. "So, when you meet them, I'll be watching you like a hawk." A satisfied smile crossed her lips. "It's not that I don't trust you," she tittered, "but like me, my friends are hot-blooded Mediterranean women."

John's eyes lit up in pretend interest. "They are, are they? Now that could prove interesting." He then winced as Mia gave him a sharp poke in the ribs.

"Look, even if they look like one of Victoria's Secret models, I would not be interested."

Mia flung her arms around him and kissed him. "Yes, and that's what I mean about you and other men. Some only have one thing on their mind when they meet a good-looking woman. Therefore, I'm glad you're not one of them."

John grinned. "Well, before things become too hot, although neither of us is religious, I thought we might visit Winchester Cathedral." He shook his head. "It's nowhere near as good as your cathedral, but it's a beautiful place."

Mia nodded. "I've heard about Winchester Cathedral, so it would be nice to see it and look inside."

He angled a glance towards her. "Well, I hope you won't be too disappointed when you do?"

A smile quirked her lips. "Don't worry, I'll be with you, so I know I'll be satisfied."

"Right, let's take Lucky out

When they later set off, a sideways glance showed Mia smiling and

looking happy.

About an hour later, they arrived in Winchester. Once parked, hand in hand, he and Mia strolled along. When they came to the cathedral, Mia exclaimed, "Wow, it looks wonderful, can we go inside?"

"Of course."

On entering, her eyes lit up at the length and width of the Nave. "Oh, this is huge. It's much larger than what I expected."

John nodded. "From what I've read, it's the largest in Europe of this style of cathedral."

Once back outside, he asked. "Do you know the story about King Arthur and the Knights of the round table?"

She cocked an eyebrow. "I've heard of it, but I don't know if it's true or not."

He grinned. "Right, we will go this way and I'll show you something interesting." After they walked a short distance, they entered what Mia read on a sign was: The Great Hall of Winchester Castle.

Inside, John pointed to a large circular table suspended off the ground.

"That's claimed to be King Arthur's famous round table."

"Well, it looks large enough."

"Yes, but there is one problem with that theory."

Mia cocked an eyebrow in puzzlement. "Oh, and what's that?"

"They made the table after King Arthur's time." He then went on to say, "As for Kin' Arthur's story, some claim it's true, while other' say it's not. Still, right, or wrong, it's an entertaining" story."

Chapter 26

On going outside, a short walk brought them to Winchester University and the College. Mia shook her head in puzzlement. "These buildings look rather ancient to be still in use?"

John nodded in agreement. "Believe it or not, those are the original buildings. It seems they are the oldest public schools in the world."

"Well, from their look, I can well believe they are."

Flashing an innocent smile, John said, "I'll tell you something else that not many people know." He shrugged. "Still, I must admit I only found this out while doing research for an exam."

Mia gave a short laugh "Oh, and what is it? You never know; I might know the answer?"

"So, did you know that Winchester was once the capital city of England?"

Mia's eyebrows rose in surprise. "No, I've never heard that before."

"Until William the Conqueror arrived in the eleventh century, Winchester was the capital city." He chuckled. "Right, that's enough history lessons for today. Shall we have lunch? Or are you not hungry?"

Mia squeezed his arm. "A snack would do me, but what about you?"

"Yes, that sounds good to me."

After finding a café where they enjoyed a coffee and a sandwich each, they continued to stroll around the city streets.

A smile quirked Mia's lip. "With old buildings and narrow cobbled streets, Winchester is full of character."

"Yes, I thought you might like it here. Anyway, have you seen enough, or shall we stay longer?"

"Longer, if you don't mind?"

"No problem, as long as I'm with you, I'm happy."

After a glance and not seeing anyone nearby, Mia gave him a kiss on the cheek. "Me too." She then went on to say, "It's funny, but this takes me back to my younger days when I used to walk along like we are now."

John cocked an eyebrow. "Oh, and what did you do then, compared to what we do?"

Mia blushed. "Nothing, if you mean what I think you do?"

John pulled her close to him, wrapping his arms around her waist. As his lips brushed her neck, he muttered, "Now, what do you think I meant." A ghost of a smile crossed his lips. "Oh, I think you mean about our making love?"

The heat of his breath made Mia's passion rise. "You are a devil John," then gave him a short kiss on the lips.

John's cheeks coloured and he said, "Okay, you win. Now, we'd best behave, or we might find ourselves in trouble."

Mia gave a subtle wink. "Yes, we'd best keep our thoughts like that until tonight."

John's eyebrows shot up in anticipation at what Mia means. When she noticed a sparkle appear in his eyes, she said, "Okay, calm down and behave."

He shook his head. "How can I do that when I have such a sexy woman like you next to me?"

"Try," she murmured. "Now, let's walk a bit more, and then we can leave."

Chapter 27

When they left Winchester, instead of going on the motorway John drove along country roads Mia sighed and cuddled into him as best she could. "I love this," she said. "It's so much better to drive on side roads than the main ones. That's of course, unless you're in a hurry to get somewhere."

By the time they arrived at John's house, the sun had disappeared. Clouds were forming and it had started to get dark.

As Mia climbed out of the car, she shuddered. "It's much colder now."

"Yes, it is," John said, as he opened the front door. "If you like, once I've lit the fire, you stay and watch TV while I take Lucky out?"

As he spoke, Lucky appeared and gave them a bark of welcome. Mia bent and stroked his head.

"No, I'll come with you, but first, I'll put on a warmer coat. I don't want to catch a cold."

"That's for sure." Once satisfied, the fire was well blazing bright, they went out. As they walked along, Lucky stopped to sniff at anything he found of interest.

"He is a good boy," Mia said. "He never seems to be a problem?"

John couldn't help but chuckle. "Of course not. I trained him."

Mia pressed a hand to her mouth to stifle a giggle. "So, are you going to train me as well?"

A sigh escaped from John's lips. "I don't think it will be necessary. I haven't found anything you do that needs sorting out."

For that, he received a short kiss on the cheek. A hint of a smile crossed Mia's face. "That's one advantage of living in this place," she said. "There are not many people around to see you if you sneak a kiss with your partner."

John glanced around, pulled Mia close and kissed her. "You mean like that?" he said, on breaking it off.

She gasped. "Yes, that's exactly what I meant." While they kissed, Lucky stood and wagged his tail as if to say, 'Okay, save that for later, let's walk.'

Once back in the house, the heat from the fire had made the lounge warm and comfortable.

"Oh, this feels so good," Mia said as she stood and warmed her hands in front of the glass doors of the fire.

After he'd released Lucky's lead, John returned with two glasses of whisky.

"Here, get this down. It will warm your inside." They clinked glasses and then sipped their drinks.

As it went down, Mia said, "I don't usually drink whisky, but as you said, I can feel it warming me already." She giggled. "Of course, it might be the fire and not the drink."

John grinned. "Well, as long as you now feel warmer, it doesn't matter which."

"You are right. Now, as we have been out most of the day, let's stay in with Lucky. I am sure there is enough food to make something for dinner?"

"Good idea. What do you think, Lucky?" A bark and a wag of his tail said he agreed.

John flashed Mia a smile. "Right, as Lucky also thinks it's an idea, that's what we will do."

After a check in the kitchen, John suggested some chicken fillets. Using these, along with vegetable and potato wedges, he made dinner.

Once finished and washed down with a few glasses of wine, they sat cuddled together on the sofa.

Mia sighed. "I love it when we are together like this. It makes me feel happy inside.

An instant later, John noticed tears pooling in her eyes. With raised eyebrows, he said, "What's wrong, darling? Why the sad face?"

She closed her eyes and summed a deep breath. "I've realised that I'll be going back to Spain soon. I don't know if you will be with me?"

John gripped her hand tight. "Darling, I don't know either, but believe you me, if I'm not, it won't be for lack of trying."

With tears running down her face, smearing her mascara, Mia sobbed. "I know, but it doesn't make me feel any better."

He pulled her close and kissed her cheek. "Hey, common, don't get like this. No matter what happens, I've promised I will join you shortly." He then kissed her wet eyes."Look, I feel sure something will come up soon to resolve this problem."

"If only I could feel as positive as you," she sobbed.

"Darling, you should always think positive, not negative. I always say, positive thoughts lead to positive results, while negative ones give negative results""

Mia nodded. "Yes, I know you are right. In my business, I always think positive. But this situation is not something I'm used to." She gave a half-smile. "If I didn't love you as much as I do, I wouldn't care, but as I do, it does matter."

John grinned. "Well, I'm pleased to hear that. I always want us to be together. Now go dry your eyes. Your tears are making my shirt wet."

An impish smile made Mia's mouth twitch. "So, you are more bothered about your shirt than me, are you?"

He laughed. "What! Never. Now go. While you are gone, I'll open a bottle of Merlot." Mia went upstairs, and on her return, John nodded in satisfaction.

"That's what I like, a smiling and pretty face. Oh, and your hair looks beautiful."

She flashed him a beaming smile. "Thank you, John. I am sorry for being tearful. It's not your fault if you can't sell your house." She shrugged. "I should know. Some houses were on our books for a year before we found a buyer." After a glance at her watch, she said, "It's late now, but I'll call Carlos in the morning. Maybe someone is interested in your house."

"Good, and I'll call Mary. Who knows, there might have been a development with the people who've expressed an interest in buying my house."

He handed Mia a glass of Merlot, then as they clinked glasses said, "Here is to some good news re a buyer."

After sipping their wine, and finishing the film they were watching, John asked, "Shall we watch another film or have you had enough?"

"No, let us watch another one. I like our being cuddled together." She then pulled him down and gave him a deep and lingering kiss.

On breaking it off, he gasped. "Wow. I'd best put on another film." Once done, he re-joined Mia on the sofa. During a break in the movie, she said, "Shall I make us a cup of coffee?"

"Yes, please. It will help me stay awake until we go to bed."

She gave a subtle wink. "So, it's sleep when we go to bed, is it?"

John's eyes lit. "We...ll, if you have something else in mind, I could be persuaded." After both laughed, they embraced and kissed.

When they later went to go up to bed, John spoke to Lucky. "Now, don't worry if you hear strange noises coming from upstairs; it will be nothing to worry about."

Mia put a finger to her mouth. "Oh, does that mean Lucky won't come to rescue me if I need help?"

John gazed at her with lust in his eyes "Not a chance," he said. Holding Mia's hand, they went upstairs and in minutes were in bed, locked in each other's arms.

After a long and tender lovemaking session, with John's arms around Mia, they fell asleep.

The following day, both wore expressions of bliss when they took Lucky out for a walk. On their return, with breakfast finished, Mia flashed John a smile. "I'll call Carlos. Maybe he has any news for us?"

John shrugged. "You can, but I don't expect he will."

She wagged a finger. "Now, what did you tell me? Be positive." A ghost of a smile crossed her face. "You never know your luck. I mean, did I expect to meet an Englishman in Barcelona who would capture my heart?"

A sigh escaped John's lips. "That's true. After all, I never expected to meet and fall in love with a cracker-like you." His smile widened and he said, "So, give Carlos a call. After all, miracles do happen."

Mia called Carlos, but with no reply, she closed her phone. They had cleared away their breakfast things when Mia's phone rang. As she picked it up, her eyebrows rose. "It's Carlos."

While John sat in anticipation, Mia and Carlos exchanged greetings. A few minutes later, she turned and with her eyes bright with excitement, gave him a thumbs up.

John then sat, twisting his hands in anticipation for Mia to end the conversation and tell him what Carlos had said.

When she finally closed her phone, with a beaming smile stretched across her face, Mia could not have looked happier.

John, his eyebrows pulled together in question, said, "Okay, please don't keep me in suspense. I can see you have some good news."

An impish smile made Mia's mouth twitch. This news is truly great, I'm so happy, I can't believe" it."

Chapter 28

J ohn's eyebrows rose in frustration. "Well, are you going to tell me or not?"

"Oh, sorry darling, of course, I will. First, an English couple came into our office to put their villa in Valencia up for sale." To John's annoyance, she then went on to say, "They had put it with an agent there, then came to Barcelona for a few days before flying home. Anyway, when they spotted our office, they decided it might be an idea to put their villa with us to try and sell it."

John spoke through gritted teeth. "Darling, if you don't get to the point soon, I'll go mad. Now, what's all this got to do with my house?"

She pressed a hand to her mouth to stifle a giggle. "Well, it seems the couple, a Mr & Mrs Walker, had seen your house in England."

At the name mentioned, John's eyes lit up. "Yes, I remember them. They were among several people who came one weekend to view the house."

"Well, after they had seen it, they went for a holiday to their villa in Valencia. While there, they decided to sell it." A satisfied smile crossed Mia's face. "Anyway, when they saw your house for sale in our office window, they thought it a sign. So, if you like? They will buy it."

John's eyebrows rose in disbelief. "Wow, that's fantastic news," he said. "And of course, they are more than welcome to buy my house."

Mia flashed him a beaming smile. "Good, as I've told Carlos to tell them yes." She shook her head. "That's not all. They've already had people interested in buying their villa." Then, after looking deep in thought for a moment, her next words surprised John

"Darling, what do you think about our buying it? Instead of living in Barcelona, we live in Valencia?"

John gazed into her eyes, then nodded. "That wouldn't be a problem for me, but what about you? How could you manage to run your business in Barcelona?"

Mia tossed her head. "Well, you never know. I have a friend in Valencia who also runs a real-estate business. If we were interested in buying the villa, maybe my friend and I could come to some arrangement?"

As they sat and pondered, Mia's phone bleeped. "Ah, it must be Carlos. He said he would send some photos of the villa." She opened her phone and found a multitude of photos.

As they looked at them, both felt impressed by what they saw. The rooms were spacious, plus, besides the small front garden, there was also a substantial enclosed rear garden.

"It looks fine, plus it has a garden for the dogs," John said. He squeezed Mia's hand. "What do you think? And more importantly, what do you think your friend would say about exchanging business locations?"

A smile quirked Mia's lips. "First, from these photos, the villa looks ideal. Plus, as you say, there is a garden for Aza and Lucky. As for what Fernando would say, I'll call him." She paused, then said, "Still, before I do, are you sure you wouldn't mind living in Valencia?"

"No problem for me. I told you I had looked at properties there before coming to Barcelona." A soft chuckle escaped his lips. "It was only you that made me decide Barcelona was a better bet."

A sigh escaped Mia's lips. "In that case, I'll call and see what he thinks. As Fernando is single, he can easily decide if it's a yes or a no."

John cocked an eyebrow. "Oh, I see."

"What!" Mia giggled loudly, unable to contain her amusement. "No, you don't. Fernando is forty and gay." When he answered Mia's call, as John could not understand Spanish, he indicated he would do a bit of work. While sat at his desk, John's thoughts were on the possibility of them living in Valencia. When he heard Mia enter the room, he looked up to see her eyes were bright with excitement.

"Well, from the look on your face, Fernando is interested?"

She flashed him a beaming smile. "You won't believe it when I tell you what he said."

John grinned. "Well, I might, if you told me?"

Mia tossed her hair back over her shoulders. "First, he is interested. Second, he had been thinking of a move up to Barcelona."

"What!"

"Yes, he said it was about time he changed his life. Therefore, my call could not have come at a better time. He thinks it's a sign the Gods had heard his prayers."

John gripped Mia's hands tight. "Darling, if you are serious about this, it would solve two problems simultaneously. It would mean we had sold my house, and we wouldn't have to go searching for somewhere to live."

Mia's smile widened. "In that case, I say we should either buy or exchange the villa for your house and move to Valencia?"

As she gazed into John's eyes, she saw him smile. "That's fine with me, but how can we contact the Walker's?"

Mia gave a subtle wink. "That's not a problem, they are waiting for your call."

John shook his head. "I don't have their phone number."

Mia put a hand to her mouth to stifle a giggle. "No, but I do. Carlos sent it to me."

After John called and spoke to Mr Walker, he turned with a wide smile spread across his face. "Right, that's it. They will buy my house, and I'll buy their villa. However, we've agreed that we would look at the villa before signing anything. In the meantime, neither of us will accept any offers on our houses." He then picked up Mia and spun her around, making Lucky jump back in alarm.

After he kissed and set her back on her feet, he said, "This calls for a drink to celebrate." As Mia went to speak, he shook his head. "First, we should book a flight to Valencia. Once we've seen the villa, we can then decide whether to live there or find somewhere in Barcelona."

A check online revealed they could catch a direct flight to Valencia from Gatwick or Stansted. With Gatwick the nearest, after he checked on flights, John booked them seats for the following morning.

Grinning, he turned to Mia. "That's it. Come tomorrow afternoon; we will have checked out the villa."

She flashed him a smile, but seeing a hint of concern in her eyes, he asked, "Darling, are you sure about this? If not, I can always cancel our flights."

Mia's smile widened, and she shook her head. "No, like Fernando, it's the answer to our prayers." She caught hold of John's hands. "Darling, I am sure, but are you? I wouldn't like you to do something you might later regret."

He shook his head. "Are you serious? This way, we will live in a villa, with a garden for the dogs. What more could we wish for?" With that, they embraced and kissed. The expression of joy on John's face then faded and replaced by a more serious look. "Um, Mia, there is one other thing."

She cocked an eyebrow. "Oh, and what's that?"

"How about your staff and Carlos? From the way you talk about him, he has been with you for quite some time."

"Yes, he has, but if Fernando and I can sort things out, Carlos would come and work with me in Valencia."

John's brow creased in puzzlement. "Oh, and what makes you think that."

"Well, for a start, his family lives in Valencia." She giggled. "Plus, I know he has a lady friend there."

"Ah, ha, so you have thought everything out, have you?"

"Only after I thought the Walker's villa could be perfect for us."

John nodded. "Well, tomorrow, we will find out." Wearing a broad smile, he said, "Now, let's get changed and go for a pre-celebration drink, plus something to eat."

A short time later, they were sitting at a table in the King's Head pub. Along with their meals, John ordered two glasses of Merlot that they sipped while awaiting their roast beef lunch to be served.

When a waitress placed them down in front of them, Mia's eyebrows shot up. "Wow, is this a normal-sized lunch?" She shook her head. "I mean, you could not get more on a plate than this."

A smile spread across John's face. "Yes, it's what one gets for lunch in a pub. Look, it's not a problem if you can't eat it all, just eat what you can." He raised his glass of Merlot and touched Mia's glass. "Here's to a successful day tomorrow."

With her eyes wide with excitement, Mia said, "I hope so."

Despite her concern about her meal's size, John thought Mia had done well when she put down her knife and fork.

When their waitress returned and asked if they would like a dessert, before John could reply, Mia shook her head. "No, thank you, that meal was more than enough."

The waitress flashed her a smile. "Yes, we pride ourselves on the size of the meals we serve." With that, she walked away.

Once they had finished their wine and John had settled the bill, he said, "How about we take a walk?"

"Yes, a great idea. After all that food, it would help to work off the excess weight I am liable to put on."

John gave a short, dirty laugh. "If you're worried about that, I'm sure I could provide you with some exercise?"

"Now that sounds interesting, but for now, let's take a walk." She winked. "I'll see if I need any other exercise afterwards."

Their laughter made the waitress look up, as did two other customers.

Once outside, after a short walk, Mia stopped. "Let us go and get Lucky. We can take him with us for a walk."

"That's an excellent suggestion. I'm sure he would agree."

After a taxi dropped them off at John's house, with Lucky on his lead, the three of them set off. Although dry, there was a nip in the air. Still, thanks to their warm coats, neither John nor Mia felt cold. Plus, the prospects of seeing what could be their new home the next day warmed their hearts.

Once back inside the house, John turned to Mia. "As we will be leaving early, I'll call Joan." When he noticed Mia's puzzlement, he explained. "Anytime I have to leave extra early, she comes and takes Lucky out for a walk."

Chapter 29

Once he had made arrangements with Joan, John sat back with a satisfied smile. "Right, that's done. She will come and sort Lucky out."

Mia nodded. "Good, now all we have to do is wait and see if the villa is as good as it looks from the photos."

"You're right. Still, as long as the structure and location are good, I don't foresee any other problems." He shrugged. "We might need to redecorate to suit our own ideas, but that won't be a problem."

"Yes, redecorating is more than likely," Mia agreed. "As for the location, I know more or less where it is. I'm sure you will approve?"

John leaned over and pressed his lips against her cheek. "Darling, as long as I'm with you, I'd be happy no matter where we live."

An impish smile made her mouth twitch. "Until we know if we will live in Valencia, I won't bother looking through any more of your design books."

John grinned. "Well, in case we don't move there, you might as well continue. I mean, apart from watching some more films, what else is there to do?"

A flicker of a smile crossed Mia's face. "John, you have a one-track mind."

"Of course. With you looking so delectable, what else should I be thinking of?"

"You are impossible," she tittered. "But perhaps that's why I love you?" She then noticed John's happy expression had changed into a frown.

"What is up, why the face?"

John folded his hands in hers. "Darling, I don't like to say, but how shall we play this?"

A worried expression marred Mia's face. "What do you mean?"

"Well, after we have looked at the villa, there is not much point in you coming back to England with me? I mean, you are due to return home next week."

"Oh, I see what you mean." She sighed. "That makes sense, but I'm going to miss you like crazy."

"Me too." John's lips turned into a grin. "Of course, I could stay with you in Barcelona for a few days? But," he said, his breath tickling her ear, "If that's a problem? I could always stay in the hotel where I stayed before?"

Mia's eyebrows shot up. "What! Don't even think about going back there." She pouted and tossed her hair. "That's unless you would prefer to stay there on your own and not with Aza and me?"

John put a finger to his mouth. "Now, let me think for a moment? We...ll, as Aza will be there, I'd best stay." He then groaned as Mia poked him in the ribs before giving him a long and passionate kiss. As they broke it off, John's face changed into a broad smile.

"Right, that's settled, I'll stay for a few days to see how things go with you and Fernando." He shook his head. "The last thing I want is for me to end up in Valencia and you in Barcelona."

"What! There is no chance of that happening. If Fernando and I cannot work something out between us, which I'm sure we will, I'll try another friend of mine. He is also in the same business." She flashed a smile. "After all, what are friends for but to help one another."

A relieved look crossed John's face. "So, you might have another possibility if things don't work out with Fernando?"

Mia wagged a finger. "Of course, don't think you will escape from me that easily."

With his lips nuzzling her neck, he said, "Now that's what I like to hear, a positive answer. Anyway, I'll pack enough clothing for a week." Then, as Mia gave a whoop of joy, he shook his head. "I'm sorry, but I can't stay longer. I have to get back and complete Mr Dawe's project."

At the mention of Mr Dawe, his daughter Sylvia came to Mia's mind. She wagged a finger. "Make sure you keep away from his daughter. I think she fancies you?"

John flashed an innocent smile. "Oh, I'd forgotten about her."

Mia tilted her head. "Yes, and I'm the Queen of Sheba."

He chuckled and bowed his head. "Of course, your majesty, whatever you say," before throwing his arms up as Mia glared at him.

"Look, how many times do I have to tell you? No one will ever tempt me away from you." He caught hold of her hands and gazed into her eyes. "At least, not unless you decide you have had enough of me."

Mia's eyebrows shot up, and she clasped him tight. "What," she gasped, "there is no chance of that from my side."

They both laughed, each hoping tomorrow would result in some good news. John had earlier said he would make them something for dinner. But, after such a large lunch, they made do with a toasted cheese and tomato sandwich.

Later, due to having to be at the airport early the next morning, they had an early night.

The following morning, after John drove and parked in the airport car park, four hours later, they were in Valencia. Outside the airport, after Mia told a taxi driver the address they wanted, they set of

As they drove along, Mia gripped John's hand tight. Like him, she hoped the villa would be suitable for them. On pulling up outside, her eyes lit as a glance showed it looked in excellent condition.

With luggage in hand, they walked in through the open gate and up the drive. A parked car showed the Walkers were at home. Before they reached the entrance door, it opened to reveal who they knew must be Mr & Mrs Walker.

"Good morning," the man said. He held out a hand, "I'm George, and this is my wife, Joyce." Once introductions were over, George said, "Right, come inside." He chuckled. "When Joyce noticed your house for sale in Barcelona, we could not believe our eyes. I knew it was a sign we should buy it." When he noticed John's surprise, he went on to say, "We fell in love with your house when we first looked it over. However, we had already decided to sell the villa, and had booked our flights here. We intended to contact you on our return to England."

As George talked, Mia who had cast her eyes around, nodded in satisfaction. John was also impressed by what he had seen. The lounge where George had taken them was of good size, although the furniture looked rather old. He then led them into the good-sized dining room.

On entering the kitchen, Mia said, "This is for you, John." She turned to the Walkers. "John is a good cook, so this is perfect for him." He nodded agreement. Then, as he looked out into the back garden, his eyes lit up.

"Yes, and the garden is ideal for our dogs." A glance out and Mia said, "We have two big dogs, so a garden is essential."

Mr & Mrs exchanged glances. So far, things looked pretty positive. George flashed them a smile. "Shall we go upstairs?"

"Yes, please." Mia squeezed John's hand. From her expression, like him, she liked what they had seen.

The first bedroom they entered, George said, was the main one. However, the sight of an ensuite bathroom made Mia's eyes light up.

Joyce, who had noticed her joyful expression, said, "We had the ensuite installed after my parents died. This used to be their house."

While they talked, John, who had taken a look around, nodded. "This is ideal."

"Me too," Mia added.

A smile spread across George's face. "Right, now let me show you the rest of the house." He then led them into the next room, which was a bedroom. Although a bit smaller, it was still a good size. It pleased John to find the third bedroom was also okay. Also, the separate bathroom was of good size.

As they returned downstairs, George shook his head. "Oh, I almost forgot." He opened a door to reveal a cloakroom fitted with W.C and a wash hand basin. On closing the door, he said, "Well, that's the house; now the only thing left is the garden." He then opened the outside kitchen door, fitted with a metal grill.

"We've never had a problem here, and as you have two dogs, I'm sure you won't either."

The garden, surrounded by a sturdy fence that had a door set in on one side pleased both Mia and John. He turned to Mia. "I think this would suit us. What do you think?"

With her eyes shining bright, she said, "Yes, it's just the type of place we wanted."

John turned to the Walker's. "Well, you heard the boss. She likes your place, as do I. Therefore, if you agree to buy my house, you can consider yours sold?"

George turned to his wife, who smiled and said, "Yes." He turned back and held out a hand. "There you are, that's a done deal. I'll call and tell my agent; I've sold the villa." Shaking his head, he said, "He won't be pleased. If he had sold it; I would have had to pay him a commission."

"Yes, and I will phone my secretary," Mia said. "I'll tell him to remove the sign in front of John's house, and notify the online sales sites."

On seeing Mr & Mrs Walkers" look of puzzlement, Mia gave a beaming smile. "It's my office where your wife spotted John's house for sale."

George shook his head in amazement. "Well, I never," his wife said, "What a coincidence?"

John laughed. "Yes, but a good one." He turned to Mia. "Well, that's this part of our trip sorted out, now for the next."

"Right, while you sort out any details you need to finalise, I'll call Fernando." With that, Mia excused herself and left the room.

While she was gone, John told the Walkers of Mia's idea of changing offices with a friend whose office was in Valencia. "Well, it would be an excellent move if you could do that," George said.

When Mia called Fernando, he said, "So, how did things go? Are we on for an exchange?"

"Yes. My boyfriend has just agreed to buy the villa I told you about, with the owners buying his house in England."

"Well! I've never heard of this sort of thing in all my fifteen years in the business," he said. "It's amazing."

Mia suppressed a giggle. "Well, I've not been in the business as long as you, but likewise. Anyway, have you time for us to meet?"

"Of course, come to the office. I'll be waiting. I would like to meet this boyfriend of yours. He must be something special to get you to leave Barcelona?"

"Yes, he is. Right, we will be with you shortly."

When she went back inside the room, Mia flashed John a smile. "Fernando is waiting for us."

He turned to the Walkers, "In that case, it was nice meeting you both. We will talk more once I return home, which should be in around four days."

Mr Walker held out his hand. "That sounds good to me. I'll await your call."

After Mia and John shook hands with him and Joyce, on leaving the house, both wore broad smiles as they climbed into the taxi Mia had ordered.

Chapter 30

On the way to Fernando's office, John said, "Darling, I've been thinking."

"Oh, and what about? Something nice, I hope," she chortled?

A crease appeared in John's forehead. "No, not really."

Mia's eyebrows shot up in puzzlement. "Oh, what is it?"

"Well, if you change offices with Fernando, aren't you going to lose a lot of money? I mean, property prices in Barcelona are far higher than in Valencia. I noticed the difference when I checked out prices before coming to Spain."

"You are right, but Fernando does good business selling to both locals and tourists. Still, I must admit overall yearly sales are far better in Barcelona than here." Before John could comment, Mia went on to say, "However, on the plus side, wages, and rents are less in Valencia." She laughed. "So is the traffic." When she noticed John's look of concern, she caught hold and squeezed his hand.

"Look, I knew all this before I suggested moving my business to Valencia, so don't worry about it. Plus, do not forget, I will not have to pay rent on an apartment." With a hand to her mouth to muffle a giggle, she said, "I'm sure I'll be able to keep us both." Mia shook her head. "I am only joking, darling. I have faith in you doing well once people hear about your wonderful house designs."

As the taxi pulled over and stopped, Mia gripped John's hand, "Well, here we are. What do you think of the location?"

A glance revealed Fernando's office was near a corner of the main road.

He nodded. "It seems okay. Plus, I noticed the seafront is not too far

away."

"Yes, it's only across from the next street." As they stood talking, the office door opened and a man wearing a dark blue suit appeared.

He flashed them a broad smile. "Well, are you coming inside, or shall we talk out here?"

"This is Fernando," Mia said, laughing as she walked up to him. He kissed her on both cheeks, then turned to John and held out his hand.

"Welcome. So, you're the man who charmed Mia and gave her the idea of moving from Barcelona."

John chuckled. "Well, I wouldn't put it quite like that," he said as he shook Fernando's hand, "but yes, guilty as charged."

"Pleased to meet you." He turned to Mia. "So, are you not going to introduce me to your friend?"

Mia's cheeks coloured. "Oh, sorry, John, this is my dear friend Fernando." The two men chuckled, then shook hands again.

"Welcome to Valencia, John." His eyebrows rose in puzzlement. "So, can I ask what brought you here?"

"Of course, but it's a bit of a story."

Fernando shrugged. "Never mind, let's go inside; we can talk there." As they walked inside, three people sitting at desks looked up.

As Mia cast an eye around, she noted the main office appeared about the same size as hers. Plus, it had a separate office that Fernando led them inside. He closed the door. "Please sit." Once all were seated, he asked, "Would you care for tea or coffee?"

Mia nodded. "I'd like a coffee, please."

"And for me," John said.

Fernando opened the door, rattled off a string of Spanish, then closed the door. He turned to John with a wide smile stretched across his face. "Now, you were about to tell me how you came to want to live in Valencia."

After John explained, Fernando nodded. Then before he could speak, a girl knocked, and came in with a tray loaded with coffees and a plate of croissants.

Fernando thanked the girl who left. He shook his head. "What a coincidence. I can see how it was a sign for you to think of moving here, Mia."

"Yes, it was." She reached out and touched John's arm. "Plus, there was no way I would have John living here and me in Barcelona."

Fernando grinned and turned to John. "Please excuse me, while I talk with Mia in Spanish."

"No problem, and may I say you speak excellent English." Fernando's eyes lit up in appreciation of John's words, then started to talk with Mia in rapid Spanish.

While they did, John looked at the photos of the various properties advertised for sale. He nodded in satisfaction when he spotted two villas for sale. Both were similar to the Walkers and around the same asking price.

When Mia and Fernando stopped talking, Mia said, "Sorry, John, but we needed to speak in Spanish."

He shook his head. "There was no need for you to apologise, I didn't expect you to discuss business in English. Anyway, can I ask how things went?"

She flashed John a smile. "We have agreed to exchange offices for two years, with the option to extend permanently. I thought two years would be enough time to enable us to decide to stay in Valencia or move back to Barcelona."

"That sounds a fair deal to me, but what about you, Fernando? Are you happy?"

"Yes. For me, it's a big chance to find out how things are in Barcelona. Also, Mia says I can move into her apartment once you

get settled here. Therefore, I am well pleased with our arrangement."
He then went on to say, "I have already mentioned to my staff the
possibility of moving to Barcelona and Mia coming here. So, it won't
come as a surprise when I tell them it's on. In addition, my secretary
Maria would like to move to Barcelona, so everything is good." He
glanced at his watch. "Look, as it's lunchtime, let me treat you to
lunch."

After a bit of friendly arguing about who would pay, John and
Mia accepted Fernando's invitation. On leaving the office, after a
short walk, he led them into a restaurant.

As they walked inside, he said, "This is where I come for lunch.
The food is excellent, and the staff friendly." A waiter greeted and led
them to a table. Once seated, Fernando said, "It's my treat, so have
whatever you want."

After ordering, a glance around Mia and John exchanged
glances. "This looks like a nice place," she said. "If the food is as good
as you say, they will have some new customers to replace those who
leave."

While awaiting their meals, John spoke to Fernando. "Once we
are here, I'm going to need an office."

"Oh yes, I seem to remember Mia said, you are an architect."

"Yes, that's right."

"Well, I don't know if it will suit, but there is an office close to my
place that is closing down. If you like, when we return to my office,
I'll go and find out if it's available?"

John's eyes lit up. "If it is big enough, that would be perfect.
Many thanks."

As Fernando had said, lunch proved excellent. Later, back in his
office, he said, "If you make yourself comfortable, I'll go and find out
about the office."

On his return a short time later, he wore a broad smile. "You're in luck; it's available." He turned to John. "If you would like to see it, we can do so now?"

John stood. "Yes, please, the more things we can sort out now, the better." He turned to Mia, "Would you like to join us?"

" Yes, why not."

Fernando led them out and along the road for about a hundred metres, then stopped. He opened a shop door and gestured for them to go inside. As they entered, Fernando greeted the man sitting behind a desk in Spanish, then turned to John and Mia.

"I've told Mr Santos you are looking for an office. He says he'll be moving out in a short while, so, if this is suitable....?"

As John took a look around, Fernando said, "Oh, there's a small kitchen and a toilet in the back."

"Ah, that's good," John said. In his mind's eye, he could see the room was about the same size as his office back in England. He nodded, thinking where he would place his drawing table and desk.

"Yes, this would do." With a smile, he inquired. "Now, how much is the rent, and how long is the lease?"

On Fernando explaining what John had said, the man shook his head and rattled off something in Spanish.

Fernando chuckled. "Well, it seems Mr Santos owns the office, but is prepared to lease it to you. Also, the rent he asks for is fair for this part of town."

"Excuse me," Mia said, "How much is he asking?" When Fernando said, she turned to John. "It's a fair price."

"In that case, I'll take it." He then held his hand out to Mr Santos, who smiled as he shook John's hand.

John flashed a smile as he turned to Mia. "Well, our trip here has been a big success. We have a house, you have a real-estate office, and I now have an office." His smile widened as he added, "Plus, we can travel together back and forth from the villa."

Mia, her eyes bright with excitement, nodded. "Yes, that would be great." After agreeing on a date for John's contract to begin, Fernando spoke. "If you like, I will draw up a contract for you and Mr Santos to sign." He glanced from one to the other. "Then, unless you want, you will not have to wait here in Valencia."

John nodded. "Yes, that makes sense," to which Mia agreed. The four of them then returned to Fernando's office, where he instructed Maria to prepare a contract between Mr Santos and John.

Once done and both had signed the contract, Marie made two copies—one for Mr Santos and one for John.

After Mr Santos had left, Mia asked, "So, what would you like to do, John? Shall we stay the night or fly back to Barcelona?"

"If it's alright with you and we can get a flight, let's go to Barcelona." He grinned. "I am sure you have missed Aza?"

Mia's eyes lit up. "Yes, I have." She turned, spoke to Fernando, who then spoke to Maria. She left and a short time later returned smiling. As John guessed, she had booked their tickets.

"Your flight is at five-o'clock," Fernando said. "So, you have plenty of time to get to the airport." He flashed a smile. "To make sure you do, I'll drive you there."

Mia shook her head. "Thank you, but we will take a cab." On noticing Fernando's eyebrows rise, she said, "If you take us, you would have to drive back during the rush hour."

Despite his protests, Mia would not accept his offer. He shrugged. "Okay, but it would not have been a problem."

After handshakes and kisses on the cheeks, Fernando later waved them off in a taxi he had called.

As they sat hand in hand, Mia sighed. "Our trip has proved more successful than I had thought possible."

John flashed her a smile. "What can I say but yes." He squeezed her hand. "For me, all is good. But I'm still concerned about you moving your business here. It's going to cost you a chunk of money."

Mia shrugged. "Maybe, but don't worry about it."

Chapter 31

After arriving in Barcelona, they were soon in a taxi on their way to Mia's apartment. When they walked inside, Sophia, who had brought en looking after Aza, had brought him back. He welcomed them with short barks of delight, jumping up at Mia and John in his excitement.

After making a fuss of him, once sat on the sofa, John took Mia in his arms and kissed her. He then let out a joyful chuckle. "It's good to be back where I can hold you in my arms whenever I want."

She winked. "Is that all you want? To cuddle me."

John gave a short, dirty laugh. "That's something you will have to wait until later to find out."

They then took Aza out for a walk. As they walked along, John stopped and waved a hand. "Darling, are you sure you won't miss being here?"

Mia's smile came soft and dreamy. "No, because Aza will have a new friend in Lucky. Plus, he will have a garden to play in and some different scenery to check out."

Once back in the apartment, Mia said, "How would you like a Chinese? I seem to remember that in London, you said you liked Chinese. If so, I have the card of one. We can either order in or go there?"

John folded her hands in his. "As we've only just come back and Aza is with us, let's have a takeaway."

While awaiting their order, John called Joan to explain that he would not be back for a few days.

To his relief, she said, "No problem, I can look after him until you return."

"Oh, thank you Joan, if you have Lucky, I'll be able to relax."

"Right, now enjoy your time with Mia and let me know when you will be back."

After he closed the phone, John turned to Mia. Joan will look after Lucky until I return."

"Oh, that is good of her." A knock on the door stopped further talk. As Mia opened it, she found a delivery man standing there.

John found the Chow Mein meal Mia had ordered both tasty and satisfying. With his plate empty, he licked his lips. "That was delicious."

"Yes, it was." She winked. "Who is a clever girl?"

He pulled her close and kissed her. "Without a doubt, you my darling,"

When they later went to bed, they embraced and kissed as though they would never kiss again.

"This is so good," Mia murmured. "I love it when I'm in your arms."

"Yes, but what else was it we enjoyed doing in bed?" The next minute, they were locked in a passionate embrace.

The next day, John accompanied Mia to her office, where while she worked, he studied a large-scale map of Valencia he had bought. On their return, he wanted to be able to find his way around.

The day before John's return to England, he and Mia were walking along hand in hand on their way to a restaurant for dinner. Their carefree stroll came to a sudden end, when a man jumped out in front of them and shouted out.

Mia gasped in alarm, then rattled off something in Spanish. Apart from the word Manuel, John did not know what she had said. With his eyebrows raised in puzzlement, he turned to Mia. "Who is this man? Do you know him?"

Mia, her lips trembling said, "Yes, this is Manuel, my former boyfriend. I've told him you are my new boyfriend." She turned and spoke again to Manuel, which, whatever she said, made him shake in anger.

John gasped. "Christ, what did you say? He looks as though he's gone mad."

Manuel shouted out a torrent of Spanish, then pulled something from his pocket. John heard a click and then saw a large knife in Manuel's hand. "Hell's bells, it looks like he intends to use that," he said.

Mia, wide-eyed said, "He says he will not allow me to be with you. I've told him what I do has nothing to do with him," she gasped.

After another exchange of words, with the knife held in a threatening manner, Manuel advanced toward them. As he thrust the point towards Mia, John jerked her away, putting himself between them. He felt a sharp pain in his chest, when, instead of stabbing Mia, Manuel had stabbed him. John cried out, then, releasing Mia's hand, fell to the floor.

When Mia, her eyes wide with fright, screamed at the top of her voice, it caused Manuel to panic. He dropped the knife and ran away, leaving Mia standing in shock. She could not believe Manuel could have done such a stupid thing. As she dropped to her knees beside John, a passer-by who had witnessed the incident, took out his cell phone. He spoke in rapid Spanish, then ran to where Mia sat sobbing, holding John's hand.

"I have called for an ambulance and the police," he said. She nodded, and between sobs, said, "Hold on, John. I'm so sorry. My relationship with Manuel finished months ago."

Through gritted teeth, John gasped, "It's alright; it's not your fault. I'm only glad he stabbed me and not you." He gave a forced smile. "Had he done so, I would have taken his knife and most likely killed him?" His eyes then closed, and with the front of his coat soaked in blood, his head slumped against Mia.

As she cried out, "Oh, no," she heard an approaching ambulance. It screeched to a halt and two paramedics came running over.

While Mia explained what had happened, one medic cut away the front of John's coat. As he removed it and started to try and stop the bleeding, a police car with siren blasting pulled to a stop.

Two police officers climbed out and pushed through a small crowd of onlookers.

On seeing John lying on the ground in a pool of blood, one asked, "What's happened?"

As Mia explained who had stabbed John, the medic had managed to stop his bleeding. Then, with an oxygen mask over John's face, the two men lifted John onto a stretcher and loaded it into the ambulance. Mia white-faced and tears in her eyes, held John's hand as the ambulance with the klaxon blasting, sped off to the hospital.

On arrival, the medics rushed John inside with Mia close behind. At the entrance to the emergency operating theatre, an orderly barred Mia from entering. She stood sobbing, and shaking in fear, not knowing if John was alive or dead.

Chapter 32

After what seemed like hours, the door opened, and a doctor came out. To Mia's utmost relief, he said, "Your friend is alright, but he will have to stay here for about a week."

When he noticed Mia's eyebrows shoot up, he shook his head. "I don't expect any problems, it's merely a precaution."

Mia grasped his hand. "Oh, thank heavens," she sobbed. "I've been so worried. I prayed he would be alright."

The doctor grinned and squeezed her arm. "Well, it seems they were answered. We will take him into the recovery room shortly. You can then see him."

"Oh, thank you, doctor. I don't know what I would have done had he died."

The doctor gave a grim smile. "If the blade had gone more to the left, things could have been much worse. Still, as it is, your friend was lucky."

As they talked, a police officer joined them. "Excuse me doctor," he said, then turned to Mia. "I need a statement from you about what happened."

By the time she had done so, a nurse had come and said she could now go in and see John. Before Mia rushed off to see him, the police officer asked that she go to the police station later, and sign her statement.

In the recovery room, the sight of bandages wrapped around John's chest made Mia gasp, "You look like a mummy. Still, thank heavens you are alright."

John, who had heard the door open and Mia speak, looked up. When he noticed her worried expression, he gasped, "I'm sorry, Darling."

"What! You have nothing to be sorry for." She shook her head. "If it were not for that maniac Manuel, you would not be here." She gave a nervous laugh. "I was panic-stricken when you fell to the floor. Then even more when you passed out in my arms."

John gave a glimmer of a smile. "Thank heavens. It explains the bloodstains on your jacket."

"Never mind me," she snorted. "How do you feel?"

"I think a horse kicked me in the chest."

Mia nodded. "Yes, no doubt. Anyway, in case of infection, the doctor says you have to stay here for about a week." Before John could speak, Mia went on to say, "I shall stay with you until you can leave."

John shook his head; "There is no..." Mia cut in. "Don't say another word. I will stay. I've called Sophia and told her what happened. She wishes you a speedy recovery, and will take Aza to her house. Therefore, there is no problem with me staying with you."

He sighed. "Okay, many thanks, darling. Oh, and don't worry about the cost of my treatment. I have full medical insurance."

"What! Forget the money," she gasped. "It is your health; that is the main thing."

John gave a half-smile. "Yes, you are right."

Once they had John settled in a private room, Mia pulled up a chair and held his hand. "I'm sorry, but you won't be catching a flight back to England for a while."

John shook his head. "Look, you didn't have to get me stabbed for me to stay on longer with you."

Mia's eyebrows shot up to her forehead. "What...t." She then noticed John wore a faint smile. "You devil, you had me going then."

"Sorry, I shouldn't make fun of the situation?"

"No, you shouldn't." Then she leaned over and kissed him.

The next day, Mia went to the police station to sign her statement. While there, an officer said, "We have arrested Manuel and charged him with attempted murder." He shook his head. "He is lucky it won't be murder. The doctor said your friend was fortunate. The wound could have been fatal."

Mia thrust a hand to her mouth to stifle a cry of alarm. She had not known how serious it had been.

On her return to the hospital, the doctor who had just come out of John's room noticed her. He flashed a smile. "Good news. Your friend is doing fine."

Mia's eyes lit up. "Oh, thank heavens."

"Yes. Now, you mentioned about Mr Philip's going back to England." He shook his head. "After he leaves the hospital, I would prefer he stayed in Spain for another two or three days before he does."

A satisfied smile crossed Mia's face. "That won't be a problem. I'll tell him." She paused, then said, "It might be best if it came from you."

He nodded. "I'll mention it before he leaves the hospital."

"Thank you, doctor, and for all what you have done for him."

"You are welcome." His lips turned into a grin. "I can tell you two are in love."

Mia felt her cheeks redden at his words. "Yes, we are. After John moves to Spain next month, we are going to get married."

"Oh, in that case, congratulations." He then excused himself, while Mia entered John's room.

On seeing him sitting up, her eyes lit up. "Good morning, darling. How are you feeling today?"

"I'm fine, but I won't be able to run in the London Marathon this year."

Mia pressed a hand to her mouth to stifle a giggle. "I should think not. Oh, the doctor said all is looking good. You should be able to leave next week."

"Good, then you'll be able to sleep in your own bed."

"Darling. I wouldn't dream of leaving you here on your own." She shook her head. "There are some pretty nurses looking after you. I would not like you to take a fancy to one of them."

John flashed her an innocent smile. "Oh, and to think I thought you wanted to be with me."

Mia giggled. "I do and always will. Oh, and my parents send you their best wishes. It horrified them when I told them what had happened." She laid a delicate hand on his cheek. "My father said if Manuel had stabbed me, he would have found and shot him with his shotgun. Therefore, although I am sorry Manuel stabbed you and not me, I'm sure he would have done what he said."

Through gritted teeth, John said, "If I were your father, no doubt I would have said those exact words." He reached out and squeezed Mia's hand. "Now, while I think about it, can you call the Walkers. Please tell them I will be here longer than planned. I will call them once I'm back." John shook his head. "There is no need to tell them I've been stabbed."

Mia's eyebrows shot up. "No problem, and I won't mention your accident."

When the doctor came to check John four days later, he was smiling. "Well, Mr Phillips, I am pleased to say all your tests have proved negative. You can leave. However, I recommend you don't do anything too strenuous for a week or two."

He turned and flashed Mia a smile. "If all my patients had such an attractive and attentive person like you to look after them, they would soon get well."

Mia felt her cheeks colour as she replied. "Thank you, doctor. John means the world to me." Then, as he went to leave, she said, "Oh, there is one thing. Is it alright for John to fly? He was due to return to England last week."

The doctor turned to John and said, "I would prefer you not to do so for another two or three days." He shook his head. "You were lucky to have escaped so lightly after being stabbed where you were. I wouldn't like you to strain yourself unnecessarily."

John nodded. "If you think like that, I'll stay here a few days more."

He then turned towards Mia, who wore a broad smile. "I can see your lady friend is happy about that. Anyway, I'll sign your release papers. You can then leave whenever you want." With that, he left the room.

Mia bent and kissed John, who folded his hand over hers. "I know you are happy I'll be here for a few days more. But for me, the longer I am with you, the better."

By the time John and Mia had left the hospital and were back in her apartment, it was four pm. Once she had John sit on the sofa with a cup of coffee, she called Sophie. After a short conversation, she closed her phone. "I've told Sophia we are home. She will bring Aza back shortly."

"It will be good to see him, and I'm sure you feel the same." John shook his head. "If Aza had been with us when Manuel appeared, would things have turned out much different from what they did?"

Mia's eyebrows shot up. "Yes, he would not have allowed Manuel anywhere near us." She shrugged. "Manuel can thank his lucky stars Aza was not with us; If he had, it would have been him in the hospital, not you." Mia sighed. "Still, I won't be happy when you return to England."

John pulled her close and kissed her. "Nor I. But, once I return here, I won't leave you again." He looked thoughtful for a minute. "Now, while I think of it, what do you think about the furniture in my house? Shall I send some over to Valencia or not? If you say no, it's not a problem. I can easily get rid of it."

Mia squeezed John's hand. "If it's alright with you, no. We can choose whatever furniture we want here."

In that case, all I'll send over will be my personal things, plus my drawing board and desk."

Mia cocked an eyebrow. "It's just a thought, but maybe the Walkers would like to buy your furniture?"

"Now, that's an idea; I'll call and talk to them about this once I'm back. You never know; after all, they have seen the inside of the house." A knock on the door stopped further talk.

"Oh, that will be Sophia with Aza," Mia said. As she opened the door, Aza rushed in, followed by Sophia. She was, John noticed, a petite, slim woman with short, dark brown hair.

"Hi, Mia." She then held out a hand towards John. "You must be John? I was so sorry to hear of your being stabbed."

"Yes, and thanks for your concern. Anyway, it's nice to meet you, Sophia." He then reached down to rub Aza's head. "Hi, Aza, it's good to see you again," who responded by licking John's hand.

Mia smiled. "Yes, I can see he is pleased to be home." After Sophia and Mia had a chat, Sophia said, "Right, I'll leave you two alone." She said something in Spanish, to which Mia giggled, then left.

As the door closed behind her, John cocked an inquisitive eyebrow. "Em, what did Sophia say as she left?"

"Don't do anything I wouldn't do."

He grinned. "Well, as I don't know Sophia, I do not know what we can or can't do." Pulling Mia close, they enjoyed a passionate kiss. On breaking it off, John said, "So, what do you think? Were we allowed to do that?"

After Mia kissed him again, she said, "Yes, I'm sure that was acceptable to Sophia."

That evening, along with Aza, they went out for a walk. This time, to prevent John from any strain, Mia held Aza's lead, with their walk shorter than usual.

A few days later, Mia struggled to hold back her tears when she accompanied John to the airport. Once he had checked in, after a quick embrace and a kiss, he waved a last goodbye. Then, as he turned to go to passport control. John stopped. He blew her a kiss, then disappeared from view.

Chapter 33

Outside the airport, as she climbed into Sophia's car, Mia wiped the tears from her eyes. One look, and Sophia knew not to say anything. After a while, Mia sat up and sniffed.

"Sorry, but I hated to see John leave. I am going to miss him like crazy and won't feel good until he is back here again."

Sophia reached across and squeezed her hand. "I am sure John feels the same way as you. Still, remember, when he comes back, it will be for good." She gave Mia a subtle wink. "Also, I seem to remember you told me you would get married?"

"Yes, on his return, John is going to ask my father for permission to marry me."

Sophia cocked an inquisitive eyebrow. "Oh, and why is that? You don't need his permission to get married."

"We don't, but it was John's idea to ask him."

"Well, as you don't seem concerned, I guess your father is happy about this?"

Mia's eyes lit up on remembering. "Yes, he gave me his blessing." She shook her head. "Still, there is one thing I'm puzzled about. My father said on John's return, he wants to talk with him." A flicker of a smile crossed her face. "Although it's nothing to do with us, he won't tell me what it's about."

"Well, as it is not about your relationship with John, I wouldn't worry too much."

"I'm not, but I am curious."

"Now, apart from your intention to get married, you said you are going to move your office to Valencia. How did that come about?"

Mia then explained about the Walkers buying John's house in England and how they had agreed to buy their villa in Valencia. When she heard Sophia sigh, she said, "Don't be like that; we'll have room for you whenever you decide to visit."

Sophia tossed her head. "Well, there is one thing in its favour; I do like Valencia."

On their arrival at Mia's home, as she climbed out of the car, Mia said: "Thank you, Sophia. We will talk later, or come around if you have the time?"

"I will." Then, with a last wave of her hand, she drove away.

Once inside her apartment, Mia sat with Aza beside her. She rubbed his head. "Thank goodness I have you. I don't know how I would manage if you weren't here?" Aza cocked his head and gazed up at her. She nodded. "If you could talk, you would know how I feel." She then bent and kissed his head.

When Mia's cell phone later rang, a glance brought a smile to her face, it was John.

"Hi darling, just to say I love you, and I'm now home." On the screen, she saw him shake his head. "But of course, I'd rather be there with you."

"As I would, too," she replied. The next minute, John moved the phone, and Lucky appeared.

"Oh; you have Lucky with you."

"Yes, I've told him we are moving, and he will have a new playmate." John chuckled. "I'm not sure if he understood, but never mind. Still, how are you?"

"Lonely."

"Likewise, but don't worry, I'll soon be back. Once I've agreed with the Walkers about when we can take possession of the villa, that's it. After I call them tomorrow, I'll let you know what's what. Oh, and I'll mention my furniture. If they're not interested, I'll check out some other options. Still, either way, it won't prove a problem to empty the house."

Mia sighed. "As long as I have you back in my arms before too long, it won't be a problem for me either."

"Darling, believe me, it will be as soon as I can make it. Oh, and when I come back, one of the first things I intend to do is to visit your parents. I would like to talk with your father."

"You know it's unnecessary?"

She saw John grin. "I know, but I said I would, so I will. Look, once I have a flight booked, I would like you to arrange for us to visit your parents. After that, we can arrange to get married." John cocked an eyebrow. "That's, if you haven't changed your mind?"

"Are you kidding?" To John's surprise and delight, Mia said, "If you like, I'll fly over to England. We can get married there."

"Wow, that would be great. But, as I previously mentioned, I want to ask your father for his permission." He shook his head. "Although I'm sure it won't be a problem, I feel I should. Now, let's talk about something else. You've spoken with your parents about moving your business down to Valencia. Are they okay about that?"

"Yes. It surprised them when I mentioned it, but said I was old enough to decide for myself. I've told them they are always welcome to come and stay with us for a holiday." She gave a half smile. "I hope that's alright with you?"

"Of course. I hope your parents and I will become friends."

"Oh, I am sure you will. I know they are looking forward to meeting you." She shook her head. "Before you ask, I still do not know what my father wants to talk to you about."

John grinned. "So, we have a mystery to be solved. That's something else I have to look forward to."

They discussed their marriage and Valencia, then ended the call.

The next day, during a phone call with Mr Walker, John mentioned the furniture in his house. To his surprise, he said, "Now there's a coincidence."

John's interest rose. "Oh, and why's that? Anything in particular?"

"Yes, while my wife and I were talking about your house, she said how she loved the way you had it furnished." He paused. "She said, should you not want the furniture, we should make you an offer to buy it." He chuckled. "As for the furniture in the villa, my wife's parents bought it many years ago. I knew you wouldn't want it, so I've arranged for a company to take it away. Therefore, the villa will be empty when you next go there. I should have asked you first, so I hope that's alright with you?"

John could not believe his luck. Trying not to let his excitement sound, he said, "Well, I am surprised you would like to purchase my furniture. But, as we decided we don't want it, I'm sure we can agree on a price. As for the furniture in the villa, that suits us fine. Look, we could meet and sort this out? Plus, I think it best we get a lawyer to draw up a legal document reference the one we signed in Valencia?"

To his relief, Mr Walker said, "I agree. If an English lawyer prepares our contract, then neither of us will have a problem in the future." He then went on to say, "If you could come up to London where we live, I have a lawyer who will make us a legal house sale contract."

"Of course, that won't be a problem."

"Right, if I phone and arrange for us to visit him, say tomorrow afternoon, would that suit you?"

"Yes, no problem. Once we have completed things, I'll return to Spain. I did mention that Mia and I are going to get married?"

"Yes. You are a lucky man. Mia seems like a lovely lady."

"She is, and as you say, I know how lucky I am."

Once Mr Walker had given his address, they arranged to meet the next day.

When John rang their doorbell, and Mr Walker opened it, his face lit up with a broad smile.

"Thank you for coming," Mr Philips. He then led John into the lounge, where Mrs Walker sat engrossed in a television program.

"It's Mr Phillips, dear."

With a start, she rose to her feet. "How good of you to come to see us."

"No problem, especially as your husband mentioned you liked the furniture in my house."

"Oh yes, I thought it suited perfectly."

"Thank you, my late wife, and I chose it."

She gasped and put a hand to her mouth. "Oh, I'm so sorry."

"It's not a problem; she died two years ago in a traffic accident." He shrugged. "It's one reason I decided to move to Spain."

Mr Walker nodded. "Yes, I can understand. Anyway, my lawyer is waiting. Shall we go?"

"Of course," John replied.

After the taxi Mr Walker ordered arrived, they were soon at his lawyers' office.

Chapter 34

His secretary welcomed them. "Good afternoon, Mr & Mrs Walker." She turned. "You must be Mr Philips?"

"Yes, I am."

"Right, Mr Jenkins is ready to see you." She crossed to a door, knocked, and opened it. "Mr & Mrs Walker and Mr Philips," then stood aside to allow them to enter.

As they did, Mr Jenkins stood. He shook the Walker's hands, then John's.

"Good afternoon, lady, gentlemen, please take a seat. Once they were, he asked, "Would you care for a cup of tea or coffee?" When all refused, he said, "I have a contract prepared that I'm sure you will find satisfactory."

He picked up two papers from his desk and gave one to Mr Walker and the other to John.

After a glance, John took out his pen and signed. Mr & Mrs Walker also signed, then Mr Jenkins took them back. He signed both papers, then asked his secretary to make copies. Once done, he handed one original to Mr Walker and one to John.

He flashed them a smile. "There we are, all signed, sealed and delivered." He looked from one person to the other. "So, is there anything else I can help you with?"

John shook his head while Mr Walker said, "No, thank you, that's perfect."

Once all had shaken hands, John followed Mr & Mrs Walker out of the office and down to the street.

"Well, that's it," Mr Walker said. "Do you have time for a spot of lunch, or are you in a hurry to return home?"

"Thank you, but I have things to sort out, so I must refuse." As John went to shake hands with them, Mr Walker said, "I've arranged a bank transfer to your account for payment of your furniture."

"Many thanks." He flashed them a smile, "I hope you will be as happy as I was living in my house. Oh, and I'll let you know when I'll be returning to Spain so you can move in." He chuckled. "It won't be long, or I'll have Mia wanting to know why."

Mr Walker nodded. "Yes, I am sure she would. Still, we hope you enjoy living in the villa, and Mia's business goes well. Plus, yours, once you have it up and running." He chuckled. "One thing you can be sure of, the weather in Valencia is much better than here."

Mrs Walker nodded agreement. "Please give Mia our best wishes and inform us when you will be getting married."

"I will and many thanks. I'll let you know once we have arranged a date." With that, John said goodbye, then flagged down a passing taxi.

On his way home, John could not have been happier. Not only was his house sold, but the contents as well. As he looked out the window, he thought, "Now, is it worth it to send my desk and board to Spain, or should I buy new ones there?" He shook his head. "No, I'll get a quotation for the cost first, then decide."

Once back in his house, where Lucky welcomed him with a bark and a wag of his tail, John rubbed his head.

"I know you've been a good boy; let's go out." After a long walk, with the sun sinking as the evening approached, they returned to the house. Once John had filled Lucky's dish with food, he wasted no time in starting to eat.

While John slumped onto the sofa, he decided to call his parents and bring them up to date. Well, not quite. He would not mention about his being stabbed. If he did, his mother would be worried stiff about his move to Spain.

When he phoned them, his father answered? "Hi dad, are you and mum, both okay?" On his reply, "Yes," John said, "I've sold the house along with all the furniture."

"Well, that's it then," his father said. "So, when are you going back to Barcelona?"

"Soon, but Mia and I won't be living in Barcelona. I've bought a villa in Valencia." On hearing his father gasp, he explained how this came about and Mia moving her office to Valencia.

His father chuckled. "Well, it seems you two have everything sorted out. Your mother and I are happy for you. Now, when do you intend to get married? Have you fixed a date yet?"

"No, but I'll let you know once we have."

"Make sure you do as we want to be there." The line went quiet, and then his father said, "What about Jasmin's parents? Are you going to tell them?"

"I must admit I've not given them much thought. What do you think I should do?"

"Hm. If you decide to say anything, for what it's worth, I would only tell them you are moving to Spain. There is no need for you to say you are going to get married out there,"

"Yes, that sounds like an idea. I'll call them. So, is mum there, or is she out?"

His father chuckled. "She is out. It's her day to play whilst."

"Ah, yes, I know she likes to play that. Anyway, give her my love. I'll let you know when I've booked a flight back to Spain."

"Thanks, son, and give our best to Mia when you talk to her."

As John closed his phone, he vowed to return every so often to see his parents. They had always been supportive of him, and especially when Jasmin died.

When he called and told Mia the Walkers had bought the furniture, she exclaimed, "Oh, that's great news. "Now you won't have the hassle of emptying the house."

"Yes, you are right." He then told her his thoughts about his desk and drawing board.

"You should wait until you find out the cost of the shipment and then decide."

"Yes, that's what I thought. Anyway, I'll soon be back with you in my arms."

"Good, it won't come quick enough for me."

After a long and love-filled talk, they blew each other kisses down the phone before saying goodnight.

The next day, after he called a removal company about his things, John called Gilbert and Wendy.

To his surprise, Gilbert answered the phone. On hearing John's voice, he said, "Hi John, where are you? Home or in Spain?"

When he said he was at home, Gilbert said, "In that case, come on over. You can then tell us all what you have been up to. Oh, in case you are wondering, I took a day off work."

When John knocked on their door, Wendy opened it and welcomed him with a wide smile. "Come in, John; we've been wondering about you."

Once inside, Gilbert said, "So, how are you John, and where is your lovely lady, Mia?" Wendy cut in saying, "Gilbert, stop talking and get John a drink."

He shrugged. "Yeah, sorry, John. What would you like, a beer or a short?"

"A beer, please." Once he had sat down, Gilbert handed him one. "Right," Wendy said, "Now tell us all what you pair have been up to."

John told them all he and Mia had done and that they had decided to get married.

Gilbert's eyes lit up. "Congratulations, that's great news."

"Yes, it is," Wendy echoed.

As they talked, Gilbert had caught a change in John's expression. He cocked an eyebrow. "So, what is it you've not told us?" He asked?

John shrugged, then told them about being stabbed by Mia's ex-boyfriend.

Wendy gasped and shot a hand to her mouth in horror, while Gilbert's eyebrows shot up to his forehead.

"Christ, John, it sounds like you were lucky, and that's putting it mildly."

"Oh my God, Wendy exclaimed. "Mia must have been in a terrible state and worried stiff."

"Yes, she was." He then told them how after accompanying him in an ambulance to the hospital, Mia stayed with him until he left the hospital."

"What about the bastard who stabbed you?" Gilbert asked.

"He is being charged with attempted manslaughter."

"Well, from what you say, he is lucky," Wendy said. "The charge could easily have been murder."

John nodded. "Yes. Anyway, enough about me. How are you two?"

Gilbert shook his head. "Well, after what you have told us, we have nothing exciting to tell you."

"No, all has been quiet here," Wendy added.

After a chat and another drink, John returned home. As he sat with Lucky beside him, he had a sudden thought. As he intended to get married in Spain, he wondered what government regulation he would have to comply with. With that in mind, he opened his computer and went online.

After a check, John made a note of what paperwork he required.

The next day, he called and made an appointment at the British Consulate in London.

Later, armed with his passport and Jasmin's death certificate, John arrived at the Consulate. He was fortunate and did not have long to wait before going in with an official. After explaining what he wanted, once he had the information, John thanked the official and returned home.

Later, when he called and told Mia where he had been and why. She giggled. "What a coincidence. I've been to our local church and asked what I need for us to get married. It will take around a month from your arrival until we can get married."

"In that case, I'd best get back as soon as possible." John said. "I have a company due to come this afternoon re my desk, etc. Once that's sorted out, I'll book my flight. Oh, and Lucky does not have to go into quarantine when we arrive. I'll get his papers sorted out tomorrow." He gave Mia a beaming smile. "So, all being well, I will be with you in about three-four days."

Mia's whoop of joy told him she was delighted at his news.

Later that afternoon, a knock on the door announced someone from the shipping company.

After checking the sizes, the man told John the cost and duration before his things would arrive in Valencia. On his acceptance, John wrote out a cheque and handed it to the man. He gave him a receipt, then said, "We can take it now if you like?"

John's eyes lit up. "Yes, please, that would be great."

The man went outside and returned with a colleague. In a short time, the two men had the board and desk wrapped and secured in the van, then drove off.

Wearing a broad smile, John booked a flight to Barcelona and arranged for Lucky to be on the same plane.

Two days later, John went to say goodbye to his parents. As he went to leave, his father shook his hand. "Now, don't forget to let us know the date you will get married."

"Don't worry; I will." He kissed his mother and hugged his father. "Right, I look forward to seeing you at the wedding."

His father chuckled. "Don't worry, son, we will be there."

Chapter 35

When John arrived at Gatwick for his flight, the vet who had dealt with Lucky's paperwork had already delivered him there. John would collect Lucky at Barcelona once the authorities had cleared him.

On his arrival at Barcelona, John's eyes lit up at the sight of Mia in the arrival's hall. When she spotted him, her face lit up in a mile-wide smile as she rushed over to him. After a warm embrace, they went to fetch Lucky. When he saw John with Mia through the mesh in his crate, he started to bark in excitement. John quietened him, and after signing various papers, a porter wheeled Lucky's crate outside to where Sophie sat in her SUV.

When she saw them coming, she climbed out and greeted John. He shook hands with Sophia, who then turned to Mia. Wearing a beaming smile, she said, "So here we all are."

Once they had Lucky's crate loaded inside her SUV and the porter tipped, they set off.

John leaned forward. "Many thanks, Sophia. Your help is much appreciated."

He noticed her smile in the inside mirror. "No problem, John, I'm glad to be of help."

When they arrived outside Mia's apartment block, Sophia said, "Let Lucky out and leave his cage in the car. I'll bring it back tomorrow with Aza."

Mia had thought it best the two dogs met outside her apartment, to which John had agreed.

Sophie kissed Mia on the cheek and shook John's hand. "Right, I'll see you tomorrow." As she drove off, Sophia waved out of the window."

Once inside Mia's apartment, John clasped Mia tight and they enjoyed a hot and passionate kiss. On breaking it off, he undid Lucky's leash and led him to the kitchen. The next minute they heard him get stuck into the bowls of food and water Mia had put out.

That night, with Mia back in John's arms, their lovemaking was long, slow, and tender.

The next day, John and Mia took Lucky out for a walk to a nearby park where Mia had arranged to meet Sophia and Aza. With John holding Lucky's lead, they found Sophia sitting on a bench with Aza beside her.

At the sight of Mia, with John holding Lucky's lead, Aza stood up stiff-legged.

Mia went and stroked him, after which, Aza sniffed and with his ears up, watched Lucky. They thought there would be a problem, but to their relief, Aza relaxed. He seemed to realise Lucky was not a threat. Then, while Mia took Azas lead, and John, Lucky's, they set off for a short walk. On their way, several people stopped to look as the two big dogs passed them by.

Once back to where Sophia sat, who had watched in interest, she said, "Well, that went well. I only hope there won't be any problem once they are both inside your apartment?"

Mia nodded. "I don't think so, but we will soon find out." After thanking Sophia, Mia, John, and the two dogs returned to her apartment.

Mia took Aza in first, who, once off his lead, went straight to the kitchen. John, with Lucky still on his lead, followed behind. Aza looked up, but when John took Lucky to where Mia had put his bowls, he went back to eat and drink. After John released Lucky's lead, he and Mia held their breath as the two dogs looked at each other.

Finally, when both dogs carried on drinking, John sighed. "Thank heavens. I was worried they might not have gotten on."

Mia nodded. "Yes, so was I, but they seem to know we want them to be friends."

When the two dogs came to join John and Mia in the Lounge, Aza lay down on his usual rug. While Lucky watched, John patted another rug.

"Here, boy, this is yours." Lucky went and lay down, with John stroking and telling him he was a good boy.

The next morning, John and Mia took both dogs out for a short walk with no problem. On their return, with both dogs settled back indoors, they went out. John had to register for a *Certificado de Empadronamiento*. It being necessary, not only for their wedding, but a requirement for buying a car, obtaining a resident permit, and a NIE. A Spanish identity card. With this in hand, they next went to an official translator, where John had all his papers translated into Spanish.

Once done, John and Mia set off to the marriage office and handed in all the papers to an official. As they stood watching as he checked them, he said "Uno problemo."

"Mia, her eyes wide, spoke to the man. He shrugged and said something to her.

SHE TURNED TO JOHN. "The birth certificate you have given does not have an official stamp on it. Therefore, he cannot accept it."

"What," John gasped, "you are joking, yes?"

Mia, trying her best not to cry, shook her head. "Unfortunately, no, I am not. He says you must provide a certificate that has an official stamp on it."

John, looked from Mia to the official. "In desperation, he said, "Look, to prevent delaying our application, please ask if he could accept the one I have given while I go and get what he wants?"

Mia shook her head "I asked him this, but he says he can't do it. If it came out that he had accepted the document, he would be in serious trouble."

John glanced at the man who put his hands up and said something to Mia. She nodded "He says he is sorry, but there is nothing he can do."

"Concern lined John's face as he gripped Mia's hands tight. "I'm so sorry darling, I did not know this would be a problem." He shrugged. "It means I'll have to return to England to get a stamped copy of my birth certificate."

"Of no," Mia cried, "can you not get one online?"

John shrugged. "I don't think so, but once back at your place I'll check." A flicker of a smile crossed his lips. "Still, you never know, we might be lucky."

With both disappointed and feeling down, they left the office and took a taxi back to Mia's office. Once inside, using Mia's computer, John went online,

A few minutes later, his eyes lit up and he cried, "Yes," punching the air with delight.

Mia gripped John's shoulder tight, her eyes bright with excitement at what he had found.

"We are in luck. I can apply for a legal copy of my birth certificate online. Also, by having it sent by express, it will only take two days to get to your office."

"Oh, that is wonderful," Mia cried. "I thought you might have to return to England to get one."

John nodded and wiped his forehead. "Yes, so did I. But, I'm more than pleased to find I don't."

Once he had applied and paid for a copy of his birth certificate, he and Mia sighed with relief.

Three days later, while in Mia's office, a courier arrived with a package address to John. On ripping it open, his eyes lit up as he held up his certificate.

"Oh, thank heavens," Mia said.

John sighed. "Yes, now we'll return to the marriage office to apply for a date to get married."

Mia pulled him tight and kissed him. Then, both wearing broad smiles, they took a taxi to the wedding office.

The man who had dealt with them before, eyes lit on remembering them. He spoke to Mia who replied smiling.

This time, after John handed in all his papers, the man checked them, took a copy of John's passport, then looked up. He beamed them a smile, then spoke to Mia. She turned to John.

"He says he is sorry for the earlier problem, and will notify us when we can marry."

After all, shook hands, when Mia and John left, they could not have been happier.

"Well, now all we have to do is wait," she said.

"I hope it won't be too long?"

Mia squeezed John's hand. "From what I found; it will be in one months' time." She cocked an eyebrow. "If it's alright with you, we could go and visit my parents. They keep asking about you?"

"Yes, that would be good." John chuckled. "Then I'll find out what your father wants to talk to me about."

Mia put a hand to her mouth. "Oh, yes, I'd forgotten about that."

When they later went to visit them, John felt nervous. It would be their first meeting.

To his relief and surprise, her father said in English, "Welcome to my home John. I am pleased to meet you at last."

As John went to shake his hand, her father embraced him. Then, as he released him, noticing John's embarrassment, he chuckled. "You are now like one of the family."

His wife flashed him a broad smile. "Yes, and thank you for saving my daughter from that manic Manuel." She shook her head. "I'm only sorry you put your own life in danger by doing so...." Her father cut in, "If I see him again, I swear I'll kill him."

Mia caught hold of his arm. "Alright, calm down, father. Manuel is in prison, awaiting trial. He will receive the punishment he deserves."

In an attempt to defuse the situation, John gave a short cough. "Excuse me, Mr Alvarez, I understand you wanted to talk to me about something?"

Her father's expression softened. "Yes, sorry, but I can't forget what that bastard tried to do." He shook his head. "Anyway, I have a proposition I would like you to consider."

While Mia gasped in shock, although taken by surprise, John nodded. "Oh, this sounds interesting. What is it?"

"Well, I own several pieces of land I gained from when I ran the business Mia now controls. They were in part payment from deals I arranged with the owners." He chuckled when he noticed the expression on Mia's face. "What is up, my daughter? Are you surprised at what I have said? Were you worried about what I wanted to talk with John about?"

She shook her head. "No, but it puzzled me."

Her father turned back to John. "Now, what I had in mind is this. If I can find people interested in buying one of these plots, could you design a house to their requirements? If so, I am sure I could find a suitable builder. We would share whatever the owner pays for the land. Plus, you will receive payment for designing the houses from the owners." He cocked an eyebrow. "How does that sound?" Before John could answer, he said, "Of course, your name would be prominent on any brochures or signs erected on the land."

John nodded. "This sounds good to me; we have a deal." He held out his hand. "The money is not so important as getting my name known. So, once I'm set up in Valencia, I'll put out adverts about this and see what response I get." He shrugged. "Although it will take a while, I am sure it will attract some business. Therefore, for me, your idea is a good one."

With that said, John took a deep breath. "Mr Alvarez. I love your daughter, and I'm asking for your permission to marry her."

To his surprise, he picked John up and kissed both his cheeks. Then, wearing a broad smile, he put him down. "There was no need to ask, but I thank you for doing so." He turned to Mia, who stood trembling, waiting to hear her father's answer.

"Of course, you have my permission. My wife and I are delighted at your news." He glanced from Mia to John. "So, when are you going to get married?"

"We have applied for a marriage licence and now waiting to be told when," Mia replied.

Her father grinned. "Now, would you have got married had I refused to give my consent?" Before Mia, who looked down, could speak, John said, "I'm sorry, but yes. I love Mia more than life."

"Good for you, my son. My wife and I are pleased to hear that." Beaming with delight, he said, "Now, this calls for a drink."

Once he had poured their drinks, with four happy smiling faces, they clinked glasses.

At the end of their visit, John, and Mia embraced her parents and said they would talk soon.

On their return to Mia's apartment, as she unlocked the door, they found Aza & Lucky waiting. While Aza gave a short bark, Lucky jumped up to welcome John. After a check revealed nothing out of place, both dogs received a treat. Once done, Mia picked up both their leads.

"Who wants to go for a walk?" Aza barked, and then Lucky followed suit. After a short walk, back in the apartment, Mia kissed John on the cheek.

"So, my father would like to do business with you." When she noticed John cock an inquisitive eyebrow, she shook her head. "No, I did not know what he would say."

"No problem. For me, it's a good deal. It will get me some free publicity."

"Yes, and they were delighted to hear we had applied for a marriage licence."

"Yes, that is much more important." John picked Mia up and kissed her. "Once we are married, I'll be the happiest man in Spain."

With her eyes shining bright, she said, "And I will be the happiest woman."

Chapter 36

John received a call one day, to say the company would deliver his desk and drawing board three days later. Given this, the next day, Mia booked them flights down to Valencia, and also booked them into a hotel.

When Mia told Sophia about her and John going to Valencia, she said, "As Aza and Lucky are getting on alright, I will look after both of them." On seeing Mia cock an eyebrow, she said, "It won't be a problem. I have a friend who will take Lucky when we take them out for a walk. Or, if you prefer, I will stay in your place with them?"

On John's agreement, Mia asked Sophia to take both dogs.

When they later arrived at the villa, John used Mr Walker's key to open the front door. On entering, as Mr Walker had said, they found the house empty of furniture.

"That's good," Mia said, with John nodding in agreement. A check revealed neither walls nor ceilings required re-painting.

A sigh escaped John's lips, "That's good." He flashed Mia a smile. "Now, while we are here, I suggest we see what we can find in the way of furniture?"

"An excellent idea." Mia giggled. "Once we have a bedroom suite or at least a bed, we could sleep here."

John laughed. "You devil, but I agree. Look, I'm sure your friend Fernando could tell us the best places to look for furniture."

"Yes, I will call him." He then texted Mia back with a list of places.

After visiting several of the shops Fernando had recommended, they agreed on a bedroom and a dining room suite. The lounge took longer before they found one they both liked. With the main rooms sorted out, they then looked for furniture for the second and third bedrooms.

While they looked, John said, "Of course, we will have to change the kitchen, plus the main bathroom."

"Yes, but we could change those after moving in." Mia paused. "Still, with a recession, perhaps we could get both fitted in a couple of weeks."

Another call to Fernando resulted in him giving Mia a phone number. She called and spoke for a while, then flashed John a smile as she closed her phone.

"We are in luck. The kitchen company he recommended has men nearby measuring up someone's kitchen. They will be here in about an hour."

"Well, how about that?" John said. "All being well, we will sort out many things in no time at all."

When the kitchen men arrived, Mia took them into the kitchen and showed them a rough sketch John had drawn.

"We want something on these lines," she said.

The man who took the paper, looked, and said something to Mia. She nodded and pointed to John. "He asked who drew this as it looked professional. I told him you are an architect."

After the men had measured up and spoke to Mia, they shook hands and left.

On returning to join John, she said, "Now, we will wait and see what price they come up with." She shrugged. "If it's too expensive, we will try another company. Still, I know this company. It's a good one."

John nodded. "In that case, as you know the prices here, if you think it fair, we will have them do the kitchen." He flashed her a smile. "Now, how about a spot of lunch?"

"Yes, after all that, I feel hungry." She cocked an eyebrow. "I know; why don't we go to the restaurant the Walker's took us to?"

"Yes, it's not far away."

Ongoing there, after finishing a tasty lunch, they returned to the villa to check out the bathroom.

Mia shook her head. "I don't know about you, but let's change everything?"

John nodded. "Yes, I agree." On seeing her look of concern, he shook his head, "Don't worry about the cost. The money for all this is not a problem. I sold my house for more than we paid for the villa. Therefore, we have enough money to do whatever we want." He grinned. "After all, it will be our home."

Mia caught hold of his hand. "I know, but I have money I can put towards things."

John's eyebrows shot up. "What! What kind of man do you think I am?" He laughed and shook his head. "I thank you for your offer, darling, but it is neither wanted nor acceptable. Now, let's find a bathroom shop." He sighed. "Once we have sorted that out, it will be enough for one day."

Mia kissed John on the cheek. "You are a darling, and I agree."

After another call to Fernando, she closed her phone. "If we go out the gate and turn left. About three hundred meters from the restaurant where we had lunch, we will see a bathroom centre." Mia let out a small chuckle. "Fernando says if we can't find what we want there, we will have to look in Barcelona."

John laughed. "In that case, let's go." They found the shop packed with a wide variety of different bathrooms and fittings. It then took them the best part of an hour before they picked out what both liked. After checking, the saleswoman spoke to Mia, who informed John what she had said.

"As I thought, they are not busy at present. So, if we like, they can arrange the installation one week later. Is that alright?"

"Yes, that would suit." John grinned. "Now, all we have to do is wait for what the kitchen company says."

"I expect we will hear from them tomorrow. It's a large company, so they should be able to install everything in a short space of time."

After Mia told the saleswoman one week was fine, John gave her his credit card. Once processed, he and Mia left the showroom and called in a café for a well-deserved coffee.

As they sat drinking a latte, Mia gripped John's hand. "Thank you, my darling. I know we will be happy once we move into the villa."

He leaned over and kissed her cheek. "Of that, I know. Now let's get back to our hotel. You can then express your thanks in another way."

Mia shook her head. "You, my darling, have a one-track mind." She winked, "Still, I'm ready if you are?"

Chapter 37

The following day, Mia and John sat waiting to see if the kitchen company would call. However, when John's phone rang, a glance showed it was his cargo company.

"Good morning," a voice said, "Would it be suitable to deliver your goods this morning?"

"Yes, that would be fine. I'll be there."

While Mia stayed in the villa, John took a taxi to his new office. After a short wait, a truck drew up outside. He went out, and between him and the driver; they carried in his desk, then the board.

Once unpacked and a check showed no damage, John thanked and tipped the driver. No sooner had he driven away when John's phone rang. It was Mia.

"The kitchen company called to ask if we could meet. I've told them, yes, and we will be in the villa."

"Now that's what I call good timing. I'm on my way."

Half an hour later, one man who had measured up the kitchen arrived. One look at the drawings he had brought showed they included all they had requested.

"It looks good, but what about the cost?" John said.

When Mia told him, John nodded. "That seems good to me. What do you think?"

"I say it's okay. Like in England, kitchens here are not cheap."

"In that case, tell him we accept. Oh, and please ask if he can give us an idea of when they could install it."

"He checked before coming. If we want, they could complete everything within three weeks."

John's eyes lit up. "That would be perfect. It means we should have both the kitchen and bathroom completed around the same time."

Mia nodded. "Yes, but I suggest we have the furniture delivered after they have finished."

"Definitely. We don't want workers tools damaging anything."

The man must have understood what John had said, as he flashed a smile then held out a hand. John shook it, then paid 50% of the total cost via his credit card. After he gave John a receipt, the man thanked them, then left.

Mia next called the furniture store. Once she had finished talking, she flashed a smile as she turned to John. "Right, that's done."

John caught hold and kissed her cheek. "In that case, we can return to Barcelona. Unless there is something, I've forgotten?"

"No, there is nothing I can think of." Mia then put a hand to her mouth. "Oh, there is one thing."

John's eyebrows rose in puzzlement. "What, I can't think of anything."

"Curtains."

"Ah, yes, that's a point," then grinning, he pointed. "As the Walker's left theirs, we can sort that out once our furniture is in place."

"Yes, that makes sense. Right, I'll make a booking to fly back to Barcelona."

On their later arrival back at Mia's apartment, after she called Sophia, an hour later, a knock on the door announced her arrival. As Mia opened the door, Aza, and Lucky rushed in with Sophia close behind.

"Now that's what I call a welcome home," Sophia said.

"It is, and thank you so much, you are an angel."

"Yes, thank you, Sophia," John added.

She glanced from one to the other. "Well, did you get everything done in Valencia you wanted to?"

Mia, her eyes bright with excitement, said, "Yes. In about three weeks' time, the villa will be ready for us to move in." She gave a short laugh. "Then we will only have one thing left to do."

Sophia cocked an inquisitive eyebrow. "Oh, and what's that?"

"We're getting married." She caught hold and squeezed John's hand. "We expect to hear shortly when we can."

"Oh, congratulations, I am so happy for you." Sophia cocked an eyebrow. "That reminds me, what did your father say when John asked for his permission for you to get married?"

"He said there was no need, but he thanked John for asking."

John grinned. "When he asked, what would we do if he had refused, I said, yes or no, we would still get married."

Both girls laughed, then an impish smile made Mia's mouth twitch. "He also had a business proposition for John."

"Ah, so now you know what he wanted to talk with John about. Anyway, what about your wedding? Where and when will that take place? That is something I am looking forward to knowing," she twittered.

John chuckled. "That makes three of us."

The following week, when a letter arrived at Mia's office from the registry office, with trembling fingers, she ripped it open. One look and her eyes lit up. "Yes," she cried. Inside was permission for her and John to marry two weeks later.

From Mia's cry and her mile-wide smile, her staff knew she had received the news she had been awaiting. Mia was ecstatic when she called John to share the news.

"Oh, that's fantastic."

"Yes, when I come home, we will arrange a date for our wedding and sort out all the details."

"Great, I can't wait, my darling. Can you get away early?"

"Of course. I will be with you shortly," she said happily.

On her arrival, John picked Mia up, twirled her around, and kissed her. As he put her down, he said, "Right, now let's sort out a date."

"Yes, and then I'll check to see if the registry office can fit us in." Once they agreed on the date, Mia called to check. As she closed her phone, her eyes were wide with excitement. "Right, they booked us in at 11-30 am on the $22^{nd\ of}$ November."

John hugged and kissed her. "That's great. I'll call my parents and tell them. I'll also let Gilbert and Wendy know, plus, Joan and her husband George." He shook his head. "Although my parents will come, I don't know about the others. Still, I must inform them."

Mia bobbed her head in agreement. "Of course, we need to know so we can arrange their accommodation." Beaming a mile wide smile, she said, "I've seen a wedding dress I like, so I'll call Sophia. I want to know what she thinks." She wagged a finger. "That, my darling, is something you will not see until the day," she chortled.

"Of course, my darling, but can I ask if it be a long or a short dress?"

She winked. "A short one. But, if you would like me to wear a long one?"

"Darling, I don't mind which. I leave it up to you. Whatever you wear, I'll be happy as long as we get married."

After she arranged to meet Sophia, Mia called Fernando. As she and John would not have time to return to Valencia for the kitchen and bathroom units to be installed, on her asking, he agreed to be present when they were.

When Fernando later called, he chuckled. "You chose well; both the kitchen and bathroom look fantastic. I've sent you some photos, so I hope you like what you see."

On later looking, like Fernando, both Mia and John were well pleased.

With Mia now having her wedding dress, the next week she and John flew to Valencia. They wanted to be present when all their furniture would be delivered. While they waited, one look at the bathroom and kitchen, and both agreed with what Fernando had said.

Mia's eyes lit up with excitement, when after a truck arrived, piece by piece, the men brought in the furniture and placed in position.

Once they had finished and gone, John squeezed her hand. "Well, darling, what do you think?"

A satisfied smile lit up Mia's face as she threw her arms around him. "Everything looks fantastic. Thank you so much darling."

"There is no need to thank me. I'm only glad you liked what we chose." He waved a hand, "I also think everything looks great." He grinned. "Now, all we have to do is get married."

Mia's smile widened and her eyes shone bright with excitement. "Yes, and that day can't come soon enough for me."

With a new kitchen and bathroom, plus all new furniture, the villa looked fabulous when John and Mia returned to Barcelona. Also, with his desk and drawing board set up, John's office was more or less ready for use.

As for Mia and Fernando's change of offices, they had agreed to wait until she and John returned from their honeymoon. This they had decided to have in Paris.

Chapter 38

On the night before the wedding, John checked into his old hotel. His parents would also stay there along with Gilbert, Wendy, George, and Joan.

Come the next morning; with John, dressed and ready to go, there came a knock on his door. When he opened it, he found Gilbert, who would act as his best man during the ceremony, standing there. He grinned as he glanced John over. "So, this is it. Are you ready to make Mia an honest woman?"

A sigh escaped John's lips. "Yes, but I'll be glad when this morning is over." Further conversation ceased, when on answering another knock on the door, it revealed his parents.

"Well, son, how are you?" His father chuckled. "From your expression, I would say you're a little nervous." He turned to his wife, "Still, the boy looks good," what do you think?"

Her eyes sparkled as she said, "Yes, but I'm sure Mia will look better." She then pulled John's head down and kissed his cheek.

On their arrival at the registry office, they found a group of Mia's friends and work colleagues stood waiting, along with Mia's mother.

After John introduced his parents to her, while Joan, George, and Wendy waited for Mia's arrival, John went inside, accompanied by Gilbert.

When he heard a cheer go up, John knew Mia had arrived. Instead of using a car, she had chosen to arrive in a horse-drawn carriage, drawn by a jet-black horse.

Her father dismounted, then helped Mia. As she stepped down, they heard a few wolf whistles.

Mia looked stunning in a long white dress decorated with tiny yellow flowers. A delicate veil covered her face, while she carried a bunch of yellow roses.

John's mother nodded in approval. "I think John has made an excellent choice; Mia looks wonderful."

Those who heard, said, "That's for sure."

As Mia entered the hall, John's eyebrows shot up. He gazed at her with open admiration. She looked breath-taking beautiful.

As she came and took hold of his outstretched hand, a flicker of amusement crossed her face. "Well, here we are at last." She raised a questioning eyebrow. "So, what do you think? Do I look okay."

John licked his lips. "You, my darling, look like a dream come true. Plus, with you soon to be my wife, I will be the happiest man in Spain."

A satisfied smile raced across Mia's face. "Thank you darling. You look so handsome; I could not be happier."

To John's relief, the service was short, and once pronounced husband and wife, he swept Mia up in his arms. After they exchanged a short but passionate kiss, John put her down.

He chuckled. "Well, Mrs Philips, how does it feel to be married?"

She laid a delicate hand on his cheek. "My darling, I am so happy I could cry. I've waited for this minute since I first saw you in my office."

John, his eyes bright with happiness, nodded agreement. "In that, I can only agree."

To the delight of those present, after they thanked the official, John carried Mia outside to their waiting carriage. With both sitting inside, smiling, and waving, the driver flicked the whip. The horse neighed, tossed its tail and plume tied up with white ribbon, , then set off for their reception at the LeClaire Restaurant.

As the carriage rolled along, several people waved and called out. On arrival at the El Palace Hotel, where after their reception, Mia, and John would spend the night, John helped Mia out of the carriage.

The reception went off well, with both service and food served excellent. Mia and John were also pleased to find their parents had got on well during the reception.

Several hours later, after numerous toasts and leading off the first dance, Mia and John thanked their guests for coming. They then left, and went up to their suite.

After he opened the door, Mia squealed with delight when John picked her up and carried her inside.

Once she had removed her wedding dress, Mia tossed her hair. "So, my husband, did your bride look good enough?"

"You, my darling, looked fabulous. Any King would have been proud to have had you as his bride today," He shook his head. "But instead of a King, you had me."

Mia held him tight and kissed him. "Darling, to me, you are my King."

With his breath tickling her ear, he said, "And you, my darling wife, are my Queen." Then, locked in each other's arms, they enjoyed a long and passionate kiss, before undressing and climbing into bed.

As John caressed Mia's breasts, he said, "Now, what do newlyweds do once on their own?"

"I have no idea," she murmured. "You will have to show me."

When they later went down for dinner, one look and anyone could see they had been making love. However, due to hosting numerous newlyweds, the staff took no notice. With neither hungry, they only ordered a snack and two glasses of Merlot. While sipping their drinks, both were looking forward to the next five days in Paris.

Once back in their suite, they made a last check to ensure they had passports and hotel bookings, then climbed into bed. Clasped in each other's arms, they lay happy in the knowledge they were now married.

The next morning, a hotel taxi took them to the airport. Here, a short time after boarding their plane, they landed at Orly airport in Paris. A taxi then took them to the K+K Hotel in Saint Germain, where they had reservations.

At the reception desk, as Mia's passport was still in her maiden name, John had brought a copy of their marriage certificate. However, with no problems, once checked in, a porter escorted them to their room.

As she walked inside, a glance out of the window made Mia gasp with delight. There in front of her was the Eiffel Tower. "Wow, what a beautiful view."

The porter chuckled. "Yes, madam. All the rooms on this side have a similar view."

Once he had left, John took Mia in his arms. "Welcome to Paris, my darling, the city for lovers."

"Thank you, my darling husband, but, where else could we be? I mean, we qualify as lovers, don't we?" She then squealed with delight as John clasped her tight and growled, "Do I have to show you?" With his tongue in her mouth that made her passion rise, she gasped, "Okay, I get the message. Calm down."

He grinned and shook his head. "But this is Paris, my darling."

Once unpacked, they went downstairs and stepped outside the hotel.

With love shining in his eyes, John said, "Well, what would you like to do, my darling wife? Take a walk around or what?"

Mia squeezed his hand. "Let's take a taxi down to the Seine. I would love to take a boat trip." She giggled. "They say no trip to Paris is complete without one."

John gave a mock bow. "If that's what my wife would like to do, then who am I to disagree?"

As a taxi pulled up to let its passengers out, John stepped forward. "Messier." When the driver nodded, John opened the rear door for Mia to enter and then climbed in behind her.

"We would like to go to the Seine, please," John said.

The driver nodded. "Anywhere in particular?"

"We want to take a boat trip."

Five minutes later, as the cab pulled to a stop, the driver pointed to a nearby kiosk. "You can book a trip there."

"Many thanks," John replied. "How much?"

The driver pointed at the metre. After John paid, adding on a tip, he and Mia went over to the kiosk. On looking at a board advertising boat trips, a check revealed they had to wait twenty minutes before the next trip. However, a glance showed a boat full of people tied up at the bottom of a flight of steep stone steps.

John bought their tickets, and holding Mia's hand tight, they joined the people already on board.

During the trip that followed, with her eyes bright with excitement, Mia clutched John's hand. "Oh, this is wonderful," she trilled as they passed under one of several bridges. "I've read so much about a trip on the Seine, and it's as exciting as they say."

John squeezed her hand. "Yes, it's a trip to remember."

At the end of their trip and back where they started, John helped Mia off the boat. He tipped their guide; then they climbed the steps back to the road.

"How about we take a walk?" John asked. "When we find a café, we can sit and have a coffee?"

Mia, her eyes bright with excitement nodded. "Yes, that would be good."

While strolling along, hand in hand with love in their eyes, they came to a café. Here, while sitting outside enjoying a caramel latte, they people watched.

Mia caught hold and squeezed John's hand. "Darling, I am so happy."

"So am I. Plus, we've been lucky with the weather." He shrugged. "After all, we are now in the last week of November."

Mia nodded. "But it's warmer in Barcelona."

"Yes, although I'm sure the temperature in Valencia will be even hotter?"

"Well, no matter what, I'm looking forward to when we go there."

"That's for sure. But first, let's enjoy our time here in Paris."

"Of course," Mia said laughing, "this is our honeymoon."

"Yes, but on our return to Spain, with all the new furniture, bathroom, and kitchen, I'm looking forward to living there."

Mia sighed. "Well, with all the money you spent, it should do."

John shook his head. "Forget the cost; it was worth every Euro to see you look so happy when we were last there."

With her eyes bright on remembering, Mia kissed John on the cheek. "What can I say except thank you?"

As they continued their way, they came to where various paintings were hung on the embankment wall. However, after a look and not seeing anything of interest, they walked on. Further along, they found a series of stalls laden with all kinds of things. Some new, while most were old.

"I guess this is an antique fair?" John said.

"Yes, we have these in Spain," Mia replied. "However, they say those in France are far better." However, after looking and finding nothing suitable for their villa, they continued on their walk.

They next came to a stall selling hats, scarves, and gloves. Here, Mia picked out a scarf she liked, which, after a bit of friendly haggling, John bought.

As he had read you could not flag down a taxi in Paris, when they came to a taxi rank, John stopped.

"Darling, shall we take a taxi to Scue Coeur?" When he noticed Mia's puzzlement, he said, "It's a large cathedral at the top of Montmartre. Apart from the cathedral, there's a wall nearby decorated with words of love in a wide range of languages. In case you didn't know, while on our boat trip, we passed under the Love Bridge. Until a few years ago, lovers could fix a padlock to the bridge and throw the key into the river. It showed your undying love for your partner. The authorities banned the practice after they realised the extra weight the locks had put on the bridge. They also removed the padlocks.

Mia gave John a suspicious glance. "And how may I ask, did you know all this?"

Chapter 39

HE GRINNED. "I FOUND out when I went online to see where in Paris we could visit."

"In that case, as there is an empty taxi, let's go."

Once there, gazing upwards, Mia said, "The cathedral looks beautiful. Can we go inside?"

"Of course."

On entering, as she gazed around, Mia shook her head. "It's incredible how they used to make these buildings." She shrugged. "Today, they mainly consist of glass and concrete."

John nodded. "Yes, how true."

Ongoing back outside, they went to where a number of artists were painting scenes and portraits. When John asked one artist where the Wall of Love was, he said how to get there.

As Mia looked at the bright coloured tiles and the writing on them, she sighed, "Oh, this looks so beautiful."

John flashed a smile. "Yes, but not a patch on my wife."

Mia's cheeks coloured as she replied, "Thank you, my husband, I love you."

After returning for another look at the various paintings on sale by the cathedral, Mia sighed. "I think that's enough for today."

"Yes, I agree," John said. "Look, I noticed a taxi rank back around the corner. Shall we go back to the hotel?"

"I'm tired, so yes, please. When John showed a driver their hotel card, he nodded.

Once back inside their hotel room, after removing their shoes and lying on the bed, John kissed Mia's cheek. "Well, my darling, I think it's been a successful day?"

"Yes, but now I would like to rest for a while."

John opened his arms to encase Mia, and in minutes, both were fast asleep.

When John later awoke, although he tried not to disturb Mia, she murmured, "I think we fell asleep?" As he turned and kissed her cheek, his warm lips sent a thrill of excitement through her.

She sighed. "Darling, I want us to always be like this."

"You and I both. Still, my darling, I have no doubts things between us will never change." He shook his head. "If they do, it will only be for the better." With that, as they embraced, Mia felt John's hardness press against her.

"Not now, darling. I'm hungry and want to eat."

John gave a short, dirty laugh. "Yes, and so do I."

She giggled. "You know what I mean." As she untangled herself from John's embrace, she murmured, "We have all night, with no dogs needing to go out for a walk."

"That's true." He kissed her, then rose from the bed and helped Mia get up.

Once she had redone her makeup, John held her at arm's length.

"You, my darling, look divine." He wagged a finger. "I'll have to keep a sharp eye on you in case some Frenchman tries to steal you away."

She cocked an eyebrow. "Oh, do you think one might?"

John growled and flexed his muscles. "They can try, but they will have to deal with me first."

Mia gave a subtle wink. "Yes, I'm sure you would protect me, my darling." Then she and John burst out laughing.

They had noticed an Indian restaurant near to the hotel, so went there for dinner. It proved an excellent choice, with the meal both aromatic and tasty.

On leaving the restaurant, after a walk to help digest their meal, they returned to their hotel. Here while sitting in the lobby bar, they relaxed with a glass of Merlot each.

Once in their room with a Do Not Disturb sign on the door; first Mia showered, then John. When he came out with a bathrobe wrapped around him, he found Mia in bed.

She fluttered her eyelashes. "Come here, my husband. I've been waiting for this since we landed this morning."

He grinned as he walked towards her. "Oh, and why's that?"

"Well," she murmured, "this is Paris, and unless I'm mistaken, we are lovers?"

"Yes, so,"

Mia threw back the covers to reveal she wore a sheer black negligee and a matching thong. With her firm breasts and hard nipples thrusting out the silky material, John's eyebrows shot up to his forehead.

"Wow! What can I say? You look fabulous?"

Mia giggled. "Yes, I can see you like what you see."

He shook his head. "Darling, I would have to be blind or gay, not too." As he removed his robe and jumped in to join Mia, he asked, "So, where did this sexy outfit come from? Not that I'm complaining."

"After I told Sophia we would spend our honeymoon in Paris, she gave me a package and said not to open it until we were here." Mia giggled. "I just remembered, so I opened it."

John ran his hands over the silky negligee, before catching hold of her breasts.

"In that case, all I can say is thank you, Sophia."

Finally, after a night of hot and steamy lovemaking that left both exhausted, they fell asleep.

Chapter 40

"They awoke, too late for breakfast, so ordered from room service. When a knock on the door announced its arrival, John slipped on his bathrobe and opened the door.

A smiling waitress wheeled in a loaded trolly, said, "Enjoy," then left. John pushed the trolly over to Mia, who lay in bed with the sheet pulled up to cover her nakedness.

As he went to hand her the tray, she giggled. "Could you please pass me something to cover up."

He passed Mia a robe, who murmured, "Is this what I can look forward to in the mornings when living in our villa?"

John gave a short laugh. "It all depends on which you mean. Our making passionate love or you having breakfast in bed."

Mia sighed. "Last night was incredible, you gave me so much satisfaction. I'll never forget the number of orgasms I had."

Love shone in John's eyes as he said, "That's good. It means I could give you what lovers do in Paris."

A wide smile raced across her face. "Darling, you did that in spades. I'm sure that many women never get the same satisfaction as I had?" She cocked an eyebrow. "But, what about you? Did I satisfy you?"

The thought of how they had given each other so much pleasure made John sigh. "It was nothing short of fantastic."

Mia shook her head. "From what I've heard, some women don't like oral sex. They think it's disgusting." Before John could comment, she went on to say, "Since having experienced it myself, all I can say is they don't know what they are missing. If they did," she tittered, "I am sure they would get more satisfaction from their partners."

He kissed her cheek. "Well, all I can say is that I love doing it to you and you with me. The pleasure I receive and what I know I give you is nothing short of fabulous."

Mia sighed at the memory of last night's actions. She shook her head. "Who knows, some women may not know what it's like to get an orgasm. Once their partner has received what he wants, they might not be interested in satisfying the woman."

John chuckled. "Maybe, but forget about them; it is only us I am concerned about."

With breakfast finished, once showered, and dressed, they went downstairs. One look at Mia's glowing expression, and it was apparent what she had been up to.

Outside the hotel, they climbed into a waiting taxi. As John had not said, Mia did not know where they were going until he told the driver, "Muse de la Romantica."

She squeezed John's hand. "Now, this sounds interesting," she whispered.

He winked. "Yes, I'm sure you will like what you see there."

When they arrived at their destination, as the taxi drove off, an impish smile made Mia's mouth twitch.

"So, are we here to get more ideas on how to enhance our lovemaking?" John shook his head. "I don't think that's necessary. Still, who knows, we might."

Inside, they found a wide variety of paintings and sculptures, all dedicated to the art of lovemaking. Some showed naked couples locked in all sorts of positions, while others showed both naked men and women.

The museum lived up to its name, with both John and Mia aroused by what they saw.

"This is some exhibition," Mia whispered. "Do you feel the same way I do?"

"If you mean about feeling horny? I would have to be a statue not to," he replied. His breath tickled her ear as he murmured, "I thought I satisfied you last night? If not, then for sure you had me fooled?"

With her voice a bare whisker, Mia murmured, "If we were closer to our hotel, I'd show you how well you did."

John sighed at what they would do once enclosed in the privacy of their hotel room. He licked his lips. "Yes, and I'm sure we would both soon be satisfied," he said with a lustful look and a lick of his lips.

"Mia sighed. "Well, we will have to wait until later."

"I know," John groaned, "but the thought of doing what some of these sculptures are doing is making it hard to wait."

"She giggled. "I know what you mean, but try not to think about it for now."

With desire burning in his eyes, he said, "How can I do that when we were doing some of these things last night. Anyway, let's leave before I rip your clothes off and make love to you." With Mia holding a hand to her mouth to prevent laughing, John led her out into the cool, fresh air.

She squeezed his hand. "We need a coffee to calm us down."

"Yes, a good idea." A short walk led them to a café where, while sitting outside under a sunshade, they enjoyed a latte. "So, what shall we do now?" asked John, interrupting Mia's thoughts.

"Let's take a walk around the shops." She shrugged. "Not that I want to buy anything. But it would be nice to look and see what's here and not available in Spain?"

John nodded. "We can, but you will find things are cheaper in Spain than here in Paris?"

"I expect you are right, but I would like to see for myself."

After a walk around the shops, Mia said, "You are right; prices here are higher than in Spain."

John grinned. "Yes. It's why I chose to live in Spain and not France."

When Mia spotted an empty taxi sitting at the curb, she clutched John's arm. "Let's go to the Champ de Elysees. I know it's early, but I've heard the Christmas Bazaar there is well worth a visit."

A short time later, they arrived to find crowds of people looking at the stalls lining both sides of the road.

"Oh, this looks wonderful," Mia said. "With Christmas light festoons everywhere, the whole scene looks fabulous."

As they walked around, they looked at the things on sale. These comprised clothing, jewellery, Christmas decorations, and women's handbags.

Mia, her eyes bright with excitement at being in Paris on her honeymoon, could not have been happier. One look at her smiling face made John swell with pride and satisfaction.

After going from one end of the market and then back again on the other side of the road, Mia sighed. "Darling, I don't know about you, but I've seen enough? Let's have a drink either in the café between the stalls we just passed, or go back to our hotel."

"That sounds good to me. I spotted a taxi rank on the other side of the road, so let's go to our hotel."

They were fortunate, and found one taxi waiting. John gave the driver their hotel address, and with Mia sat nestled against him, they set off.

Once back in their hotel lobby bar enjoying a glass of Merlot, John asked, "Well, what did you think of today?"

"It's been fabulous, my darling husband, and it's all down to you."

Chapter 41

On finishing their drinks, they went to their room, showered and dressed, then went out for dinner. There were several restaurants nearby, so they chose one and went inside. After a look through the menu, Mia ordered a mixed seafood salad, while John chose pork chops with French fries and a side salad. When he ordered a bottle of Merlot, he noticed Mia's eyebrows rise in question. He grinned. "After all the walking we have done today, we deserve more than a glass?"

Mia nodded. "Yes, you're right."

Once they had finished, John licked his lips. "That was delicious. How about your salad?"

"Excellent, we will dine here again?"

"Yes, not only was the meal good, but the service as well."

On leaving the restaurant, after a short walk, they returned to their hotel room. With both tired, curled up in bed and locked in each other's arms, they fell asleep.

After breakfast the next morning, Mia suggested they take a bus tour of the city.

"Now that's an excellent idea," John said. "I remember when you took me on one in Barcelona."

Mia sighed. "Darling, how could I forget. It seems we only met a short time ago, and now, here we are married."

He folded his hands over hers. "Any regrets?"

Mia's eyebrows shot up. "Are you serious?"

"Of course." John chuckled. "Here we are on our honeymoon in Paris, what else could I want? Nothing."

"Me neither. I love you so much, and as you say, we are in the city of lovers."

Ongoing to the reception desk, they booked a day tour of the city that included a visit to the Louvre.

"Oh, that would be wonderful," Mia said, "I've always wanted to go there."

John nodded, "So apart from seeing various sites around the city, we can take a look inside."

While talking with the receptionist, she indicated that they could also buy a two-day bus pass.

"With this, you could also visit the Versailles Palace.'" She glanced from one to the other. "It includes a visit to Marie Antoinette's Estate."

"In that case, please cancel our first ticket," John said." As he paid for their two-day bus pass, the receptionist said, "A coach for a city tour will be outside the hotel in fifteen minutes."

"Perfect," John turned to Mia. "We both have our phones, so we can use them to take photos of anything we like."

The tour proved great. Among the various sights, they passed the world-famous Moulin Rouge and Notre Dame. Unfortunately, a fire had destroyed the roof and one tower. Their guide announced that rebuilding works were now ongoing. They also made a circular trip around the Eiffel Tower. As they did, Mia, her eyes wide with excitement, said, "This looked great from our hotel room, but up close, the tower looks enormous."

For Mia, the tour's highlight was when they went inside the Louvre. However, although fascinating to see paintings by world famous artists, it proved a tiring experience.

Once back at their hotel, John and Mia went straight to their room, took off their coats and shoes and then collapsed on the bed.

"Well, I'm exhausted from walking through the Louvre," Mia sighed. "But after seeing such a vast collection of paintings from the old masters," it was worth it."

John, raised a bleary eyelid. "I'm not much into art, but I enjoyed the experience."

After a well-deserved rest, as both still felt tired, they decided to have dinner in the hotel's restaurant. A waitress greeted and led them to a table. After a look at the menu, Mia decided to have tomato soup, with grilled chicken, peas, and potatoes for the main course. John ordered duck pate for a starter, followed by grilled salmon with potatoes, green beans, and asparagus. To wash it down, they ordered a bottle of white wine.

As they sat relaxed while enjoying their meal, John said, "How would you like to see the Palace of Versailles tomorrow?"

Mia sighed. Reaching across the table, she took hold of his hand. "Darling, it would be nice, but not tomorrow. After today, let's have a quiet wander around here. We could go there the following day?"

"No problem. Whatever you want is fine by me."

"Good, tomorrow, we can look around the shops." Her smile came soft and dreamy. "We could then sit outside at a cafe for a coffee or snack."

"Right, that's settled. Now, how about a dessert. You have a choice of Crème Brule, yoghurt, and fruit, a piece of tart or a slice of gateau?"

Mia cocked an eyebrow. "What's going on? Are you trying to make me put on weight?"

He shook his head. "No, of course not. I love you just as you are."

"Well, I could have fruit and yoghurt. That's if you are going to have anything?"

"I'll have the cream, Brule."

The waitress who had noticed them looking at the menu came over. May I get you something else?"

"Yes, please," John replied. "Could we have one yoghurt with fruit, and a Creme Brule?"

"Certainly, sir."

A few minutes later, she returned with their order. As she went to leave, John said, "Sorry, we'd like two caramel lattes?"

She flashed a smile and then walked off.

Once they had eaten their deserts and sat sipping their lattes, a satisfied smile crossed Mia's face. "That was excellent."

John grinned. "So, you're satisfied, are you?"

"I am now." Mia fluttered her long eyelashes. "But, by the time we get inside our room, I might feel the need for something else."

John's eyes lit up. "In that case, before going there, a short walk to help our dinner go down would be ideal."

Mia put a hand to her mouth to stifle a giggle. "Oh, why's that? Do you have anything specific in mind?"

A ghost of a smile crossed his face. "Yes, I do."

"Is it something I will like," she murmured?

John gave a short, low, dirty laugh. "Oh yes, I can guarantee that."

On their return to their room, after a quick shower, John joined Mia in bed. As he pulled her close, she said, "Now, what is it you can guarantee I will like?"

While locked in a hot embrace with his tongue tangled with hers, Mia's passion rose. While brushing his fingers over her mound, he realised Mia had put on Sophia's present. The touch of the silky thong made his cock harden, which Mia felt as he pushed his leg between hers.

"Oh, yes, I know what you mean," she said, catching hold of his erection.

His fingers caressed the front of her thong and then entered her pussy. As he fingered her, pushing deep inside and around, he could feel Mia's wetness.

Her lips quivered and she sighed, "I love it when we make love, you give me so much pleasure."

"If you like that, then you will love what I'm going to do next." He threw back the bed cover, and slid down her thong, revealing her pussy's lips showing through her mound of soft, black hair. As his head went down between her thighs, Mia spread them wider.

When he slid his tongue inside her pussy and licked her wetness, she sighed. "Oh, yes, I love what you're doing." The more John licked and sucked her clit; the louder Mia's moans of delight became.

When he stopped and looked up, Mia's eyes were half-closed with the tip of her tongue licking her lips.

"I'm pleased to see you are enjoying what I'm doing." He grinned. "I also take great pleasure in giving you satisfaction."

She opened her eyes and winked. "Good, now don't stop again. I love what you are doing."

As John continued to pleasure her, she felt his thumb rub over her clit. "Oh, yes," she

cried. "With your mouth and fingers playing with me it feels wonderful." She then pulled John's head down and with his mouth jammed tight against her pussy, her climax burst. To her delight, John continued to lick and lap at her clit until she came again. Finally, lifting his head, she gasped, "Enough, I want you inside me."

In a flash, John moved up the bed. He slipped on a condom, mounted her and slid his cock deep into her wetness. Each time he thrust in, Mia pushed her hips upwards, so his balls became jammed against the lips of her pussy. As they speeded up, faster and faster, she cried, "Oh, oh, this feels so good." Then, when she climaxed again, before she could tell John to stop, with a last thrust he came. As he collapsed on top of her, still trembling with excitement, Mia gasped, "That was fantastic."

John, with a fine sheen of sweat on his forehead, raised his head. "Darling, whenever we make love, it is always wonderful. You give me so much pleasure."

Holding him tight, she sighed. "As do you, my darling."

After lying joined together for a while, John eased himself off Mia. Once both had visited the bathroom, they enjoyed a long and tender kiss. John grinned, when he noticed that although her eyes were closed, Mia was smiling.

Chapter 42

The next morning, the sun was shining bright when Mia and John boarded the bus to visit the Versailles Palace. On their arrival, as they climbed off the bus, Mia gasped at its enormous size. With the façade covered with beautiful ornate mouldings, it gave an insight into what they would see inside.

As their tickets included a guided tour, they set off behind one. To their amazement, he said, "There are 2,300 rooms." On noticing their look of concern, he chuckled. "Don't worry; we won't be going into all of them."

The tour that followed was fantastic. Even without furniture, the rooms were beautiful. With decorative ceilings and ornate mouldings, it gave an impression of how luxurious they once were. In addition, with large paintings, both hanging and painted onto the walls, it made an incredible sight.

When they entered the Hall of Mirrors, John shook his head. "Now, this is something."

"Yes, it is," Mia replied. "I have never seen such a beautiful building as this."

By the time they had seen the Royal Apartment, the Royal Opera House, the Gallery of Great Battles, and the Royal Chapel, John, and Mia were exhausted. However, both were delighted at seeing such an array of beautiful sights.

Once finished, the guide led them to a café. After buying a drink and a snack, they collapsed on a bench.

Once rested, they went to look around the gardens. These were huge, containing lakes, ponds, an orangery, numerous sculptures and even a maze. As they wandered around, they came to a sign that read "Trianon." A check on the map they had, showed two. "The Grand Trianon," and the Trianon. The latter overlooked the Versailles Grand Canal, being smaller and covered in pink marble. A sign at the entrance stated, "The Emperor and his family used to stay here to escape from the pomp and ceremony of the main palace."

From their guidebook, they learned Marie Antoinette once lived in the Trinion before being beheaded.

Mia gasped in horror. "Oh, what a terrible way to die."

John nodded. "In those days," he said, "they beheaded numerous people, including several Queens."

When they later drove away from the Palace, Mia sighed, "Darling, what an incredible experience. Both the Palace and the gardens were amazing."

"I've seen the inside of the palace on television, but to see it first hand was something else."

On their last night in Paris, before returning to Spain, John suggested they take an evening cruise on the Seine. "We can have dinner on board if you like."

Mia's eyes lit up with delight. "Oh, yes, please. It would be a fabulous ending to our stay here."

John kissed her cheek. "Yes, I thought you would agree."

In the evening, a taxi dropped them off down by the Seine. As they boarded the cruise boat, a waitress handed them a glass of champagne.

"What a wonderful way to start the evening," Mia said as she accepted it.

As they set off, with a combo playing and a female singer singing love songs, it set the scene for a romantic evening. Also, with the bridges and various buildings floodlit, the trip made Mia's eyes sparkle with delight. That and candles lighting the tables as waitresses served them a three-course dinner, made it a spectacular evening.

As each held a glass of wine, John and Mia toasted each other.

"So, what do you think of my idea for our last evening in Paris," he asked?

"Wonderful, my darling. It is an evening I'll not forget in a hurry."

"Yes, and I love the pictures the photographer took of us."

A satisfied smile raced across Mia's face. "Yes, they are excellent. We will have them framed once we are home."

At the end of the cruise, as they climbed off the boat, John handed a large tip to the official standing by the steps.

"Many thanks. That was a fabulous evening."

Mia flashed him a smile, "Yes, wonderful."

With a line of taxis waiting by the top of the steps, a short time later, John and Mia were back at their hotel.

No sooner had John closed their room door when he swept Mia up in his arms. They embraced and kissed as they removed their coats and kicked off their shoes. John then carried Mia to the bed, where they continued to kiss and embrace. By the time they broke off, both were breathless but happy.

Once stripped off and in bed, their lovemaking was long, slow, and tender.

The following day, a taxi took them to the airport for their flight back to Barcelona. A short time after boarding, it seemed only a short time after taking off, they landed, and were back inside Mia's apartment.

As she cast a look around, Mia sighed. John caught hold of her hand. "Are you sorry about leaving here?"

"No, I know we will have a fabulous life in Valencia." She kissed John on the cheek. "Instead of living here with only Aza for company, I will be with my beloved husband in our own villa in Valencia." Her smile widened. "Plus, Aza will have a friend to keep him company while we are at work."

A relieved look crossed John's face. "That's good, as I'm looking forward to being there." He shrugged. "Although it will take a while to get my business up and running, I love a challenge. Oh, and the thought of doing business with your father adds more excitement."

"Yes, I'm sure it will work out well for both of you." She then went on to say, "My father has many contacts. With you preparing plans for anyone interested, it could prove beneficial for both of you."

"Yes, but if nothing else, the publicity could be a big help to my business."

Mia's smile came soft and dreamy. "Darling, I only have good vibes about my moving to take over Fernando's office. Plus, I know he cannot wait to move to Barcelona."

Right. Now, what's the plan about moving all your things to Valencia? Also, what about the dogs?"

"That's not a problem. Fernando has arranged for a company to bring his things up to Barcelona. Once his are offloaded, they will load my things and take them down to Valencia." She shrugged. "Regarding the dogs, it takes about the same time to drive as going by train. But as you can only take one dog per passenger, Sophia will bring them down in her car."

John nodded. "That's good of her, and of course, I will pay for her fuel." He flashed a smile. So, with the dogs sorted out, all we have to do is pack up your things?"

"it would be best if we say goodbye to my parents before we leave."

"Of course. You can take that for granted. Call them."

A short time later, Mia flashed a smile. "They are expecting us tomorrow."

The next day, when John knocked on Mia's parents' door, it opened to reveal both standing there.

Her father beamed them a smile. "Welcome, Mr & Mrs Phillips." He first hugged Mia, then John, before saying, "Come inside."

"They will if you let them pass," Mia's mother said, laughingly. She then embraced Mia as she passed her father. "Oh, it is so good to see you." After kissing John on both cheeks, she led the way into the lounge, with Mia's father bringing up the rear.

Once all had sat, her father said, "Now, before you tell us all about Paris, let me get you a drink. John, would you like a beer or a glass of wine? I know Mia will have wine."

"A beer would be fine, thanks."

With everyone holding a drink, her father said, "Welcome my son and daughter."

"Yes, welcome, son, Mia's mother echoed. Her eyes lit as she said, "Now, tell us all about Paris. Did you have a good time there?"

Mia, her eyes wide and bright, said, "It was wonderful."

Her father chuckled. "I should hope so; after all, you were on your honeymoon." Mia blushed, then told them all the places they had visited, except the Museum of Romance.

After a tasty dinner and a chat, several hours later, John and Mia said their goodbyes. As they went to leave, John said, "Now, don't forget, we look forward to welcoming you to our new home in Valencia."

"Yes. Don't leave it too long before you come down," Mia added.

"Don't worry, we won't, but we will give you time to settle in first," her mother said.

Her father said, "Oh, John, I almost forgot. I've put the word out about our proposed project." He shrugged. "We will now have to wait and see what response we get."

"That's good," John replied. "Once I've got my office up and running, I'll put out some adverts about the project."

"Yes, and I'll put a notice in my office window," Mia added, "plus put it on our company website. Oh, and Fernando said he will do the same. Given all this, I am sure things will prove successful."

The following day, Mia packed up her personal things from her office and took them to her apartment. John then helped her pack all her belongings into a suitcase and a few cardboard boxes. Once the truck had arrived and loaded her belongings, she and John would drive down to Valencia in her car. They would be at the villa when the truck arrived.

Mia had earlier introduced Fernando and Maria to her two staff members who would stay and work with them. After Carlos had helped Fernando and his secretary settle in, he would drive down to Valencia in his pickup truck.

When the truck arrived with Fernando's things, he and the men took them up to Mia's apartment. Then, after a short break, they loaded Mia's things into the truck. Once done, Fernando shook hands with John and kissed Mia on the cheek.

"Well, this is it. I feel sure this will prove a good move for all of us."

Mia, her eyes bright at the thought, nodded. "Yes, I am sure it will be."

John chuckled, "I have only good thoughts for both of you. I'm also sure that once I get set up, things will go well for me, too." He shook hands with Fernando, who hugged and kissed Mia on the cheek.

With John and Mia looking forward to starting a new life as husband and wife in Valencia, they drove off.

Chapter 43

Thirty minutes after their arrival at the villa, Fernando's truck arrived. John helped the men take all of his and Mia's belongings inside and up to their bedroom. Once finished and the truck left, he and Mia unpacked and put everything away.

Mia sighed. "Well, after all that exercise, we deserve a spot of lunch."

"Yes, let's go to the restaurant we went to before. He gave a wry grin. "After all, I don't expect you to start cooking as soon as we arrive here."

Mia gasped, then noticed John silently laughing. She shook her head. "You devil, you had me going for a minute."

He laughed, then pulled her close and kissed her. "After we've had lunch, I suggest we call in a supermarket and stock up. Or at least, get in the basics."

"Yes." Mia flashed him a smile. "Then you will not have an excuse not to have dinner ready for me when I come home from work."

John grinned and shook his head. "Well, as we will be coming home together, that's not liable to happen. Still, whenever I come home first, I will have dinner waiting for you."

Both laughed, then enjoyed a loving embrace.

After Mia drove them to her new office, John helped carry in her computer and bits and pieces. He then walked to his new office, where he made a list of required items. Next, he called the number of an office supply shop Fernando had given him. He had also suggested John contact a builder he had recommended.

"They might put some work your way," he said.

While awaiting the shop to deliver his order, John wrote out an advert he wanted placed in the local paper. After completing one about his architectural services, he prepared another one. This mentioned building plots for sale, with house plans of the buyer's choice included. To arouse more interest, he left out where these plots were. At the bottom, he added, interested parties, please call this telephone number.

Once satisfied with what he had written, John fixed several of his old house plans to his office window. He had just finished when he heard a van pull up outside. A glance showed it was from the office supply shop. After storing everything away, he checked to see what else he required, then locked up.

Ongoing to Mia's new office, he found her smiling and looking pleased with herself.

"Well, from your expression, things are going, okay?"

She flashed a wide smile. "Yes, they are." She turned and motioned the two girls sitting at their desks. "John, let me introduce you to Zoe and Daniela. They used to work with Fernando, but have agreed to work for me."

John went and shook hands with them. "Hi, and thanks for staying with Mia." He flashed a smile, took out two of his old business cards and handed them one each.

"These are in case you know of anyone who would like a house built." When he noticed Mia's puzzlement, he shrugged. "You never know, and I need to get the word around. Oh, and I've written your telephone number on the back of them."

To their surprise, Zoe said, "My father is a builder. I'll tell him about you."

John chuckled. "There you are. From little apples, mighty oak trees grow. It's the same with business. A word from one person can lead to a big result in sales."

Mia turned to the girls. "I'm sure my husband will reward you for any business you put his way."

"That's for certain," he said, then turned to Mia, "Right, now can I help you with anything?"

"No, thank you. Oh, did you get the supplies you wanted?"

"Yes, all done. I've also written two adverts I need to place in the local newspaper." To their surprise, Daniela said, "I can arrange that. I have a friend who works in advertising with the paper."

"That would be great," John exclaimed." Thank you." He took two papers from his inside coat pocket and handed them to her.

"Please have them put in for two weeks." He shrugged. "By then, I should know if I need to rewrite them."

Mia then led John into her new office. It was, he noticed, similar to her old one in Barcelona. She closed the door, and once seated, said, "The girls are friendly, so I'm sure we will get on well."

John nodded. "That's good, plus I thought it good of Daniela to get my ads put in the newspaper." He glanced around. "Well, you seem to have settled in pretty quickly?"

"There was not much to do. It's not as though I was starting from scratch." She shrugged "I'm sure Fernando will find it the same as well." A flicker of a smile crossed her face. "Now, I have an idea about your business."

John cocked an eyebrow. "Oh, and what's that?"

"The girls have told me where there is a print shop."

"Ah, now that sounds interesting?"

"Yes, I think we should visit them. You can get new business cards printed, and also order some printed headed paper."

"Yes, I need both. I'll also buy some larger size printed paper to put details of what services I can supply."

"Good idea. Plus, you also need a sign for your office. I'll keep the name Fernando used, but I'll put a sign that says it's now under new management.

John nodded. "You are right. Regarding my sign, I'll use the name Philips Architectural Designs. What do you think?"

"Yes, that sounds perfect."

On checking online, John found a local sign company. He called, and spoke with someone, who said a representative would visit him in an hour's time. John gave them his address, then he and Mia went to his office to wait for their arrival.

When a man later arrived at John's office, after greetings, John gave him a drawing showing the name he wanted.

The man glanced at it. "No problem." Once he had measured up the existing sign box, he told John the cost. When he noticed Mia nod, John said, "Good. How long will it take to make and install?"

"Ten days, is that okay?"

"Yes, no problem." John wrote out a cheque and handed it to the man who gave him a receipt, along with his business card.

Once he had gone, John chuckled. "Well, I don't know what you think, but why don't we call it a day?"

A flicker of a smile crossed Mia's face. "Yes, I told the girls to lock up and go home, so let's go."

A short time later, they were inside the villa. "Would you like a glass of wine, Darling?"

"Yes, I'll fetch it," Mia said as she went to the sideboard.

On her return with two glasses of red wine, John knew it was Merlot, their favourite brand. As they sat looking out of the front window, John touched his glass to hers. "So, Mrs Philipps, are you happy to be here? Or would you rather be back in Barcelona?"

Mia's eyebrows shot up. "Are you kidding?" She pulled John's face to hers and kissed him. To his surprise, she sighed, "Although I am delighted to be here, there is one thing missing."

John cocked an eyebrow. "Oh, and can I ask what?"

The corner of Mia's mouth curled up into a mile wide smile. "I miss having Aza and Lucky with us."

John swept a hand across his forehead and breathed a sigh of relief. "Thank heavens. You had me worried for a minute. I wondered what was wrong?"

Mia giggled. "Don't be silly. I am more than happy to be here with you. Plus, the villa is so much better than my apartment."

"That's for sure, Still, like you, I'll feel better when the boys are with us." After touching his glass to hers, with both happy, they sipped their drinks.

Once settled into the villa, and Mia in her new office, she called Fernando. "Hi Fernando, is everything alright up there?"

"Oh, hi Mia, I was just about to call you."

A worried expression marred Mia's face. "Oh, is there a problem?"

"It's nothing major. But it seems you have to sign a paper re my taking over your office. I will have to come down and do the same for you."

Mia sighed with relief. "What a coincidence. My mother is not feeling well and I'm flying up tomorrow to see her. If she is ok, I'll stay at my parents," house for a couple of days. Then, with my friend Sophia, we will bring the dogs down here in her SUV.

"I'm sorry to hear about your mother and hope she recovers soon." He then said, "Now, I seem to remember your parents live outside the city? If you like, I can meet you at the airport. Then, after we get the form signed, I will drive you to their house."

A satisfied smile raced across Mia's face. "Well, if it's not too much trouble, then many thanks. I'll call my father and tell him he won't have to fetch me from the airport."

With this agreed, Mia called Sophia. As expected, she was sorry to hear about her mother, but delighted when Mia said she would travel down with her and the dogs.

"Oh, that would be good. Anyway, you will be pleased to know both dogs and I are okay. Once you are here, you can tell me how things are going down there."

"Yes, but for now, all I will say is that everything is going well. The two girls who worked with Fernando are getting on well with me and Carlos."

"Oh, that's good. Now, after seeing your parents, let me know when you are liable to get here. I don't want to be out with the dogs when you arrive."

Mia laughed. "Will do, and I look forward to seeing you later, bye-bye."

When Mia told John about her mother and having to go to see her, he said, "Of course, you must. I only hope it's nothing serious. Please give her and your father my best wishes. Anyway, I'm sure you and Sophia will have a good chat on your way back here with the dogs."

Mia laughed. "Yes, I'm sure we will." she said.

Chapter 44

On her arrival at the airport, Mia found Fernando in the arrival's hall. He greeted her with a kiss on the cheek, then said, "I'm sorry to hear about your mother. I hope it's nothing serious." He shook his head. "Also, about dragging you up here to sign the paper re our transferring businesses. I'll be down in a few days to sign my paper."

Mia nodded. "Well, I was coming anyway, so it's not a problem." Once in his car, Fernando drove them straight to the government office. After he and Mia had signed the necessary papers, he drove her to her parents" house. On arrival, he said, "I won't come in, but please give your mother and father my best wishes."

"I will, and thank you Fernando. If I have time, I'll call in and see you before Sophia and I drive down to Valencia with the dogs."

As Fernando drove off, Mia knocked on the door. To her surprise, her mother opened the door.

Mia's eyes lit up. "Oh, I'm so pleased to see you up and about, mother."

"Welcome, Mia. Thank you for coming, but I'm afraid you have come for nothing." She then went on to say, "Since we talked, I went to the hospital and had several tests. They all came back negative." A flicker of a smile crossed her face. "The doctor said he thought it was due to stress caused by you and John getting married and moving to Valencia."

Mia sighed in relief and hugged her mother tight. "Oh, that's wonderful news. You don't know how happy I am to hear you are alright," She shrugged. "As for coming, I had to come to sign a paper about Fernando taking over my office. Still, I would have come anyway. Is father here?"

"No, he has gone to see a potential customer." When she noticed Mia's puzzlement, she said, "The man is thinking of buying one of your father's plots of land. He is interested in taking up the offer of John designing him a house."

Mia's eyebrows shot up. "Oh, that would be wonderful."

"Yes, but we will have to wait until your father returns before knowing." She cocked an eyebrow. "Are you going to stay the night? If so, I'll make up your bed."

"I am, but I'll make up the bed, not you." Despite her mother's arguments, after taking her case upstairs, Mia made up her old bed.

As she did, it made her think back to when she had gone to take over and run her father's old business. She sighed. Had she not done so, she would never have met and married John. The thought of his arms around her and his lips on hers made Mia sigh with pleasure. He was a wonderful man, and in her heart, she knew they would always be happy.

About an hour later, while Mia and her mother sat talking, they heard the front door open.

"Quick, hide Mia. We will surprise your father." Just as she did, she heard her father say, "How are you feeling?"

"I'm fine," her mother answered. "Now tell me your news."

Once he had put on his slippers and poured himself a glass of wine, he sat down in his favourite armchair. As he sipped his wine, his wife said, "Enough. What news do you have?"

Mia waited with bated breath to hear his reply. "Everything went well," he said. "The man is interested and has given me details of the kind of house he wants. If John can do what he wants, it will be good for both of us."

On hearing this, Mia could hardly control her emotions. She crept into the room, put a hand over her father's eyes and kissed the top of his head.

As he felt her hands and lips, he said, "What the..." Then, as Mia uncovered his eyes, he shook his head. "Oh, I see your mother played a joke on me. So, how are you, my daughter?" He cast an eye over her, then nodded. "I can see married life is good for you."

"Thank you, father, and yes, it is. I came to see how mother was, and was relieved to find she is alright?"

"Yes, after the hospital ran several tests, it showed all was fine." He chuckled. "So, you heard what I said about a possible project for John?"

"Yes, and I'm sure he will be able to supply plans to suit the man's requirements."

"So am I, my daughter. From what you have told me, John can design all kinds of houses."

Mia nodded. "I have seen references from many of his clients. All said how satisfied they were and recommended his services."

"Well, I will give you the man's details, and you can pass them on to John. It will be a good surprise for him, don't you think?"

"Yes, it will also give his confidence a boost about the future."

A ghost of a smile crossed her father's lips. "Yes, but first John will have to convince the client he can supply what he wants." He shrugged. "Anyway, I will talk to John after he has them." Turning to his wife, he said, "Now, what do we have for dinner?" Without waiting for a reply, he glanced at Mia. "I never asked, but I expect you are going to stay the night?"

"Of course," she chortled. "How could I turn down one of mother's delicious dinners?"

After he hugged and kissed her cheek, her father poured them all a glass of wine.

Once the meal was over, they sat in the lounge with Mia, telling them how different life was in Valencia to Barcelona. She also called John to say her mother was alright.

"Oh, that's great news. Please give her my best wishes, and your father of course."

As her father had said not to, Mia made no mention of a possible project for him. She did, however, say she and Sophie would be down on Friday with the dogs.

After spending two days with her parents, Mia said goodbye and took a taxi to Sophia's apartment.

When she knocked on her door, Sophia opened it, with Aza and Lucky letting out barks of welcome at seeing her.

Mia stooped, ruffled both their heads, and kissed them. "Hi Aza, Lucky, it's good to see you too."

She stood and kissed Sophia, who stood wearing a beaming smile. After a warm embrace, they went into the lounge with the dogs following close behind.

Once seated on the sofa, Sophia cocked an eyebrow. "So, how are things going in Valencia? I know it's early days, but I'm sure you have a good idea?"

"Yes, John and I are happy there."

"That's good, but what about John's business? How are things going?"

Mia shrugged. "As he said, it will take a while to get the word out before he gets any business. Still, he has ordered a new sign for his office and placed adverts in the local paper about his architectural services. I've also placed a sign in my office window about John's services." She then put a hand to her mouth. "Oh, I almost forgot, John has an appointment next week with ReAza. They are one of the biggest real estate companies in the world. It seems they might have a proposition for him."

An impish smile made Mia's mouth twitch. "Anyway, never mind that. How have the dogs been, and what have you been up to?"

"They have been no trouble and been out every day for a walk." A smile quirked Sophia's lips as she said, "Oh, did I tell you I have a new boyfriend?"

Mia's eyes lit up, and her smile widened. "No, you did not. So, where did you meet him? How old is he? What is his name, and what does he do?"

Sophia laughed and put her hands up. "Whoa. Anything else you want to know?" Not giving Mia time to say any more, she said, "A friend introduced me to him at a birthday party. His name is Hugo. He is twenty-six and works in advertising."

Mia caught hold and hugged and kissed her. "Oh, I am so happy for you." She cocked an eyebrow. "I hope he treats you well?"

"Yes, he does. Although we've only known each other for a short time, we get on well. Oh, and Hugo likes dogs. He came with me on several occasions when Paula was too busy."

"Well, in that case, I look forward to hearing all about your Hugo."

Sophia laughed. "Yes, I am sure you are. Anyway, would you like a drink, wine, or coffee."

"Let's have wine." As they sat and sipped their wine, Mia said, "I'll call and tell John what time we expect to arrive."

When he answered and she saw his face, her eyes lit up. "Hi, darling. I'm with Sophia, who sends you her greetings. Yes, my mother is good, and Fernando and I have signed the transfer papers. So, how are things down there?" In a quieter tone of voice, she whispered, "Have you missed me?"

"Of course, but have you missed me?" He went on to say, "Without having you here, and the boys, I've been living like a monk. Still, I'll show you how much I've missed you once you are here in my arms."

Mia felt her cheeks flush. She knew what John meant. Trying hard to control her voice, she said, "Oh, that will be nice. Now, Sophia expects us to arrive at the villa around 2 pm tomorrow."

"Great, I look forward to your arrival. Oh, it will be interesting to see what the boys think of their kennels."

"Yes, Aza has never had a kennel before. I wonder what he will make of it."

"The same applies to Lucky. Like Aza, he has always lived inside the house. Still, it was a good idea to buy them. If they are out in the garden when it rains, they can shelter inside. Still, once you are here, we will soon find out if they like them or not. So, what other news do you have?"

"Sophia has a new boyfriend."

She saw John' shake his head and his eyebrows rise. "Poor girl. It means you are going to ask her all about him."

"Not everything. I already know his name, age, and his job."

John laughed. "Now, why am I not surprised to hear that." After a chat, before closing their phones, both said, "I love you, and blew each other a kiss.

The next day, come 2-0-clock, John fidgeted as he stared out of the front window. When 3-0-clock had passed and no sign of Mia, Sophia, and the dogs, he Smile changed to a frown. He rang Mia, who said, "Hi Darling, we will be with you in about 35 minutes...." Before she could say more, he heard a loud crash and Mia scream. Then, besides the dogs" howling, there was silence.

Chapter 45

Fear flooded through John's veins as he cried out, "Mia, what's happened? Please speak to me."

The next thing he heard was Sophia's voice. "Are you alright, Mia?"

To his relief, in a shaky voice, he heard her reply, "Yes."

When he heard her speak, John, who had held his breath, breathed out. Then after what seemed like a lifetime, Mia gasped, "Sorry, John. Some crazy idiot hit us and I dropped the phone."

"Never mind that, are you and Sophia alright? Are you injured?" He heard Mia tell the dogs to be quiet, and then speak to Sophia. When she said, "No, we are both okay," John said, "Thank heavens. What about the dogs?"

"They went crazy when the car hit us, but I've managed to calm them down. They are okay."

"Thank god you're not injured." He then heard a car door squeak open, and Sophia say, "What a mess. We will not be driving anywhere in this."

"Is it that bad?" Mia asked.

"No, but one wing is pressing against the wheel and your door's damaged," she said. "Those idiots caused a big pile up. They should have their licenses revoked for racing on the main highway...." John cut in, "Mia, where are you? I'll come and fetch you."

"We are at Sagunto, on the A23 highway. It is about 37 KM from where you are."

"No problem, but I'll need a larger car than ours to take you all."

"That should not be a problem. I'll call Carlos. He has a Nissan twin cab pickup with the rear section covered. I'm sure he won't mind coming to fetch us."

As they spoke, John heard a police siren, followed by the clanging of an ambulance.

"The police and ambulances have arrived," Mia said.

"Yes, and breakdown trucks will soon arrive to clear the road," he heard Sophia say.

A few minutes later, Mia came back on the phone. "John, Carlos will come to pick up the dogs. So, if you come in my car, you can take Sophia and me." She paused. "Look, I'd best call you once I know where we will be. We might get taken to the hospital?"

John's voice trembled as he spoke. "Hospital, I thought you said you and Sophia were uninjured."

"Yes, but Sophia says I have a cut on my forehead, and her left arm hurts."

"Right, I'm leaving now. Once you know where you will be, call and let me know where to find you."

"I will, but there is no need for you to panic and speed. I don't want you to have an accident on your way here."

"Don't worry; one accident today is enough. Right. I love you and I'll soon be with you."

Despite what he had told Mia, as John sped along, Mia called. "Carlos has arrived. He has our cases, and the dogs in the back of his truck. Oh, and Sophia and I are now at the hospital. "

"Wow, that was quick of Carlos to get there."

"Yes, it seems he was out near here when I called."

After Mia told him how to get to the hospital, a short time later, John arrived.

Ongoing inside, his eyebrows shot up in alarm when he spotted Sophia sat on a chair, but no Mia.

He rushed to her side. "Sophia," "Is Mia alright? Where is she?" he gasped.

She caught hold of John's arm. "There is no need to worry, Mia is okay. She suffered a slight cut when she banged her head. The doctor wanted to check her over."

As they spoke, Mia appeared with a plaster strip on her forehead. On seeing blood on the front of her coat, John's eyebrows shot up as he rushed to her side.

"Darling, are you alright? Sophia said the doctor wanted to check you over."

Mia threw herself into John's arms. "Oh darling, I'm so sorry to worry you."

He clasped her trembling body tight. "Never mind me. What did the doctor say?"

She shrugged. "After checking, he found nothing wrong. So, after cleaning the cut and applying a plaster, he said I could go."

"Thank God. I guess that's how the blood came to be on your coat." Turning to Sophia, he asked, "What about your arm? Mia said it hurt."

"It does a bit, but it's not broken."

John glanced from one woman to the other. "So, what happened?"

Mia spoke. "We were doing fine until we reached Sagunto." Sophia then went on to say, "Two idiots driving souped-up cars were racing. I spotted them in the outside mirror weaving in and out of the traffic as they came flying up towards us." She shook her head. "When one car hit the other, it crashed into our car and sent us sideways into the safety barrier." She shrugged. "I must have hurt my arm while trying to control the car. Anyway, although the dogs went crazy with fright, neither them nor us were badly injured." She then went on to say, "When the police arrived, after I and some other drivers had given a statement, they arrested the two drivers. As for my car, the front wing, and the passenger door were badly damaged."

John's shoulders slumped as he expressed his apologies for the damage to her car. He also expressed gratitude that neither of them was injured. I would have felt terrible had you been doing us a favour."

Carlos, who had been talking with someone on the phone, came over.

"Hi, John." His smile then turned to a frown as he turned to Mia and Sophie. "I'm sorry to say, a woman passenger in one of the other cars involved in the accident has died."

Sophia and Mia gasped in horror as Carlos went on to say, "She was in the front seat with her husband driving when one car hit theirs." He shook his head. "She died from a heart attack. As a result, the two men who caused the accident are being charged with causing death due to dangerous driving." He shrugged. "It means the police will want you both to give evidence at their trial."

"Oh my god, that's terrible," Mia sobbed. "That poor woman's husband. I feel so sorry for him."

"Yes, so do I." Sophia shook her head. "The accident would never have happened if those two idiots had not been racing."

"That's true," Mia said. "But, if you were not bringing down our dogs, you would not have had an accident."

To prevent further discussion, John cut in. "Look, Sophia, you can fly home, at my expense. As for your car, once repaired, I'll drive it back to Barcelona."

Mia spoke to Carlos, who said, "No, I'll drive it, John. You don't know the way."

John nodded. "Thanks Carlos, but first, I think we should all go to our villa. We can relax there with a drink and discuss this."

"Good idea," Sophia said. "I'll come with Carlos. Once at your place, I'll call and inform my insurance company of the accident.

They will decide where my car gets repaired. As for the dogs, you can take them in the back of Mia's car or leave them with us."

Mia shook her head. "No. We will take them. They will be calmer with us."

Mia drove, with John beside her and the two dogs sitting on the back seat, they drove to their villa.

Once inside, John led the dogs to the kitchen. After they had a drink and something to eat, they wandered off to explore the house.

When John joined Mia on the sofa, she shook her head. "Well, this is not how I expected our weekend to start."

"Me neither, but thank goodness neither you nor Sophia suffered any injuries."

"Yes, and her car was not too badly damaged. Plus, of course, both dogs are okay."

As they sat talking with the dogs laid out on the floor, the doorbell rang. When Mia opened the door, Sophia, and Carlos came in.

After Carlos greeted her and John, he said, "Right, if you don't need me anymore, I'll say goodbye and see you all on Monday." He grinned. "My girlfriend is waiting."

While John shook his hand, Mia kissed him on the cheek. "Thank you, Carlos, and please give our apologies to your girlfriend for spoiling your weekend."

"Likewise," John added.

Sophia kissed Carlos on both cheeks. "Thank you so much for your help, Carlos. I appreciate it."

He flashed her a smile. "You are all welcome." With Mia accompanying him to the front door, he left.

Once Carlos had gone, Sophia slumped down in an armchair. Despite what she had said, her downcast expression showed she was still in shock. No doubt from hearing that a woman had died in the accident.

John caught Mia's eyes and nodded his head in Sophia's direction. Mia rose and went to sit beside her. She put her arms around Sophia, and with tears in their eyes, they held each over close.

John left them alone to comfort each other. He went to the kitchen, with the two dogs following behind.

On his later return, he was pleased to find the two women sat talking. Not wishing to disturb them, he settled in an armchair. While checking his phone for any messages, Mia spoke. "Darling, it's not been a good afternoon, so how about we go out for dinner? Wearing a mischievous smile, she said, "After all, it will save you cooking."

He chuckled. "Well, if you insist, what's a poor husband to do but agree with his wife's suggestion."

With the three of them laughing, it helped ease the tense atmosphere. A few minutes later, Sophia said, "If it's alright, I would like to take a shower."

"Of course," Mia replied. "I'll take you up to your bedroom. You will find fresh towels in the bathroom. John and I will also take a shower. It will make us all feel more refreshed."

As the two women went to pick up their cases, John said, "I'll take them."

"No problem, darling, we can manage," Mia said as she led Sophia towards the staircase, "Why don't you take the dogs out for a walk?"

"Yes, then, while you are getting ready, I'll have a shower. It won't take me as long as you to prepare to go out."

He called the dogs, slipped on their leads, and after putting on a coat, took them out.

Once the dogs had performed and had a short walk, John returned to the house. He made sure both had food and water, then went upstairs, where he found Mia sat in the bedroom drying her hair.

"Oh, you were quick," she said.

John chuckled. "Yes, I thought I might catch you in the shower."

A flicker of a smile crossed her face. "Behave, we have company." In the dressing table mirror, he noticed Mia flutter her eyebrows. "Still," she murmured, "providing we don't make too much noise, we might manage something later."

Chapter 46

By the time John had showered and dressed, he found the two women dressed, looking smart and talking downstairs.

His eyes lit as he glanced at them. "So, I have two gorgeous women to escort. People seeing us will be jealous. They will wonder how I manage."

Sophia's cheeks flushed, while Mia shook her head. "Take no notice, Sophia. John is always like this. Now, where are you taking us for dinner?"

"Well, after today, none of us wants to drive anymore. I thought of the restaurant Fernando took us to? I mean, it's close, so we can walk there."

Sophia shuddered. "That suits me. I don't want to drive anywhere," while Mia added, "Me neither."

On arrival and seated in the restaurant, John asked, "What would you girls like to drink?"

Mia glanced at Sophia, "Would you like a short or wine? If wine, white or red?"

"Neither, thank you. I'll have a gin and tonic, please."

Mia turned to John. "Right, shall we have Merlot or a bottle of Bordeaux?"

"Whichever you prefer, darling?"

"I'm going to have Paella, so Bordeaux would suit, but what about you?"

"No problem, I'll have the same, so Bordeaux it is." Once all had a drink in their hand, Mia touched her glass first to Sophia, then John's.

"It's not been the kind of day I imagined, but we are all safe and well, and that's all that matters."

"Yes, that's true," Sophia said. "As for my car, the insurance company will sort that out."

"Thank heavens for that," John said as he touched his glass to Sophia's.'

"Yes, but that's why we pay for insurance," Mia said laughingly. She then cocked an eyebrow at Sophia. "Now, what about your boyfriend, Hugo? Have you told him about the accident?"

"Yes, I called him while I was getting ready. When he heard of our accident, he wanted to come and see if I was alright," She shrugged. "I convinced him there was no need, and that I would see him on my return to Barcelona."

Mia wagged a finger. "So, he must think a lot of you to want to come and see if you were telling him the truth?"

Sophia's sudden change of colour told Mia she was right in what she had said. Her eyes then lit as she said, "Alright, I must admit Hugo is a bit special."

"Oh really," Mia said laughingly, "now this sounds interesting."

To Sophia's relief, she was saved from further questioning by their waiter's arrival with their meals.

"Enjoy," he said, then walked away.

John chuckled. "Alright, Mia, I think Sophia has had enough excitement for today?"

"Thank you, John," Sophia said, shaking a finger at Mia. The three of them laughed, which caused some other diners to glance in their direction. John put a hand up to acknowledge they were making too much noise. Then, red-faced, the three of them started to eat.

By the time they had finished their meal and returned to the villa, Sophia looked more relaxed. As they sat drinking coffee, John said, "So Mia, your mother is alright. I'm sure your father was relieved when her tests returned negative."

"Yes, he was concerned, but delighted when the doctor put her problem down to stress." Then, unable to hold back her excitement any longer, wearing a mischievous smile, she said, "I have something for you."

John looked puzzled. "Oh, what is it?"

Mia opened her handbag, took out an envelope and handed it to him. "My father said to give you this. He thought you might like to see what's inside."

John shook his head, wondering what it could be. He opened the envelope and took out some papers. Then, as he glanced at them, his face lit into a beaming smile.

"Oh, this is great news." He pointed a finger at Mia. "You devil, you knew what was inside the envelope..." Mia cut in, "So, what do you think? Can you do what he wants?"

"Yes, of course. No problem."

Sophia, looking puzzled, glanced from John to Mia. "Would one of you care to tell me what's going on? I feel a bit left out."

John looked suspiciously at her. "Are you sure Mia never told you?"

"No, but from the look on your face, it must be good news."

John kissed Mia on the cheek. "Yes, it is, or at least it could be." He then explained his arrangement with Mia's father and held up some papers. "A potential customer wants to know if I could design a house for him. These are to help me design what he wants."

"Oh, that's wonderful," Sophia exclaimed, "I'm so happy for you."

John shook his head. "Thank you, but before we celebrate, I'll have to convince the man I can deliver what he wants. So, first thing tomorrow, I'll start preparing sketches."

As it had been a stressful day, Sophia said, "You will have to excuse me, but after today's events, I'm going to have an early night."

Mia faked a yawn. "Yes, that's a good idea."

Sophia kissed them both on the cheek, said goodnight, and went upstairs, with Mia and John not far behind.

Once inside their room, John took Mia in his arms. As they embraced, he said. "You don't know how long I've been waiting to do that." His smile then faded. "Darling, when I heard the crash and you scream, I almost stopped breathing. My heart was in my mouth until I heard you tell Sophia you were okay."

Mia shuddered at the memory. "I was terrified when the other car crashed into us. I dropped the phone and had to release my safety belt before I could scrabble around on the floor to find it."

A smile crossed John's lip. "Right, now let's get into bed. I've missed holding your gorgeous body next to mine."

Once in bed, he held Mia close and kissed her eyes. He then kissed the tip of her nose before their lips met, and they enjoyed a long and passionate kiss.

"Darling," Mia muttered, "I've missed you terribly."

Although a bathroom was between theirs and Sophia's bedrooms, John and Mia's lovemaking was quieter than usual. However, with it being long, and slow, both felt well satisfied.

As they lay in each other's arms, spent but happy, John muttered. "Wait until we are on our own. Then you can cry and moan as loud as you want at what I will do to you."

"Oh, now that sounds like something well worth waiting for." She kissed his cheek, and then, in a spoon position, they fell asleep.

Chapter 47

The following day, with breakfast over, while the two girls took the dogs out for a walk. John stayed behind. He started to prepare sketches for what he hoped would be his first client. On their return, he said, "What with all the excitement, I forgot to say my new office signs installed."

Mia's eyes lit up. "Oh, that is good." She cocked an eyebrow. "Are you pleased?"

"Yes, it's just what I wanted. When you see it, you can tell me what you think."

"Well, I intend to take Sophie to see my new office this morning. We will take a look while we are there."

John nodded. "Yes, but you also want to see it at night when it's illuminated."

Mia's eyebrows rose. "Oh, you never mentioned you were having it lit up."

"Sorry, I thought I had, but never mind."

While Mia took Sophia to her office, John continued to prepare his sketches. When they later returned, he said, "Well, I've finished. But before I send them to the man, I need your help, Mia."

She cast an inquisitive eyebrow. "Oh, in what way?"

"Well, you know I've been learning Spanish?"

"Yes. You speak it quite well now."

"Thank you, but I would like you to add a note on my email to him."

"Of course, no problem." She winked at Sophie, then turned to John. "So, do I get a commission if the man approves your project?"

He grinned. "Yes, but as you are family, you will receive less than normal."

At this, the three of them laughed aloud.

Once Mia had written what John dictated in the email, he attached copies of his sketches and sent it to the man. He shrugged. "Right, now we have to see what reply he sends back."

A flicker of a smile crossed Mia's face. "I'm sure you will receive a satisfactory reply. Oh, and we looked at your new sign. It looks great, and I am sure it will look even better when illuminated."

"Thank you, I thought you would like it."

Mia's smile widened. "Yes, and I had an idea. I took a photo of the sign that I'm going to send to Fernando. He may know people he could send it to?"

John nodded. "Now, that sounds good. By the way, I never told you how I got on with ReAza. If you remember, I had an appointment to see them earlier this week."

Mia's eyebrows shot up in anticipation of what John was about to say. "Yes, I do, so

how did your meeting go?"

"We had a long chat, and I showed them some of my designs." Mia stamped her foot. "Alright, but what happened? Don't keep us in suspense."

"Okay. They were interested and will contact me after speaking to a few other architects."

"Yes," Mia exclaimed, "but what do you think? I am sure you had an idea when you left them?"

"Well, from what I gathered during our meeting, I could be in with a chance." He shrugged. "Still, until I receive an offer, nothing is certain." His colour rose when Mia flung her arms around him and kissed his cheek, while Sophie sat wearing a bemused smile.

"Darling, I feel sure you will receive one." Mia's smile then widened. "So, you have a possible house project, and now things are looking good with ReAza. What a great way to the start of our living here," she chortled.

John nodded. "Yes, but I'll be happy when you sell some properties, I mean, one of us has to earn money."

Mia wagged a finger. "Don't worry about me. I am sure I will be able to support you, darling."

John laughed, with Sophia and Mia joining in.

After Sophia called her insurance company and explained about the accident, she sighed as she closed the phone. "That's a relief. They will check out the damage and then get the car repaired. Most likely in Barcelona."

"Oh, that is good," Mia said. "Yes, it is," John added. "Now, don't take this wrong Sophia; you are welcome to stay as long as you want. However, once you decide when to return home, "I'll book you a flight."

Sophia shook her head. "Thank you, John, but there is no need, I'll..." "Not a chance," John said, cutting in. "I shall pay. It's the least We can do after all you have done for us."

"That's a definite yes," Mia said. "Now, let's not hear any more about it." She wagged a finger at Sophia. "The only thing you have to do is decide when you want to leave."

Sophie glanced from one to the other, then shrugged in resignation. "Okay, and thank you. On Monday, I'll call my boss and explain why I won't be in for a few days." A flicker of a smile crossed her face. "It won't be a problem."

After Sophia spent an enjoyable two days with Mia and John, they drove her to the airport for her flight home.

Once checked in, Sophia said, "Thank you for having me."

John shook his head. "No, it's us that thanks you."

"Yes, it is, "Mia said. "I'm only sorry about the damage to your car."

"It's not a problem. I know the garage that will repair it. They have a great reputation, so I know it will look as good as new when I get it back."

After giving them a last kiss and a hug, Sophia vanished through passport control.

Chapter 48

When John later checked his email, his eyes lit up, and he punched the air. "Yes, great news, darling."

Mia came in from the kitchen, her eyebrows raised in puzzlement. "Oh, what is?"

"It's from the man I sent the sketches. He likes what I sent him and wants me to send him a contract." Wearing a broad smile, he said, "Once he signs and sends it back, I'll start preparing full architectural drawings."

"Oh, that's wonderful, darling."

"Yes, and I know your father will also be pleased." John nodded. "Who knows, this could be the first of several such projects. Still, either way, it's a good sign for the future."

They were still excitedly talking when John's phone rang. After he opened and spoke, he gave Mia a thumbs up.

"Thank you, I'll come to the office this afternoon." He closed his phone, turned, picked Mia up, and swung her around and kissed her.

As he put her down, with her eyes bright in anticipation, she said, "Well, I can only guess that was ReAza."

"Yes. They want me to work on a large project of theirs." He gave a hint of a smile, then continued. "Not only that, I said if we reached an understanding, I would want to continue with my own projects."

"So, from the way you act, I guess they agreed?"

"Yes. It means I can do this man's project, and any others that come my way."

Mia's smile widened. "That's fantastic news, darling. I am so happy for you."

"Well, that's two pieces of good news. Still, they say good things come in threes, so I wonder what the third one will be? Anyway, in the meantime, I'll fetch the bottle of champagne I put away for such an occasion."

He left, returning with the champagne and two flutes. With the bubbles still rising, John poured out two glasses. With both happy and smiling, they clinked their glasses.

"Here's to a successful future," John said.

"For sure, it's a great way to start the year." Mia gave a mischievous smile and caught hold of John's hand.

"I might have that third piece of news you mentioned." The subtle rise of his eyebrows put a giggle in her belly. "I only hope you get the same pleasure when I tell you as you received from the first two?"

John's eyebrows shot up in puzzlement, and then his face lit up in a mile-wide smile.

"Darling, if you mean what I think you do, forget about ReAza and the man's project."

Mia kissed his cheek. "Yes, I am pregnant."

"Oh, that's fantastic news." With tears of joy running down his cheeks, he said, "I've always dreamed of becoming a father. Now, thanks to you, my wish will come true." As he held Mia at arm's length, John's smile turned into a frown. "Well, as you can see, I'm delighted at your news, but how about you?"

With her eyes wide with excitement, she said, "I'm thrilled, but I am concerned as to if I'll be a good mother?"

"What! Don't be silly. You will make a wonderful mother." John beamed her a broad smile. "Now don't you worry. I'll do everything I can to help you."

With love shining in their eyes and arms linked, they sipped their champagne.

The following week, Sophia called. "Great news. I have my car back. Plus, as I expected, it looks as good as new."

"Oh, I'm so pleased," Mia replied. After a chat about this and that, she said, "John also had great news. The man he sent sketches about designing a house has accepted. John is now going to prepare detailed plans. Oh, and another piece of news, he signed a contract with ReAza. They want him to work with them on a large new housing project."

"That's fantastic news. I am so happy for you both."

Mia, who could hold back, no longer said, "Oh, one more thing I almost forgot to mention. I'm pregnant."

Sophia's squeal of delight made Mia hold her ear. "You devil, for not telling me sooner. So, are you pleased? And what does John think about your being pregnant?"

"He says he will do all he can to help me get through these next months." Mia sighed. "I only hope I'll make a good mother?"

"What, don't be silly, of course, you will. Anyway, I am so happy for you. Please give my congratulations to John." Sophia laughed. "Well, once you have a baby, I'll be down to take it out for a walk in its pram."

"What! I expect you to be down before that."

Sophia laughed. "Of course, I will. I'll try and get down next weekend. Oh, Hugo and I are getting on well. We go out several times a week."

"That's good, but make sure you don't end up like me."

Sophia giggled. "In what way? Married or pregnant?"

"You know what I mean, so don't play the innocent," Mia said laughingly.

"Right, I must go," Sophia said, "Some of us have to work for a living."

"Cheeky. I also go to work every day." They both laughed, then after saying they would talk later, closed their phones.

Mia then called her parents to say they would be visiting them two days later.

"Of course, that will be wonderful," her mother said. "It will please your father when I tell him." After a chat, although Mia was bursting to tell her mother she was pregnant, she managed not to.

When John and Mia arrived at her parents' house, the door was flung open by her father. He had heard their car pull up. Beaming with delight, he said, "Welcome, my son, and daughter, it is good to see you both looking so happy." After he hugged John and kissed Mia on both cheeks, his wife, who stood beside him, kissed Mia, then John.

Once all were sat in the lounge, her mother went to prepare tea. While it was brewing, she came in and sat down. Mia's father, who had been talking, said, "So, what do you think, my dear. Do they not look happy?"

She gave a short laugh. "I should hope so. They have only just got married." After going to the kitchen, on her return, she carried a tray loaded with a pot of tea, cups, and saucers. Plus, a plate of biscuits and some small cakes.

Her father chuckled. "Your mother has been busy since you called to say you were coming." He grinned. "I was pleased to hear that you have your first client requiring house plans, John."

"Yes, so am I."

"Well, you will be pleased to hear I have more good news. Another person read about our little deal and called this morning. I gave him your email address, so, expect to hear from him shortly. His name is Felipe Sanchez."

"That's great news," John said. "Yes, it is, but I too have news," Mia said, cutting in.

Her parents looked up in expectation of what she was about to say. Then, before she could speak, her mother, wearing a broad smile, asked," Are you pregnant?"

Mia, who could not hold back her calm expression anymore, said, "Yes, I am."

Her mother leaped across to where Mia sat and kissed her. "Oh, that's wonderful news, I am so happy for you."

Her father, beaming with delight, strode over to John, who looked as though he had won the pools.

"Congratulations, my son." He wrapped John in his arms and kissed him on both cheeks. "As you can tell, we are delighted at your news." His smile then changed to a frown. "But what about you two?"

John, grinning ear from ear, said. "I was over the moon when Mia told me."

With her eyes bright with excitement, Mia said, "I too am delighted. Once we know if it's a boy or a girl, we will get its bedroom decorated."

"Well, this calls for a celebration," her father announced. He shrugged. "I don't have champagne, but I have wine." As he went to leave the room, he turned and pointed to Mia. "You, my daughter, can only have a small glass. We don't want you to risk anything." He chuckled. "Especially as you are carrying me and your mother's first grandchild."

Mia nodded. "We don't, but it's early days yet."

"Never mind," her father called back, "Only a small glass."

On his return, he carried a tray with four glasses and a bottle of Merlot. After pouring out their drinks, he gave one, having less wine to Mia.

"There you are, my beloved daughter. Once you have given birth, I'll give you a large glass of champagne."

They all raised their glasses. With Mia's father, who could not have looked happier, saying, "Here is to my daughter and may she give birth to a beautiful and healthy baby."

With that, they all clinked glasses and echoed his words.

On finishing their drinks, Mia's mother said, "I have made your bed upstairs." She glanced from Mia to John. "I hope you are going to stay the night?"

As Mia went to answer, John said. "Of course, we are."

Her father nodded. "Your mother must have known you would. It explains why she spent so much time cooking a dinner fit for a king." He cocked an eyebrow at Mia. "Did you mention to your mother about being pregnant?"

"No. I wanted to see your expressions when I told you."

He chuckled. "And there was me thinking I must have done something right to deserve such a meal."

His wife shook her head. "Now, why would you think that?" Then, while he thought of an answer, she said, "Come Mia, let's take your bag upstairs." Mia thought this strange, but followed her mother up to her old room.

As she pushed open the door, Mia gasped. In place of her old bed was a brand new double sized one.

Her mother, beaming with delight at Mia's surprise, said, "Now you are married; we thought it best to buy this for you and John."

Mia hugged and kissed her. "Oh, thank you mother."

She shrugged. "Nonsense, we want to see more of you now that you are married." She pulled Mia close and kissed her cheek. "And with you being pregnant, even more."

After a large and delicious dinner, they sat talking out on the patio. All were happy and smiling while they discussed Mia's pregnancy.

Her mother said, "They say a new house, a new baby." She hugged Mia, then added, "Well, no matter, your father and I could not be happier about your news."

That night Mia and John cuddled together in bed, happy and content. They did not make love, as neither wanted to embarrass her parents by making too much noise.

Chapter 49

The following morning, after a nourishing breakfast, John and Mia said their goodbyes to her parents. They drove into town to call in at Mia's old office. She was eager to find out how things were going for Fernando.

When he saw them enter his office, his face lit up in a broad smile. "Hi, Mia, John, it's great to see you." He kissed Mia on both cheeks and pumped John's hand in a firm handshake. After Mia had spoken a few words to Fernando, she went to say hello to the two old members of her staff. She was pleased to hear that both were happy, and said Fernando was an excellent boss. After a chat with them, she returned to talk with Fernando.

"So, how are things going in Valencia?" he asked.

"Everything is going well," she said. "How about you?"

"Great. I knew I would like it here in Barcelona. So, thank you for suggesting we exchange offices. Business is going well, and your two girls and I are getting on well. Oh, and your apartment is great. For me, life is good. Now, how are things going with you John? Have you got any new business yet?"

"Yes. Things are starting to pick up. I've had several inquries, plus one new project and a possible second one...." Mia cut in saying, "Yes, but don't forget ReAza."

Fernando's eyebrows shot up. "Oh, and what about them?"

"I have a contract to help design a new housing project of theirs."

"Wow. Well, that is great news. Once word gets out you are helping ReAza, I'm sure you will soon find yourself with plenty of work."

Mia, her eyes bright with excitement, could not hold back any longer. "I also have a piece of news."

Fernando's forehead creased in puzzlement. "Oh, and what is that?"

"I'm expecting a baby."

Fernando, his eyes wide, leaped up from his chair. "Oh, that's fantastic news. I am so happy for you." He kissed Mia on both cheeks and then pumped John's hand.

"Thank you, Fernando. It delighted us when the doctor informed Mia." John grinned. "As we have a fenced-in garden, it will be perfect once the baby is older."

"Yes, and with Aza and Lucky as guardians, it will always be protected," Mia said, laughing.

On leaving, Fernando, John, and Mia drove back to Valencia. By the time they arrived, it was getting late. However, as the dogs were in the garden and had their kennels, they decided to have dinner out.

Once they had finished a large seafood pizza, they returned home full and satisfied. As they climbed out of the car, the evening breeze wafted the scent of warm sea air. John sniffed. "Although I love the smell of the sea, "it could never match your delicious scent."

Mia cocked an eyebrow. "Oh, does it mean you want something, my darling?"

"Yes, I want to take your naked body in my arms and make love to you." He chuckled. "I mean, I don't have to worry about making you pregnant."

"That's a point." She winked. "Still, let's wait until bedtime. I think a shower followed by a cuddle on the sofa would be nice for now?"

"Whatever you say, my darling. As long as I can hold you in my arms, I'll be happy."

After going inside, they could hear the dogs barking in excitement at their return. Zoe, who had a dog of her own, had been looking after them while they were in Barcelona. When John opened the gate, both dogs charged in wagging their tails. While Mia made a fuss of Aza, John did the same with Lucky.

"So, you have missed us, have you," Mia said. Both dogs seemed to understand what she had said, as they responded with a short bark. John then gave both a treat, which disappeared in no time,

Later, after Mia and John had showered and sat on the sofa in the dressing gowns, Mia sighed, "This is so relaxing."

John kissed her cheek, then grinned. "Well, we had better make the most of it while we can?" When he noticed Mia's eyebrows rise in puzzlement, he said, "Once we have a baby, we will be spending a lot of time feeding and changing it." He shrugged. "Plus, of course, we will be up at night to either feed or change its nappy."

Concern marred Mia's face as he asked, "Darling, you are not sorry about my pregnancy, are you? As you say, it will mean we won't be able to relax as we do at present."

John's face lit up into a mile wide smile as he clasped Mia tight. "Are you kidding? For us to have a baby, it will make my life complete." He squeezed Mia's hand. "I have no regrets and only hope you feel the same?"

She looked at him with raised eyebrows. "I do, but my only concern is that I'll make a good mother."

John shook his head. "Don't worry, I have no doubts about that, so relax. Anyway, between us, I'm sure we won't have any problems bringing up our baby. Now, shall I put on some soothing music, or would you prefer to watch a film?"

A film. I'll pick one out," Mia said, rising to her feet. She picked out a romantic film, put it on, which they watched while curled up on the sofa.

After the film finished and the dogs had been out in the garden, both John and Mia were tired as they climbed the stairs. In minutes, both were fast asleep in bed.

Chapter 51

As Mia's stomach swelled during the next six months, so did John's business. Both were happy with how her pregnancy was going, until one day, John received a phone call from Mia. To his shock and horror, she said, "Darling, I started bleeding. Carlos is taking me to the hospital."

"Oh no," he gasped, "I'll be there as quick as I can." As John went to dash out of his office in ReAza, he called to a colleague, "I have to go to the hospital."

Once in his car, as he sped off to the hospital, John was a bundle of nerves. His hands shook on the wheel, and his eyes opened wide at the thought of his not being with Mia in her time of need.

On arriving at the hospital, John screeched to a halt and switched off the ignition. Not bothering to remove the keys, he jumped out and ran inside. Still trembling in fear, he found Carlo sitting by the reception desk.

He stood, gripped John's shoulder and to his relief, said, "It's alright; John. Mia and the baby are okay. The doctor has examined her and is waiting to talk with you. You go and see her. I'll wait here."

John gave a half-smile, and then followed a nurse who had joined them. She led him into a room, where he found Mia lying on a bed with a white-clad doctor standing beside her. One look at John's wide eyes and trembling lips, and he shook his head. "There is no need to worry, Mr Philips. Your wife is alright."

Mia gave a tired smile. "Sorry, darling, but I thought it best to get here right away.

The doctor nodded, "Your wife did the right thing. In these circumstances, it's better to be safe than sorry. As it is, there is nothing to worry about. Now, your wife tells me she has been working in her office." He shook his head. "I've told her to forget about work until after the baby is born. She needs to lie down and rest." As John went to speak, he said, "I'll see her next month, and then decide if she can go the full nine months. She might need to have a caesarean birth." When he noticed John's eyebrows shoot up, he shook his head. "Don't worry, Mr Philips, this won't be a problem for your wife." Glancing down at Mia, he said, "She then won't have any problems giving birth."

After he shook hands with John, who still could not get over the news of Mia's bleeding, the doctor spoke. "Please stay in bed for another hour Mrs Phillips, and then you can go home." He wagged a finger. "Oh, and don't forget, no more work." With that, he left.

John leaned over and kissed Mia's cheek. "Thank heaven you are alright. I almost died of shock when you said you were bleeding."

Mia caught hold and squeezed his hand. "I know how you felt, darling. Still, the doctor checked and said all was well with the baby." She shrugged. "It seems what happened is not that unusual with pregnant women."

A relieved look washed across John's face. "Maybe, but as the doctor said, you will not return to work." Before Mia could comment, he put up a hand. "I don't want anything happening to you or the baby, so that's the end of it."

Mia sighed. "You are right, of course. Still, I can deal with most things on the phone, and Carlos can handle anything else in my absence."

"Good. As for ReAza, I'll explain what's happened. With the main project complete, they won't need me for a while unless another one comes in. Anyway, I can do most of my work from home." He grinned "I'll bring my drawing board; and any other bits and pieces I require. Therefore, my darling, I'll be able to make sure you do as the doctor said."

Mia laughed. "Oh, that would be nice. The garden needs weeding, and I can't help you.... She left the end of the sentence unfinished, with them both laughing.

John nodded. After all the stress and panic he'd experienced, he would be happy to work in their garden with Mia resting inside the house.

After talking with Carlos, John arranged to meet him outside his office the next day. He would bring his drawing board etc; to the house.

The following morning, once he had Mia sat on the sofa watching the television, John said, "I won't be long." He wagged a finger, "Don't get any ideas of doing anything while I'm gone." He made sure she had her phone, kissed her goodbye, and then left. When he met Carlos, he asked, "How is Mia?"

"She's fine, and thanks for taking her to the hospital yesterday."

"It was nothing, but I'm glad to hear she is alright." John unlocked his office, and the two men entered. After clearing his drawing board, he and Carlos soon had it in the back of his truck. Once John had collected up papers and other bits and pieces that he put in his car, he and Carlos drove to the villa.

With the truck close to the entrance door, it took less than ten minutes to get the board inside and set up in the lounge.

As they worked, Mia said, "Many thanks, Carlos. Is everything alright at the office?"

"Yes, no problems. The girls send you their best wishes and say for you to take it easy." He grinned and pointed to John. "With John's set up here; he can keep an eye on you."

John nodded. "That's for sure. We don't want any more scares like yesterday."

Mia's lips trembled. "You are right. I don't want to go through that again, either."

Once Carlos had left, and John finished setting up his drawing board, he said, "Right, that's finished. Now can I get you anything, darling?"

"No thanks. I think I have all that I need. TV control, phone, notebook, pen, and a book to read."

"In that case, how about a cup of tea or coffee? Which would you prefer?"

"Coffee, please."

When John returned carrying a tray with two cups of coffee, Mia's eyes lit up when she noticed a few chocolate biscuits on a plate.

"What's this? Are you trying to spoil me?" she tittered. "Still, as I'm heavily pregnant, I suppose it's to be expected."

He bent and kissed her cheek. "Anything for you, my darling."

She looked up and fluttered her long eyelashes "I am only sorry I can't give you anything in return."

"That's not a problem. When you give birth, I will have everything I ever wanted and more."

Chapter 52

During the next two weeks, while John worked at home, Mia relaxed on the sofa. A visit to the hospital resulted in the doctor saying, "All is well, but I think it best you come in the day after tomorrow. It's time for you to give birth."

Mia looked at John, who squeezed her hand. "Don't worry, darling. I'm sure all will go well. Plus, once you've had the baby, I will be with you in the hospital until you leave." He grinned. "Also, instead of your lump, you will have a baby to take care of."

She gave a nervous smile. "Yes, and then I won't have to waddle around like a duck." Both the doctor and John laughed, then the doctor said, "Right, if you come in Wednesday morning, you will have a baby before dinner." He shrugged. "As you never wanted to know what sex the baby will be, I only hope you won't be disappointed."

John shook his head. "Not a chance. We will be happy whatever it is. Is that not right, darling?"

"Yes, as long as it's healthy, I don't mind."

The doctor nodded. "Well, from what I've seen on your ultrasound results, the baby has no problems. So, there is only one thing you and your husband have to sort out."

John and Mia exchanged puzzled glances. They had no idea what the doctor meant. He chuckled. "I mean, what will you call the baby? Will it have a Spanish first name, or English?"

"Ah, yes. That is something we have not yet agreed on," John said. "We have names for both a boy and a girl, but will decide once we know if we have a son or a daughter." He turned to Mia, "Agreed, darling?"

"Yes, but I'm sure we will pick something we both like."

On leaving the hospital, John and Mia returned home. After getting Mia comfortable on the sofa, he said, "Well, we have to pick a boy's and a girl's name before you give birth."

"Yes, so if you get paper and pen, we will sort this out." A flicker of a smile crossed Mia's face. "If you remember, we made a list of names." She cast a glance at John. "I know my parents would like us to choose a Spanish first name, but it's what we decide that counts."

John shrugged. "It's not a problem for me. Plus, if I remember rightly, we can use some Spanish names in Spanish or English. Anyway, just a minute." He left, then returned with pen and paper. "Now, we said Marco, Roberto, Tomas, and Alexandra for a boy, and for a girl, Sofia, Gloria, Jade, and Nina."

After some discussion, they could not agree on a boy's name. Mia wanted Filippo or Alexandra, while John preferred Tomas or Marco. As for a girl, it was a toss-up between Nina and Jade. Mia preferred Nina, while John fancied Jade.

An impish smile made her face twitch. "Well, although we don't agree, I think we have made a good choice of names."

John kissed Mia on the cheek. "Yes, I agree. Still, we will have to wait to find out what you have inside. Only then can we make a final choice."

Come Wednesday morning, John put a small case in the car's boot containing some things for Mia and himself. After he helped Mia into the car and made sure her seatbelt was fastened, he climbed in beside her. Squeezing Mia's hand, he said, "Right, let's go and get this baby."

A smile quirked Mia's lip. "Yes. I'll be glad when it's over, and I can hold it in my arms."

At the hospital, once checked in, after John kissed Mia and wished her well, a nurse wheeled her off to the delivery room.

During the next two hours, John paced up and down, looking nervously at the door. After years and Jasmin unable to have a baby, his dream of having his own family was about to come true. He could not sit still. His thoughts were on Mia and how she was. Despite the doctor and his parents saying she would be fine; he could not relax.

Finally, after what seemed like forever, the door opened, and a nurse pushed a bed into the room. John's eyes lit with delight when he saw Mia sat up, holding a bundle. He leapt to his feet and rushed to the side of the bed.

"How are you, darling? Did everything go off alright?"

"Yes, it went off better than I expected." She gave a tired smile. "I never felt a thing."

John, who could hardly control his excitement, asked, "So, do we have a son or a daughter?"

Mia flashed him a huge smile. "We have a beautiful baby boy." She cocked an eyebrow. "I hope you are not disappointed?"

"What, don't be silly. We agreed we'd be happy, whatever it was." After the nurse made sure mother and baby were comfortable, she said, "I'll be back in a couple of hours. But, if you need anything, press the red button. Someone will be right with you."

After Mia and John thanked her, she left.

"So, Mrs Phillips, are you happy?"

"Yes, thank you, daddy," she said, flashing a tired smile.

John leaned over and making sure not to disturb the baby, kissed her cheek.

Mia eased away the blanket covering the baby's face. "There, what do you think?"

"Oh, he looks so cute, just like his mother."

"Yes, well," she tittered, "remember those words, in case he turns out to be naughty."

"What! "John said, laughing; "there is no chance of us allowing that to happen."

"No, and I'm sure our parents would also make sure of that." Her smile came soft and dreamy. "Oh, we must phone and inform them they are now grandparents."

While John phoned his parents, Mia phoned hers. It delighted both when told Mia and their grandson were good. Mia's parents said they would come to the hospital the next day to see their first grandchild. John's parents said congratulations and they would be over later.

As she had said, the nurse later returned to check on Mia and the baby. Come night-time, with John sleeping in the same room. After Mia had taken a prescribed painkiller, she slept with a smile on her face.

The following morning, Mia's parents both wearing broad smiles, entered the room. Her father pumped John's hand and then hugged him, while her mother went to Mia and kissed her. With congratulations over, Mia uncovered the baby's face.

"Oh, he looks beautiful," her mother said. "Yes, he does," her father agreed.

After staying awhile, her mother said, "Right, we will go now and leave Mia to rest." Her father nodded in agreement. "Yes, but we will come back down once you are home and feel up to our visit."

"We will look forward to seeing you," John said, with Mia adding her agreement.

When Mia, John, and their son they had named Alex left the hospital, John could not have been happier. Finally, his dream of having a family of his own had come true.

As time passed, Alex turned into a happy child, who brought joy and laughter to his doting parents. He was also the delight of his grandparents, who paid frequent visits to see him.

Things could not be better for Mia and John. Her business was doing well, with John's name now known for high-class house designs. Alex became inseparable with his two four-legged guardians, Aza, and Lucky. Whenever the weather was suitable, they were always out playing together in the garden. Also, whenever Mia took him out on her own, with Aza and Lucky beside her, she had nothing to worry about.

The End

Also by Colin Guest

1
Desperation Rules the Day
Suzy's Dilemma

Standalone
Desperation Rules the Day
Fatal Love
An Unforgettable Cruise
A Dangerous Love Affair
An Expats Experiences of Living in Turkey
Impending Disaster
Terror Holiday
It Happened in Barcelona

Watch for more at https://www.colinguestauthor.com.

About the Author

Colin Guest is English, now retired and living in Istanbul. He has written eleven books, including memoirs, thrillers and romance stories. His latest book is Unforgettable Cruise, a romance story. Colin is passionate about wild animals and has adopted a tiger for the past twelve years.

Read more at www.colinguestauthor.com.

Milton Keynes UK
Ingram Content Group UK Ltd.
UKHW010001240823
427351UK00001B/70

9 798223 767824